Love on a Train

by

Colleen L. Donnelly

Love on a Train

Cover Art by *Diana Carlile*

The Wild Rose Press, Inc.
PO Box 708
Adams Basin, NY 14410-0708
Visit us at www.thewildrosepress.com

Publishing History
First Vintage Rose Edition, 2016
Print ISBN 978-1-5092-0526-4
Digital ISBN 978-1-5092-0527-1

Published in the United States of America

"Want to see a picture of the girl I plan to marry?" Raymond's face appeared, forced its way into my mind—the way he'd looked when I first met him, and the way he looked again when he asked me that question, both of us riding the train into Kansas City for our respective jobs. *"Just got back from doing my part for the war,"* he said in our very first conversation, and he meant the big war, the Second World War. *"I build bridges. Right now I'm working on the Madison Bridge, not far from downtown. I'm building bridges for the city and building a whole new life for myself at the same time."* And then he smiled, looked at me in a way that told me there was so much more to what he'd said than just that he worked and built. We were the same inside, and I knew it that very moment. Hearing his voice and seeing his expression ignited tiny flames inside me. Flames that had flickered quietly far too long, done little more than lick the surface of my imagination. Until that day. Each time he spoke after that, something in me flared to life and heated me up from within, bringing what Mama called an unladylike glimmer to my eye. A glimmer that was identical to the one I saw in his eyes, but she never knew that. I never talked about Raymond to her. I didn't dare. *"I love words,"* I said back to him that first time we spoke. *"I have a secretary job, and sometimes I take dictation. Mr. Arnold, my boss, says I'm good at it."* I didn't tell him Mama said it wasn't proper for me to write my own words and stories, and that's why I just copied everyone else's.

Copied everyone else's until I met him. After that, my own story erupted in full force. I couldn't stop it. That's when it finally began to grow.

Praise for Colleen L. Donnelly

"*LOVE ON A TRAIN* is a romantic ride through a post-World War II world. The characters are layered, the setting is intriguing…will appeal to readers who like a lead character willing to strike out and make her dreams come true."

~*Lori Robinett, author of* Denim & Diamonds
~*~

"An excellent read. I felt like I was one with Martha as she was going through life, trying to do what everyone else expected of her and at the same time knowing down deep what she needed to do to make her own life right for herself."

~*Kacee Everhart, Pastor*
~*~

"Very good story; each of Colleen's books is better than the last. Can't wait for the next!"

~*Judae Jamison, avid reader, critique source*
~*~

"Exciting, good story, hard to put down…nice ending."

~*Wilma Stainbrook, avid reader, author support*
~*~

"How often have you thought about your ancestors and what their lives must have been like? The author's ability to make me visualize the dynamics within the family brought a depth to the many personalities that are not easy to achieve, and her skills with the written word have me searching for more of her books. And now if you will excuse me, I have another book to add to my 'keeper shelf.' After I read it again…"

~*MelR7, The Romance Studio (5 Hearts)*

Dedication

To my mom,
who never fails me as a valuable critique partner.
To my critique group—
you have taught me to think like a writer and to grow.
And to Nan, my Editor at The Wild Rose Press,
who continues to encourage and support me.

Chapter 1

Mama said it couldn't be done.

I glanced at the stack of books on the table beside me and the line of women in front of me—a row of eyes glued my direction, copies of my book in their hands.

Love on a Train by Martha Cole.

Mama said it shouldn't be done. She said a book like this should never be written. Not by a respectable young woman, and certainly not by me, her and Daddy's only daughter.

"You've heard of Mills and Boon, maybe. Those publishers of sappy emotional tales out of England?" Mama's lectures about the pitfalls of romance and stories that told about it generally began the same way—an undermining of the literature, followed by a promise that if I ever believed or read such nonsense I'd ruin every chance I had for a future of wedded contentment. "Stay away from anything with their name on it." Mama'd tsk as she forged the path that was to usher me from childhood to being the wife and mother I was supposed to be. "Garbage. That's what their books are. Silly stories that fuel young girls' wild emotions with false notions about marriage, replacing what's real with dreams of romance instead."

I always stood and listened to everything Mama had to say. Only once did I ask her how, how something that talked about love could be so wrong and cause people so much harm. She didn't answer with her usual speed; she stumbled first over a look that was there and gone too quickly for me to grasp. "Love?" she'd finally said, recovering, and looking straight down at me. "Don't be thinking that every little pitter-patter of your heart is love, Martha, because it's not. Love isn't that way, and places like Mills and Boon should be closed down for making women believe any different."

I glanced at Mills and Boon's logo on the spine of my book, ran my finger over their emblem, thinking how right Mama had been in the end. I never did read such stories. It turned out they were inside me, instead—not just waiting to be read or written, but to be lived.

Mama'd picked up on that inclination in me, somehow noticed the tiny spark flickering so deep within that even I didn't know it was there. By the time my tendencies sprouted, matured enough to seep into conversations or onto scraps of paper, she was ready. She had braced herself for that day, and from that moment on she doubled her efforts against wildly palpitating hearts, targeting my heart in particular. "A real husband doesn't sweep a woman off her feet," Mama lectured every chance she got. "He builds her a solid home, instead. Just like your father has done—work and provide, all day every day, nothing more and nothing less. Marriage is about family, not romance. And a fitting wife never gives way to ridiculous fairytales."

Mama's efforts were commendable, but in the end not powerful enough to stop what I couldn't stop, either. For all her work, she missed her target. Someone else found it instead. Someone who for a moment had awakened my heart, made it believe Mama was wrong when she claimed stories like mine were purely fictitious and could never be lived. Not by anyone. Not even by me. Not ever.

"Is it true?" a hushed voice asked above me, bringing me back to the bookstore and the stack of books I was here to sign. I glanced up at the next woman in line. "I mean, did this really happen?" She inched one of my books across the table until it stopped in front of me. Her fingers pressed on its cover, pinning it there, her nails turning dark pink with half-moons of white under the pressure.

She was somewhere around my age, both of us in our early twenties. We were marrying age—or slightly beyond it, as Mama often commented—my book an impediment to my future, according to her. Even more of an impediment than the war we'd just come through, and the shortage of available young men as a result of it. I glanced at the faces behind the young woman, a line from my table to the bookstore's entrance, each expression expectant—exactly like hers was today, and mine used to be—no matter the differences in features, ages, or marital statuses. The similarity that bound all women together was in the eyes. Love. And the hope for it. The raw need for love on a train, on a bus, wherever she worked, or wherever she lived. Love cropping up somewhere, with someone—that one someone every woman was certain she was meant to be with—that one someone who would stay with her forever.

That one someone who had sat beside me on a

train, taught my heart to sing and to write as I'd never written before. And then disappeared.

"It's a work of fiction," I replied. I placed my fingers near the young woman's, and she let my book go. I glanced at the cover before I drew it open, at the profile of a young girl, a pencil sketch of a face so similar to mine... *"Want to see a picture of the girl I plan to marry?"* His voice exploded in my thoughts. I could hear it as if he'd asked me only yesterday. A voice I intended to never hear again after today. Mills and Boon, Mama's worries, my book and all of its memories—everything gone as soon as I signed and sold all that was left of them. All that was left of him.

"Oh. I see," the young woman answered from above me. "Even if it's just a story, it can still happen, right?" Hope rang in her voice.

I looked up from the book's cover. The lights that dangled on chains from the bookstore's high ceiling created a halo around her head—innocent expectation, all too familiar, all too easily destroyed. I stared at the hazy splinters of light, then batted my eyes until she looked normal again. "This sort of love has happened for real," I admitted. "I know for a fact it did. It just isn't this story."

"Want to see a picture of the girl I plan to marry?" Raymond's face appeared, forced its way into my mind—the way he'd looked when I first met him, and the way he looked again when he asked me that question, both of us riding the train into Kansas City for our respective jobs. *"Just got back from doing my part for the war,"* he said in our very first conversation, and he meant the big war, the Second World War. *"I build bridges. Right now I'm working on the Madison Bridge,*

not far from downtown. I'm building bridges for the city and building a whole new life for myself at the same time. " And then he smiled, looked at me in a way that told me there was so much more to what he'd said than just that he worked and built. We were the same inside, and I knew it that very moment. Hearing his voice and seeing his expression ignited tiny flames inside me. Flames that had flickered quietly far too long, done little more than lick the surface of my imagination. Until that day. Each time he spoke after that, something in me flared to life and heated me up from within, bringing what Mama called an unladylike glimmer to my eye. A glimmer that was identical to the one I saw in his eyes, but she never knew that. I never talked about Raymond to her. I didn't dare. *"I love words,"* I said back to him that first time we spoke. *"I have a secretary job, and sometimes I take dictation. Mr. Arnold, my boss, says I'm good at it."* I didn't tell him Mama said it wasn't proper for me to write my own words and stories, and that's why I just copied everyone else's.

Copied everyone else's until I met him. After that, my own story erupted in full force. I couldn't stop it. That's when it finally began to grow.

The first time I saw Raymond Haynes, I believed he was the man God intended for me. I barely managed to stagger past him down the train's aisle that morning, smitten in an instant with his dark good looks. I dropped into a seat not too far away, wishing he'd turn his head from the window, and the older gentleman he was conversing with, and glance my direction. What I could see of him, beyond his dark eyes and chiseled tanned features, was a spring of optimism. He looked eager for life, far more eager than most. And his voice, as it relayed the few words I could hear, was full of sunny determination. Everything about him was affable, so pleasant and pleasurable it was almost in contrast to the stark ebony of his hair and his ruddy complexion. He sat tall and he looked slender, the strength of his shoulders still evident as he leaned the older gentleman's way. My heart had exploded that day—beat hard enough I was afraid he could hear it as I watched him—studied the first and only man I'd ever had a longing for, the only man I thought I ever would.

The young woman waiting for me to sign her copy of my book let out a sigh, almost a gasp above me, a burst of ardor I watched bubble to life in her eyes. I knew that look. I understood the glint I saw beneath the bookstore's low light. She leaned close. "Tell me about it," she insisted. "Tell me about the real love story that happened."

I glanced from her to the long line behind her, her gaze following mine. She frowned as she straightened. Her smile disappeared, and a tiny grimace of disappointment took its place. "I wish you'd written about the real love story in your book. Maybe you could do that in your next one."

I picked up the fountain pen the bookstore had provided me. It quivered as I dipped the golden nib into the bottle of ink. "Who do I address this to?" I asked, tightening my grip on the pen. Mama was right. I should never have written this story, at least never finished it like I'd decided to do. I should never have agreed to sit in this bookstore calling it a work of fiction instead of the story I thought I was meant to live—the story someone else ended up living for me.

I'd waited forever for Raymond to finally notice me on that train. I was mostly average the way I looked—only fairly pretty, tall with light brown hair, slender, and dressed the same way every other young female dressed after the war. Mama said any young woman—all young women, in fact—who wanted to be a bride and to catch a good husband in this shortage of men had to look the part of an upstanding lady in order to be chosen. I figured that was why Raymond never noticed me at first. I blended in. Nothing about me was spectacular enough to catch his eye, not the eye of someone as handsome and striking as he was, handsome and striking enough he could have any woman he wanted.

"What in heaven's name is that thing in your hair?" Mama's voice escalated an octave above her norm the day I tried to sneak out of the house with a spangly new comb I'd bought. I missed breakfast, standing in front of my mirror that morning creating a smart new wave in my hairdo. She spotted it before I made it through the front door and told me to take it out. My comb disappeared into her apron pocket as she patted my hair back into place. "There," she'd said, as she sent me off plain and simple, blending into the scenery. Hadn't Raymond just come home from a war where everyone blended in? He would never notice me. His eye had been trained to detect the one thing that was different, the unusual, the thing that stood out from scenery that all looked the same.

"Amelia." The young woman in front of me rescued me from my thoughts. "Amelia Long. And wish me lots of love when you sign the book, will you?" A faint blush dotted her cheeks. "I really did adore your story, even if it wasn't real. As soon as I read your first line, 'Want to see a picture of the girl I plan to marry?' I was hooked. How did you ever think of that? You're very clever. And talented. Are you married?"

I bent over her book. "To a lovely young woman, Amelia Long," I wrote. The sharp nib of the pen scratched out the sentiment, etching it into her book forever.

"That's nice." Amelia tipped her head sideways and read the salutation.

"May love find you or you find it, whether on a train, a plane, or on the sidewalk outside your own home. Sincerest wishes, Martha Cole."

"That's beautiful!" Amelia took the book from my hands and twisted it her way to read it again. Her face glowed far brighter than the lights that hung above her, far more than the lamps situated on small tables around the store. "Thank you." She clutched the book to her breast and hurried away.

"You didn't answer her question." The next woman stepped forward, her eyes exactly like Amelia's, exactly like mine were at one time. This woman was slightly older, wizened in a tired sort of way, but that longing still evident as it spilled from her glance. "She asked if you were married."

"Engaged," I replied, taking the copy of my book she handed me. "I'm engaged to a man named David. David Tidwell."

Chapter 2

David Tidwell. A good man, according to Mama. A reliable man, one who would provide well for me and our future children.

I signed the book the woman handed me. I glanced up and smiled as she took it from my hand. I smiled at the next woman in line, also, and then the next, and the next. "To Helen...To Maxine...To Betty...To Gayle..." I addressed their books the way they asked me to, and I promised each of them love in the sentiments I added between their names and mine. With every book they set in front of me, I did my best. Did my best to assure them of what they believed in, and my best to avoid looking at my book's cover. At that sketch, that profile—the memories I was here to put away—images of Raymond I was replacing with David.

No, I don't want to see a picture of the girl you plan to marry. I hadn't said it to Raymond that day he asked me, but I'd heard it loud and clear in my mind as I pressed back against the inside wall of the train, wishing I could jump out the window and run away.

I'd spent weeks choosing seats fairly close to his before he finally noticed me. I picked them near, but not so near that Mama's voice would ring in my head reminding me how young women were supposed to behave. Raymond would have needed field glasses to spot me if I stayed beyond Mama's suggested boundaries, so I budged her limits a little until at last I caught his attention—met those eyes, dark and black as coal, when he looked my way and acknowledged me. I caught a flicker of recognition in the first brief glance. I saw it and he must have felt it, for he followed it with a quick nod that sent my heart reeling outside my chest. Not long after that he smiled. Eventually he said hello. And at last he paused before he sat, choosing a seat fairly close to mine. That was the day we finally swapped names and what our jobs were, stepped beyond just looking at each other to at last sharing who we were.

With time he began to save a seat for me. Not right next to him like I longed for, but close by. Most of the time he saved the one in front of him. The first time he did, he held it for me by dangling his hands over its back. I fell into that seat, my knees giving out the moment I saw his ruddy smile and dark eyes above it. I hit the cushion with a thump, dreaming I was falling into his lap instead. I had to keep looking forward for a moment, compose myself before I turned and gazed into his handsome face. *Martha Haynes, Martha Haynes, Martha Haynes*, I'd thought until at last I'd turned, fanning my face with my hand as I did, visions of us bound together forever making me hot inside and out.

Martha Cole. Martha Cole. Martha Cole. I signed the book in front of me with a noisy flourish, scratched a wavy line beneath my name, and looked up at the young girl I'd just signed it for.

"Thank you," she whispered. She leaned my direction, then peered over her shoulder. "If my mother catches me in here, or even reading a book like this, she'll whip me sound." Her eyes were huge when she turned back my way, full of youthful daring above an impish grin. I watched her stuff my book into her satchel.

"No," I said before I thought. "Could you give the book back? Please?" I stretched my open hand her direction. The girl twisted to the side away from me, yanking the satchel behind her. I hadn't been as determined when I was her age, nor as daring, yet I'd ended up the same place she intended to go. Then lost. I closed my hand. Telling me "no" had done Mama no good, and telling this girl "no" was just as futile. No woman ever wanted to hear that word. "Please? It will be okay." It would. I'd do my best to make it so for her. I used a soothing tone she wasn't quick to trust. She studied me in a way that made me feel nearer her mother's age than hers.

At last the satchel eased forward, her gaze never leaving me until a corner of the bag appeared from behind her back. "You're not going to keep it, are you?"

I clasped my hands together and rested them on the table. "If you learn nothing else from what I've written, learn this. That book is like love. No one can take it from you—you have to give it to them. And hope they give it back to you."

Her eyes lit up. Tiny lights in the dark of her pupils, undisturbed by the subtle warning in what I'd said. This wasn't the sort of excitement a young woman gets over new bracelets or two-wheel bicycles, the things her mother most likely hoped still stirred her little girl's heart. No, this girl's heart craved much more than new toys or jewelry. Her eyes were alive with the type of desire that gives as well as takes, shares in ways she never fathomed as a child. Ways her mother and mine would say are wrong, a caution I should, but couldn't, bring myself to say. She drew the satchel in front of her and clasped it against her stomach, the fingers of both hands splayed as she guarded it. The intensity of her eyes burned as she gauged me. She opened it then, lifted the book from inside, and laid it in front of me.

I dipped the tip of the pen into the ink, and opened the front cover. What I'd written before to her looked tinny and cheap. I touched the pen to the page below my previous words, and added, "Let those love now, who never loved before; let those who always loved, now love the more." I set the pen aside and stared at the page.

"What? What does that mean?" She cocked her head to read it. I glanced up, and saw her frown.

"It's an old quote, hundreds of years old, actually, from a man named Thomas Parnell. It tells us that hearts never really change. We all desire love, and those who don't believe in love or who haven't experienced it yet, should find it. And those who do love already should have an abundance of it." I turned the book her way. "I wish both of those things for you. No matter how, or where, or when."

Her face lit up. She lifted her book, and stared at the words before she slid it back into her satchel. She closed the flap and ran her hands down the front. "Thank you." Womanhood blossomed right there in front of me on her childlike face. She reminded me of myself, the me who'd forgotten everything Mama'd ever said, the boundless flush of virgin passion the first time Raymond sat next to me.

****

My heart had nearly jumped out of my chest that day. I melted and froze all at the same time as he slid in next to me instead of staying in the seat behind me. His eyes were alight with more wonder than I'd ever seen as he smiled down at me. I could feel the lean strength of his thigh as it pressed against mine, my skirt so full and in the way that I gathered the bunches of its fabric into my lap so I could sense his leg better. Mama would have dragged me off that train by my hair if she'd seen me do that, but I didn't care. He was there beside me; he was staring at me, his eyes shining with the same sort of light that glowed in my heart. He swiveled my direction, and his knees leaned into mine. I let them, my face so warm I worried it looked like it had leapt into flames.

"Want to see a picture of the girl I plan to marry?" he asked me. My heart stopped the moment I heard those words. Its glow disappeared, and I could feel the color drain from my face. I stared at him, at his exuberance, and I suddenly understood why he had taken so long getting to know me; why he had never asked me to dinner, never held my hand, never made a move to say he felt the same way about me that I did about him. He reached into his shirt pocket as I sat there cold and numb, and he withdrew a folded piece of paper. The train vibrated my back as I flattened myself against its side, my head and teeth jarring as I pressed against the window. I would have sprung to my feet and jumped from that window if my legs hadn't turned to mush. I sat there, instead, a sob building in my chest. Be brave, I told myself, go on and look at this girl's

picture. Be happy for him even if his happiness doesn't include me. Each fold that he opened was like a hammer to my heart, one after another, until the paper was even. He pressed it smooth on his long thigh, then held it up for me to see. There she was—this light-brown-haired girl, her profile penciled onto the page. I gasped. I'd looked from her to him, and saw the twinkle of excitement in his eyes. He loved her, and she was me. That was my profile, a likeness of me he'd drawn from memory, his face alight with the passion I'd so longed to see for me as I looked back to him.

****

Books continued to appear in front of me, streaming past the same way memories of Raymond did with each one I signed. Every woman was hungry for a share of my story, *Love on a Train*. Each one read what I wrote to her, then glanced down at me as if I had the power to guarantee those sentiments, make the story real, bring it to life, and assure her of perfect and lasting love. I wanted to cry instead of smile. Signing my name as I signed him away was much more difficult than I'd thought.

Martha Cole. Martha Cole. Martha Cole.

I wrote it over and over beneath each promise, a name I hadn't thought I'd be writing by this time. I'd believed it would be Martha Haynes. At least I'd believed it until the morning I boarded the train and the porter handed me a lunchbox. It was Raymond's lunchbox. I'd seen it dozens of times.

"Your friend left this on here. Said he was going somewhere, and he was pretty excited about it. Kind of nervous, too, so I suppose he just forgot all about this lunchbox. Maybe you can get it to him?"

I'd taken the pail from the porter and dropped into a seat. Raymond was going somewhere? The train lurched forward as my thoughts yanked backwards. Going somewhere? He had mentioned bridge jobs, talked about the house he was buying, described pieces of the future I'd assumed would be ours, though now I couldn't recall if he'd ever used words like "we" or "our." Maybe my girlish fascination had deafened me to what he really said. Maybe I'd been wrong to tell myself we were building our marriage on that train, meeting the same way every day so we could set a firm foundation for what lay ahead when we were finally off the train. Together. Instead of going somewhere, apart.

I rested my hands on the black lunchbox, the cool metal chilling my palms while I thought how much I'd wanted to believe Raymond had just been too afraid to hurry us very much, that the tiny pauses, the fleeting frowns, were merely decisions and plans being cemented regarding our future. I'd told myself he hadn't wanted to jeopardize what we had by taking me to dinner, taking me to his house, before we really got to know each other. My hands looked wobbly as tears blurred everything I thought and saw. How I had longed to be somewhere alone with him. Every day I imagined how he would hold my hand, talk more intimately than he could with scores of people around us. Each afternoon I waited, breathless as we parted, wondering if this was the day, the moment he would finally ask, ask me out for a genuine date, and begin cementing our lives together for real.

"Raymond caught me like an expert fisherman lands a fish," I told my best girlfriend, Karen, the only person I ever mentioned him to. We laughed at the

analogy, neither one of us fishermen, but both of us understanding the lure of the right man. *"He baited me, he teased me, he made me want the morsel so much that I was ready to chomp on it, hook and all, the moment he finally tossed it out."*

There was no laughter when I sat alone with his lunch pail on the train, cold creeping from my palms up through my hands. It penetrated my arms, stole on toward my heart. Raymond hadn't dragged me to shore like I thought he would. He acted almost surprised as I came alongside him. I'd brushed that away as shyness on his part, but in the shell of the train, alone with just his lunchbox, I knew better. I undid and lifted its lid. Litter lay strewn in the bottom, debris left behind from his last noon meal…waxed paper, a cloth napkin, a spoon. I moved it aside, and there, beneath it all, lay an envelope. My fingers trembled as I clasped it, lifted it out, and closed the lunchbox. I opened the flap and saw a small stack of his sketches. Pieces of paper, differing sizes, different scenes he had drawn to show me his work, his world. I thumbed through them, my heart making more noise than the train. Until I saw it.

My heart stilled the moment I spotted the photograph tucked between his drawings. I'd fished it out and laid it on my palm. It was a profile, a picture of a young woman so much like me she could have been me. But she wasn't. She was the woman in the sketch, the real woman in the sketch. She was the girl Raymond planned to marry.

"David's outside."

I glanced up from the book I was supposed to be signing. The bookstore owner's wife, Gretchen, stood at my side. "He sent this in to you. He's talking to someone out there that he said wants you to sign it."

Gretchen slid another copy of my book toward me, the one from David—actually from whatever fan was standing outside talking to him. I finished autographing the book I had, wished the woman my best, and handed it back to her. I took the book Gretchen had laid on the table. It felt thicker than it was supposed to. It was bulky and worn as if it had been well used, and I could see it had become a repository of odds and ends pressed between its pages. I drew open the cover with one hand, holding everything else in place with the other. That was when I saw what made this book different from all of the others. His name. There on the page beneath *Love on a Train* by Martha Cole, he had written, "Illustrated by Raymond Haynes."

I stumbled as I came to my feet. "Where is he?"

"He's outside, like I said, talking to the guy waiting for you to sign that book." Gretchen nodded toward the front.

I stretched, stood on my toes, strained to see over the heads of the women waiting in line. "Not David. I mean…"

"Sit back down before you fall over." Gretchen placed her hands on my shoulders, pressing me back toward my seat. "Sign the book, and I'll run it out to them while you take a break. I'll have David come in as soon as he sends the fellow off, and the two of you can relax together. You've been at this too long; you need a little rest."

I shook loose from Gretchen's clasp. "Excuse me," I said to the woman next in line. "If you can excuse me for just a moment…"

The woman wanted me to stay. I saw the

disappointment in her eyes, and I knew I should.

"I'll be right back," I promised. The front door bell jingled as I clutched Raymond's book. I heard it close as I rounded the table. David appeared. He was there in front of me before I could move farther, his cheeks flushed from the cool of the outdoors.

"Where is he?" I asked. I pressed the book against my chest, looking past David, listening for footsteps or the door's bell to ring again.

"He left. Oddest thing. He didn't wait."

"What did he say? Is he coming back?"

"Don't know for sure. Guess it doesn't matter much to him, or he would have stayed." David came near, glanced toward the front door, then back at me.

I looked at his face, the rather ordinary face that was composed the way Mama said a good man's face should be. Staid. Expressionless, businesslike, bent toward doing right, never wavering, never veering any unexpected way—never away at all. Always here. He removed his hat, revealing a neat circle creased around his straight blond hair where the hatband had rested. He handed the hat to Gretchen, then removed his coat and laid it in her arms.

"Honestly, all he did was ask if you were in here signing books, when I came up to the store. Said he had one, so I told him he could get your signature easier if he let me get it for him. That way he could save some time and spare himself a little embarrassment."

I heard, and I wondered if Raymond had heard, the hint of dismissal in David's tone, the thin tolerance of the book I'd written and insisted on publishing. I looked past David toward the window glass of the front door. I circled around his puzzled look, walked to the front, and stood with my face close to the glass, small dots of steam forming where I breathed as I watched. Raymond had been here. But then he had gone. Again.

"More women here for Martha's book signing than I expected," I heard David say to Gretchen. They'd moved with me and were standing behind me now, not too far away. "I would never have believed it. In fact, when I came here instead of going to lunch, I wondered if she'd already be gone." David paused. I could feel his eyes on my back. "I think the guy was probably relieved not to have to come in and get that book signed for his wife. Or girlfriend. He never said which one. When I told him why I was here, and that I could get it for him, he looked down at the book and started flipping through it. Messed with the pages, like he'd changed his mind. I think he would have left without getting it signed if you hadn't stuck your head out the door. I decided for the poor guy, then. Just took it and handed it to you. When you disappeared into the store with it, he just left. I doubt he'll be back to pick it up."

Four women hurried along the sidewalk and approached the door, copies of my book clutched in their hands. I held the door open for them, wide, letting the scent of the city rush in, the energy of the people, the sound of a train. *Want to see a picture of the girl I plan to marry?* I smiled at each woman as she entered, breathing deep, wondering if it was there—his scent— but it wasn't. The women disappeared into the bookstore, their happy babble blending with the soft tones already there. The door closed behind them as I glanced once again at the street. A wife. A girlfriend. Raymond hadn't said which.

David stepped alongside me. I felt his arm drape

Colleen L. Donnelly

around my shoulders. We stood there, watching people pass by on the walk. "You'll be done by five?" he asked. He stood a little closer, his arm wrapping a little tighter. "I'm coming back to pick you up then and take you home. Your mother's making a special supper tonight. Special supper, special night."

I glanced at him, saw a slight flicker in his eyes. David had a plan. In Raymond's eyes it would have been a flame; he would have had a surprise. I looked away from David's flicker and put away Raymond's flame. "Of course. Go on back to work for now," I said. "There are enough books to be signed to keep me busy until five o'clock. I'll be looking forward to this evening."

David took his coat from Gretchen and slipped it on. He set his hat on the creased ring that was still in his hair. "Until this evening, then, my dear," he said as he opened the door. "It will be good."

Chapter 3

"It's almost time to close and lock up." Gretchen leaned against my table. The crowd had thinned, and only four books were left—three on the table and the illustrated one in my bag. "I've never hosted such a well-attended book signing before. Ever. Your book is a marvelous success."

Gretchen lifted one of the three off the table, ran the palm of her hand over the cover as if she was absorbing it. "It's a really good book. Too bad my husband didn't read it." She sighed.

I knew her husband, John, and he would never read a book like mine. In fact, he'd avoided the signing—left Gretchen with specific instructions as to how it should be run, then gone. I smiled at her. She'd done an excellent job, even without him there.

"You chose one of my favorite parts to read aloud this afternoon," she said, laying the book back on the table. "The part where your hero, Jacob, saw Eloise's flaw as his instead of hers. He became a true prince at that moment, for me."

I'd given my heroine, Eloise, a flaw—one leg just slightly shorter than the other—the difference exaggerated by the padding her mother packed in her shoe every day, and the endless coaching her mother gave her on how to walk, how to stand, how to do her best to look just like everyone else.

"We can all identify with hidden flaws," Gretchen tapped a finger on my book's cover. "That one little thing we're so sure will drive our prince away." She straightened and looked around the store. "I'll start cleaning up. You want the rest of the cookies to take home to your mother and father?"

The bookstore's clock chimed, one sound to let us know it was a quarter to five. I looked away from Gretchen to the clock's ornate face and hands. The day was done. Fifteen more minutes and the doors would be locked. Fifteen more minutes for Raymond to return for the book I was to sign for his wife. Not his girlfriend. David didn't know him, didn't know it was for Raymond's wife.

But I did.

I looked back at Gretchen. "No, you keep the cookies for you and John. I'm sure he'll enjoy them." Mama wouldn't appreciate having those cookies in her house, and neither would I. Not now. Daddy'd be happy to have a few, but what he didn't eat would lie on the cabinet top until they dried out, after which Mama would throw the rest away. The sooner my book and anything associated with it was out of her life and mine, the better. I shook my head, imagining Mama's face if I brought them home, as I warded off Gretchen's second offer. I glanced at the clock again—4:48 p.m. Twelve more minutes. "I'll help you clean up."

"No, no. You sit. Someone might still come in." Gretchen protested as the clock continued to tick.

My heart picked up its cadence, tried to hurry it along. Tick-tock. Tick-tock. Tick-tock. I hummed as I stacked the three books at the end of the table, capped the ink bottle, and cleaned the pen. I hummed louder than the clock as I helped Gretchen box the cookies, rinse the cups and saucers, and replace the chairs that had been arranged in an arc around where I had earlier read.

Gretchen brushed her hands together as we stood near each other and looked the bookstore over. "Looks perfect." She scrutinized the area. "No one would even know the best signing I've ever had took place right here." She looked at me. "You're writing another book, I hope."

The bell on the front door tinkled, a breeze from the chilly early evening air swept inside. I looked the direction of the door. Stared through bookshelves and tried to breathe. *No, no more books. I've already decided that. Unless...* I listened, waited to see who had come through the door. *I could...maybe I could write another book.* Footsteps entered the store. The door closed, and the footsteps came our way. I watched. I waited. *A sequel, maybe, one with a true happy ending, one that really happened and that I didn't have to make up just so I could move on.*

"You're ready. Good. Your mother will have supper waiting. We don't want to be late." David rubbed his hands together and smiled his approval.

Gretchen touched my shoulder. "You go on. Sounds like someone has some special plans. All that's left to do here is count the day's income and lock up, and John will come help with that." She walked around David toward the front door. I went for my coat. *No more books. I am done.* I put my coat on, shrugging one arm in and then the other. I lifted my satchel, and walked to David.

"That fellow come back for his book?" he asked.

I shook my head as I pressed the satchel against my side, the small rectangular shape of Raymond's book beneath my hand. Just like the one I'd signed earlier today for the young girl—love, or the hope of it, tucked and hidden away in a bag. Where no one can take it from you—you have to give it to them. And hope they give it back to you. Which they don't always do.

"I didn't think he would." David turned toward the bookstore's front door. "Too late now."

David steered me out of the store. It was too late. Raymond hadn't come back. Just like before. He left me behind with only pictures. And memories. He didn't return, just like he hadn't returned my love.

Just like before.

Chapter 4

I paused as David and I entered the front door to my parents' house, my house also until next spring, when David and I would be married. No one said a word. I listened and waited for a shout, a "Surprise," even a "Congratulations," but there was nothing. Nothing special like David had hinted. We removed our coats in the quiet. No one approved of what I'd done today, except maybe my father. He was generally quiet, but not the sort of quiet that felt like disapproval. We hung our jackets on the nearby rack. I leaned behind it, tucked my satchel out of sight on the floor, straightened, and glanced at David.

"Didn't you say tonight was…" I leaned close in a whisper.

"Time to eat," Mama broke into my question from the back of the house. David nudged my elbow, and steered me into the dining room, where Mama and Daddy were standing behind their chairs at opposite ends of the table. Mama clutched her hands together and grinned. "Well, let's everyone sit down."

David rounded the table and took the chair across from me, the one Mama had decreed as his ever since Daddy first brought him home from work over a year ago.

"Long day?" my father asked after we were settled. He handed me a bowl of mashed potatoes, and I caught the meaning in his blue eyes. Long meant good to Daddy, it was his definition of a day well spent, a day enjoyed, and one that was successful. I smiled at him, and the gentle specialness he brought to the end of a day that had indeed been long. And hard.

"Too long," Mama cut in before I could say anything. "Let's fill our plates and ask the blessing."

I gave Daddy a private nod. He didn't need to know my day hadn't been the sort of long he hoped.

Platters and bowls circulated the table as we filled our plates. When every dish had been around, we bowed our heads as Daddy prayed. When he finished, our mealtime noises resumed—the rattle of glass, the heaviness of pottery, the clink of silverware against one or the other.

"Got a special order today," my father finally said, without looking up. I caught the word "special" and glanced his direction. I watched him scoot corn toward his mound of mashed potatoes with his fork and press the kernels into its side like an artistic strategy against erosion. "Not the first one, but this one was large. Medals. For the war heroes, but still, at least it's not ammunition casings. Thank God those days are over."

David nodded, and he gave an "amen" to my father's sentiment. David hadn't fought overseas; he'd joined my father as an apprentice while the battles were going strong. My father was a master craftsman of metal work, a skill he used for small ornate items in times of peace, but one that had been converted to war purposes not long after the conflict began. David's assistance during the extra load created by the combat made him invaluable. By the time it was over, David's ability to manage a company had shone through, and so he stayed—a permanent fixture in my dad's business, at my mother's table, and now, in my future.

I arranged my corn the same way my father did, a mosaic of vegetables, as David picked up on the news Daddy had shared about the order and why it was special. "This is the beginning of good times ahead; at least that's what my father would have said if he was still alive and watching this small turn toward a post-war economy." David paused. I could see numbers and calculations in his thoughts. Whereas my father was an artisan who worked from the heart, David was a businessman who worked from his head—or his father's head. David and my father were opposites, but the blend was beneficial and caused my father's business to grow and flourish.

Mama's eyes glistened, and her head nodded with approval as David started up again to run on about the benefits of such an order. I glanced at my father, happy for his and David's long day, understanding now why our suppertime was so special. Daddy was focused on his corn, his fork cementing the last few kernels into the bank of potatoes as he listened to David's predictions for future transactions. Daddy nodded. Not vigorously, but he nodded again, until finally he stopped nodding and took a bite. David was good at what he did. I could see it in Daddy's willingness to listen to what he said and Mama's satisfaction that David fit her definition of what a suitable man was. I looked up and listened, and nodded also, until David was finished and our meal was done.

"So," David said, as he wiped his mouth with a napkin. Mama clasped her hands together again, her eyes sparkling as she looked from David to me. "All of this, and more, leads us to why tonight is special."

I nodded. "I can see that. I can see why it's special. Those orders are wonderful news, and I'm very happy for both of you."

Mama reached over and squeezed one of my hands. "Shush for a bit. You listen to what David has to say."

I frowned. I glanced across the table to see David watching me. Daddy cleared his throat to my left. I heard his silverware settle on his plate, and when I glanced his way he was folding his napkin in little triangles until it was thick enough to wedge under the edge of his plate.

"As I was saying," David continued. "Special orders and significant endings lead to special events." David stood. He gazed down and across the table at me, his arms straight, his fingertips perched on the table's top. "Because of this positive turn in business, because of the end of the war, and because today you finally put all of your notions about writing aside, I see no reason to wait until spring to be married. I know we had plans to have the wedding next April, but I've moved it to three weeks from today. Well, three weeks and a day, if you count the wedding day. Before the holidays. Martha, you and I will be married November twentieth."

My mouth fell open. I felt the unladylike gape that Mama, for once, didn't try to correct. I stared at David.

"Everything's been taken care of." Mama spoke from my right. "Once David knew you truly were going to be done with that book, he had me check the church for availability, and it's free. Ida Mae already had your gown cut out for April. She just has to get it sewn together a little sooner."

David smiled down at me. "Your mother took care of practically all of the major things. There are still lots of little things to do, so you'll have plenty to keep you busy, but all of the big obstacles are out of the way. Primarily having financial security, and you moving forward to more important things than novels. So November twentieth is the day. You'll be Mrs. David Tidwell, and I'll be the same excellent husband and provider my own father was. I promise."

Chapter 5

David led me to the sofa after our special supper and his special suppertime announcement. I no longer gaped outwardly, but I did inwardly, words lost—none would come. In my silence, Mama could be heard, two rooms away, where Daddy stayed with her to take my place and help clear the table and scrub the dishes. Mama's voice was clear, enthusiastic as she hailed our new plans and a little gritty as she closed out my old. Almost as gritty as those scouring pads she swore by, when she mentioned my book. Scrubbing away, doing her best to rub out any lingering stains so I could shine in three weeks and a day when I became David's wife.

I glanced at the coat rack as her timbre wafted into the room, gazed at my satchel behind it. Mama really didn't need to work so hard to rid me of something that was already gone.

David reached for my hand, a gentle cupping motion as he draped his fingers over mine. He never held on tight like he was saving or protecting me. It was more of a gesture of right, like signing his name on a document and managing what was his. Mama said this was real love. Right. Responsible. What a family was made of.

Mama's monologue continued from the kitchen, the next three weeks and a day becoming a verbal rosy path toward the big event she'd worried would never happen. Warmth from David's hand seeped into my skin, a tiny canopy of radiance as we both listened.

"I think you'll like the latest furniture I bought," he said.

I glanced up. Mama's noises faded into the background as the big event loomed to life. I'd be living in his house with that furniture in three weeks plus one day.

"I think the sofa would be better across from the front windows rather than under them," he said. "I like to look at the light, not have it at my back. I think I'll move it."

Three weeks. One day. Mrs. David Tidwell. "I can come help you…"

"No, I can manage. Of course once it's moved, we'll need to put that lamp you set by the chair somewhere else. Maybe near the sofa, since there will be less light to read by on that side of the living room."

"Should we get another lamp?" I turned my hand over so our palms faced each other. I threaded my fingers through his, letting his warmth dry the clamminess on mine.

"I'll pick one out," he said. "But you could contribute your book money to that, if there's enough." He turned to the side and looked at me. "I doubt you made much, but is there enough for one lamp?"

One lamp? I bit my lips, pinched them together. I'd made enough for a dozen lamps. Maybe more. I nodded.

"Once we use up your money on the lamp, this book stuff will be completely over for good," he continued. "It's okay to use it to buy a little something to help us get started. Of course we'd have had more to spend if you'd just gone to your secretarial job today. In any case, from now on you can focus on being my wife. And eventually on being the mother of my children." He squeezed my hand. "The money-making will be up to me after that, and I'll take good care of us."

"Gretchen did ask if I'd write another book." I stared at our hands.

David tipped his head back. I glanced up to see him peer down his nose as if he had to get a better look at me. "Well, no, to that," he said, a tiny frown crinkling his staid expression. "I assume you told her that."

I looked back down at our hands and the way they were entwined. "I didn't, but it doesn't matter. I'm not writing another." To David and Mama that part of my life was sealed and done as of today, when in actuality it had ended the moment I saw the photo in Raymond's lunchbox. I stopped writing my romance that day, stopped writing altogether until I finally forced myself to finish the book, creating pure fiction from that point until the end so I could put it all away forever and cleanse myself of Raymond. I laid my other hand on top of David's. I had no more words of my own to write. From now on it would just be others' words at my secretarial job. Until I became pregnant, expecting our first child. After that, there would be no more others' words, either, just life and living, and taking care of the people I was responsible for.

Our hands blurred. Tiny half-moons of moisture gathered in my lower lids.

"Fresh start and new life," David said. He smiled as he let go of my hand and stood. I watched him lift his coat off the rack and slide first one arm and then the other into it. "Just twenty-two more days. They will go fast." He shook his head as he fastened his buttons. When he finished, he turned to me and extended his arm and open hand my direction.

I latched on and rose to join him at the front door as he opened it. I glanced outdoors, the porch and the yard all glowing in that same crescent of moisture, cradled in a hazy curve of unwelcome tears.

"I'll give you money for the new lamp tomorrow," I promised, batting the dampness away. "It's late, or I'd get it for you now…"

"Tomorrow's fine." He clasped me by the shoulders and pecked me on the forehead. "Sweet dreams."

I closed the door behind him, listened until his footsteps faded down the front steps and along our walk. I waited, then turned to where my satchel lay behind the coat rack.

The half-moon of moisture returned as I clutched the bag, brought it to my side, and made my way through misty steps up the stairs to my bedroom.

"Goodnight," my father called. His voice made it sound like a question, instead of a wish, as I passed his and Mama's bedroom door in the upstairs hall.

"Goodnight. Pleasant sleep." Tears pooled on my lower lashes, making them cool and heavy as I hurried on to my room. I kicked off my shoes as I closed my bedroom's door behind me, and I crawled into bed without undressing. Leaning back against my headboard, I tented the blanket over my raised knees, drew from my bag the book I had written and Raymond had illustrated, and propped it against my legs as if they were a lectern. I gazed at the cover before I opened it, staring at his name. Then I flipped through the pages, watching his drawings flick past, until everything dissolved in tears. I turned off the light and burrowed under my blankets, letting our book drop to the floor beside my bed. I cried away the dewy crescent, my illusions of writing, my delusions of Raymond, and all the qualms over whether I was ready to make David a suitable wife.

Chapter 6

"How about this one?" My best friend, Karen, held up a blue floral tablecloth. "This would look nice on the reception table, don't you think?" Her nails, filed down to mere nubs, lined up in a perfect row where her fingers clamped over the package's top. I glanced from her nails to her face. "Gear shifts are tricky," she said, tucking her fingers tighter into the bundled fabric. "And we're not here to discuss how my nails look. We're here because you have a rapidly approaching wedding." She extended the tablecloth in my direction, her fingernails hidden from view. I tried not to smile. Karen wasn't fastidious, but she was always well-groomed, her auburn hair in a smart wave and shining, her clothing well-fitted and making a statement that was one half-step bolder than the young women around her. And her nails were generally long.

"You really are learning to drive?"

"You know I have to. Until my father gets back."

Back from the postwar work he'd been called to overseas. She omitted that because we both already knew he'd accepted a position that left Karen and her mother with challenges neither one ever expected to face on their own. He'd left them with what money they had, and the promise he'd send what he could, and that everything would turn out fine. "Everything will be fine," Karen told me often. "He won't be gone that long." But now she was learning to drive, and her nails were no longer the lengthy beauties they'd always been.

I turned from staring at her to gazing at the tablecloth she held up, from pondering her nails and the fact she was learning to drive to the changes that faced both of us. I tilted my head, first to one side and then the other, narrowing my eyes as I studied the cloth. Three weeks from today. Mrs. David Tidwell. I shook my head. "I'm not sure it's the right shade of blue."

Karen peered over the package at me. I could tell by her eyes she'd puckered her lips. It was her way, a slight pursing that said she was considering me, not judging me.

I unclasped and re-clasped my pocketbook. "I know, I can't afford to be choosy this close to the wedding."

Mama'd told me that this morning before Karen came by to help me shop for the last few items I needed.

Karen set the tablecloth back on the stack. She sorted through the others, searching for just the right size, the right shade, the right everything to make this wedding successful.

"Maybe just white?" Karen dragged a plain tablecloth from the bottom of a pile. She held it up. There was nothing to see, really, nothing to make it a difficult decision. I shrugged. I nodded. Then I shrugged again. She tucked it under her arm. "Okay, plain white. Maybe some colored napkins to set it off."

"Sure, colored napkins. That's a fantastic idea." I nodded as I spoke, both attempts to comply, both a little too vigorous. Karen glanced up, the tiny frown on her face bringing a quick end to my efforts. "I'm sorry. I'm not quite myself. Kind of overwhelmed by all of this rush. Thank you for being a good maid of honor. I don't mean to make things difficult for you." I waited for her to smile and nod. We'd always moved in perfect synchronization, Karen and I, side by side throughout childhood, supporting and understanding each other without arguments or lengthy discussions. The frown stayed longer than it should have as she turned back to the linens and moved farther down the display. She paused at the napkins and flipped through the first stack, searching for the right color to go with the invisible tablecloth.

"Mama took care of the big things for us, thank goodness." I fidgeted with the stack next to hers. She didn't look up. I really didn't need to say anything; it was information Karen already had. "She took care of the church, the flowers, found a friend to take pictures, even enlisted her Ladies' Aid group to provide the cake and the punch. I don't know what I'd have done without her." I trailed Karen, doing my part to help by sorting through the wedding itinerary as she rifled through the next stack of napkins, the white tablecloth squeezed tight under one arm.

Karen paused at a bundle of bright red napkins. She glanced back at me, one eyebrow arched, her fingers on the crimson pack. "Ruby red?"

I shook my head. "Mama'd never survive that color."

"Near-death experiences are good for people. At least they're supposed to be." The arch of her brow leveled into a pensive frown.

"Near-death experiences are good for people? What do you mean by that?"

She looked at me, leaving the napkins behind. "You know—when something shakes us out of our shells. Makes us go places and do things we never expected. Makes us bigger and better than we were."

Her expression told me what things she was talking about. Things I'd done while Raymond was still fresh in my heart, things I'd done to avoid letting that passion die. Things that hadn't helped in the end, and that I was leaving behind. I thought of Karen's broken nails along with my broken heart. "Like driving?" I asked, fidgeting with a package of pale mint-colored napkins.

"Like driving." Karen's lips pursed again, then straightened. "When you're afraid to. And like writing when no one wants you to, like chasing after someone or something you lost, like going to and surviving a war, like watching your daughter succeed as a writer when you're against romance, like falling in love and getting married in three fast weeks. Painful, like ruby red, but supposedly good."

We stared at each other. I lifted the pale mint-colored napkins and held them up for her to see. Karen took them from my hand and deposited them back on top of the pile.

"What's wrong with mint?" I asked, reaching for the napkins.

Karen blocked my hand with hers, splaying her fingers across the top of the stack. Her hand didn't move, and neither did her eyes as she continued to stare at me. "Mint is nice and white is safe." She nodded toward the tablecloth still pinched under her arm. "I know time is short, but neither one is you. It's like being embalmed before you're really dead, that's what's wrong with mint. Take your time; choose what you want; no one will actually die. Not even you. And everyone should be the better for it in the end."

I stared at the stacks of linens, the assortment of colors pinned under Karen's hand. My shoulders drooped. I folded like a tired accordion as I looked from the napkins down the aisle—everywhere except at my friend. "It's just for a wedding. Mint and white make good wedding colors, and that's all I need for now."

Karen removed her hand from the stack, leaned against the counter, and shook her head. "You, Martha Cole, wrote an amazing book. There was nothing bland or ordinary about it. If you weren't mint green and white when you wrote the book, why would you be mint green and white for your wedding?"

"Because I'm changing..." It sounded like a question. I fidgeted with the stack of napkins in front of me. "Like you are with driving. You have to change."

Karen tilted her head to the side. I saw it in my peripheral vision as I ran my finger around the top package's edges. "I have to drive," she finally said. "To run errands, to save train and streetcar fares, to have a way for Mother and me to get somewhere if we suddenly need to. And I'll have more of these before I finally master it." She raised a stubby-nailed finger for me to see. "I'm terrifying my mother and myself in the meantime. I'll probably dent the car, and I've offended our neighbor man, who told me it was wrong for women to learn to drive. It's far more near death than I ever wanted. But"—she lifted her finger again—"these will grow back, and I'll wear them the way I want. But stronger next time, and with the added ability to shift gears around them."

"What I had won't grow back," I said. "It's

different." What I had was gone—not just near death, but dead. What I'd thought was love hadn't been. What I had now wasn't stronger or with any added abilities, but it was right. Different. Changed.

Karen frowned. She drew the white tablecloth from beneath her arm and held it up between us. "See this? This suits your mother. Maybe even David." She fished the red napkins from their stack and held them up alongside the bland tablecloth. "But these are you. These are the heart of passion that lived, wrote, and signed your book. The object of your book may be gone, but you aren't. Your heart's been through a lot, and that means it's ready to pump harder and beat stronger. And if you don't let it, it's going to bleed out and soil this white tablecloth."

I stared at the red on the white, the heart I couldn't let bleed or pump like it had when I began my book. The one that was hammering inside my chest, the one that had finished everything pertaining to *Love on a Train*, and the one that would never live or write something like that again. "I'm going to be a wife now, and wives don't write books. Not like that. They don't let their emotions get in the way of what's sound. Wives are white and mint green, not red."

"Most women don't write at all," Karen said. "But you did. And we're talking about you." She laid the tablecloth and napkins on top of the piles.

I stared down at them. The heart that wrote *Love on a Train* could never raise a dozen children. That would take a different sort of heart. One that was capable of arranging furniture, purchasing napkins, and baking cookies.

"I know you don't intend to keep writing after

you're married," Karen continued. "But you still have to be you, even when you're a wife." Her gaze softened. "I always thought you would, though, you know, keep writing somehow. Finish *Love on a Train* for real. For yourself, not just to sell. Write your own happily-ever-after instead of the fictional one everyone loved."

"That's what I'm doing." I swiped a tear from my eye, one that appeared from nowhere. "I'm changing so I can live my happily-ever-after, instead of writing one."

The for-real ending Karen wanted was already done. Lived and written, it just hadn't been by me. I'd seen it last night when I looked at Raymond's version of my book—words and sentences he'd added alongside some of his drawings, especially toward the end. I couldn't bear to read them. I couldn't even bring myself to look at his sketches. It was enough to know it was over. The story. The hope that had lived in my heart—that little piece of Raymond that had never gone away even though I'd thought it did. The whole book—his parts, my parts, my feelings I'd mistaken for love. Everything was tucked inside my nightstand's drawer until I could throw it away. Sometime soon.

Sometime between buying mint green napkins and saying, "I do."

Chapter 7

"Martha Cole, I'd like you to meet Harvey Wilson." My boss, Mr. Arnold, gestured toward the tall man who rose from one of Mr. Arnold's office chairs. "He is working on, well, sort of a patent, an innovative construction idea through a local law firm that specializes in patents. It's based on bridge designs, like the structures he observed when overseas during the war."

"Miss Cole," Harvey said, extending a hand to shake mine. "Mr. Arnold highly recommends you for your dictation skills. He says you're the best in his office, and I need someone like you. I hope you'll listen to my proposal and consider devoting your time particularly to me and this project."

Mr. Wilson's hand was huge and powerful as it wrapped around mine. I was grateful for its strength as I leaned into it. Bridges. War. Overseas. It was as if Raymond had stepped into the room—those words, his voice, overriding what I really heard. I left my hand in Mr. Wilson's as I forced myself to focus. I listened to him the way I'd learned to as a secretary, the back of my mind recording his words while my forebrain pieced together what they meant. Bridge project. That's what my forebrain tackled first. That's what it homed in on. Memories of train rides and getting to know Raymond, days when he talked about his job, the construction he did, the excitement that danced in his eyes when he spoke of bridges and how they were pieced together.

"Have a seat, please, Martha." Mr. Arnold drew a chair near the front of his desk, pointed it so that it angled toward him and Mr. Wilson. I let go of Mr. Wilson's hand and sat with a pad and pencil on my lap, bridges and Raymond still plaguing my mind.

Mr. Wilson folded his lengthy body into the chair not far from mine. He inched it forward, his eagerness like Raymond's, that enthusiasm shining in his hazel eyes the same way it had burned in Raymond's dark ones. "I was in the war," he began, "not a fighter, but an officer. I plotted and planned. I had the advantage of observation through thousands of other eyes, and the ability to sit back and piece it all together."

I wondered if Raymond had been one set of those eyes as Harvey broke down the details of European bridge construction compared to ours. He explained their strengths and their weaknesses, and his plan to incorporate what he'd learned into a new design.

"Higher is stronger," I said. Mr. Wilson stopped. He and Mr. Arnold stared at me. I blushed. It was something Raymond always said, and there it was, in my mind and out of my mouth as if he'd said it to me only yesterday. On a train. Near each other… I glanced at the two men. I should tell them about Raymond and that he explained higher-is-stronger as a law of physics for bridges, at least his law of physics. I should lay Raymond out there as a fact, a tool, another piece of engineering Mr. Wilson could use and then put aside. I glanced down at my blank pad where I hadn't taken a single note. I blushed even more. "I'm sorry," I said, willing my cheeks back to their normal color. "Forgive me for interrupting you. It won't happen again. But, before you go on, did Mr. Arnold tell you I'm getting married soon? Just short of three weeks from now. I only told him recently; the change is sudden. I'll be gone for that..." I refrained from mentioning the honeymoon and how long I'd be away from work, knowing the inference would make my cheeks flush even hotter.

Mr. Wilson nodded, then looked at Mr. Arnold, and nodded again. He turned back to me and leaned forward, propping his elbows on his knees, bringing his face close. Close enough I could see the flecks of amber in his eyes.

"You're exactly what I need," he said. "I can see that now. And I'm willing to work around your wedding. My wife would have me hung if I didn't." He grinned. "Just come with me for now, and take notes while I visit attorneys and engineers. After you get married and come back from your...well, after all of your wedding and such, we'll resume. We'll even begin traveling to other locations. I'll make it well worth your while financially."

He'd respected my modesty, hadn't made mention of the honeymoon, but, still, I would protest his offer. I would decline, even knowing David would be in favor of more income for a while, maybe even proud. He liked success. He would appreciate the extra money, money earned in this legitimate way instead of by writing another book. He would consider it a plus until we started having children. After which we'd stick to our agreement that I'd become a full-time mother. "I don't think..."

"Of course, of course," Harvey straightened in his chair. "Ask your husband-to-be first, by all means. I'll give you a figure before I leave. Let you know what I'm willing to pay you above and beyond Mr. Arnold's salary, which he will continue. You show your fiancé that, and I'm sure he'll agree."

I nodded. But no amount of money could brace me enough to go to locations, places where bridges were being built, places Raymond may have been. Or may be again. Not even a new last name could gird me for that. Nor could any wedding ring on my finger or Raymond's, either. "Yes, sir," I replied. I couldn't. I wouldn't. No matter that my heart pumped madly. No matter what David said. I'd never work with Harvey Wilson.

Chapter 8

"Of course you should take this job." David's hands were stuffed into his coat pockets. He watched the sidewalk in front of us as we walked quickly, side by side in the brisk evening air, to a wrap-up meeting at the church where we were to be married. "They understand you won't be working there once our family begins, right?" He glanced my way, puffs of steam bringing emphasis and visibility to his words in the air.

"Yes, I've made that clear. Mr. Arnold knew even before he recommended me." I looked down at the sidewalk, our feet hurrying us from Mama's supper table to my family's Lutheran church, where Pastor Reynolds waited. He had insisted we meet with him before he agreed to marry us. David was Baptist but was willing to convert. Pastor Reynolds had set out to be certain, already having spent much time with us laying out the Lutheran doctrine, making sure that at least spiritually we were one.

"Evidently Mr. Arnold thinks a lot of your work." David's voice sounded approving. I felt him gaze down at me as he moved a bit closer, still plowing us forward as he did. The church's sign appeared less than a block ahead, its name on a plaque imbedded in a stone slab, the same type of stone the church had been built from. "It will be a little extra money for us. Help us get ready for having kids."

"It seems silly, though, don't you think? I mean, the job sounds so specialized, it's a shame to train me when I won't be there that long." I tugged at my lower lip, hoping, praying, David would see the sense in what I said.

"I know women aren't cut out for jobs the way men are," he said. His footsteps slowed. "But this is a tribute to you. Your boss and Mr. Wilson know what they're doing. If they chose you, then take them up on the offer. Just do your best until the first baby makes its presence known. That's it, after that. Your secretary days are over from that moment on."

David slowed his pace even more. I moderated mine to match his. I was thinking of babies, of our future together, of what sort of mother I'd be, and what sort of father he'd be. Mama'd always said he was designed to be a good husband, that he had everything it took. I glanced to the side at him, studying the everything I knew about him—his precision, his determination, the way he scheduled and organized life. He said it was the way his father had done things. His father was gone before David came to work for Daddy, so I'd never met him. But I'd met David's mother. She seemed organized also, the way I felt organized when David was around.

I shoved my hands deeper into my pockets as we turned onto the church's walkway, went up the front steps, and into the foyer. What if David's organization and Pastor Reynolds' indoctrination weren't enough? What if Karen was right, and I was still red while David was white and mint green?

"David," I whispered. He was loosening his coat. I wrapped a hand around his arm. I whispered his name again, keeping it low so my voice wouldn't echo in the empty foyer. "David?"

He glanced down at me with his staid expression, the one that was always prepared, always on the right path at the right time.

One I could trust. One determined to help me along.

"Never mind," I whispered again. "It's nothing."

Pastor Reynolds stood when we entered his office. I'd never noticed before how much it reminded me of John's and Gretchen's bookstore. I paused just inside the doorway, noting the warm cozy lighting, walls lined with spine after spine of reading material, the soft scent of yellowed pages and dusty light globes filling the air. I turned, looked at all the books that stood like soldiers, row after row, and wondered how my book would look there—*Love on a Train.*

"Come in. Hang your coats, and please sit down."

My face flushed at Pastor Reynolds' voice.

We hung our coats on a rack in the corner, then each took one of the cushioned chairs facing Pastor Reynolds' desk.

"We've covered nearly everything in our previous sessions," Pastor said as he straightened papers and books on top of his desk. "Doctrine, and how it impacts church attendance, tithing, submission in the home, and children." He glanced at each of us before straightening his stacks again. He leaned his elbows on the desk in the clearing he'd created, and stretched forward. "And I have a full commitment on both of your parts to all we've discussed, right?"

I saw David nod to my left. My commitment had been cemented years ago as a child. It was David's that

Pastor Reynolds was interested in, but I nodded along with him because we were about to become one.

"Good. I thought as much, but I wanted to give you the opportunity to express any doubts. So tonight I'll give you the chance to ask me questions, if you have any. Certainly about anything we've already discussed, but also..." He cleared his throat. "But also about, well, whatever else might be on your minds. More personal types of questions, if that's the case, matters that might present some difficulties if left undiscussed."

I swallowed. I was sure everyone heard it. I stared at my knees with nothing to ask and nothing to say, but I could still see Pastor Reynolds looking from David to me, then back to David again.

"Whatever you say or ask will never leave this room," his voice assured us. "I'm here to help make sure you are both sound before God and in the church, so now is the time to ask the hard questions, the ones you may be afraid to voice any other time."

"You're referring to her book, aren't you?" David straightened in his seat. "That's what you're worried about."

Heat flashed along with the shock that streaked through me. My book? But I was done with that. It was over, and David knew that. The color drained from my face as I listened for David to continue and tell the pastor not to worry. My color receded farther in the silence, even my fingers and toes turning cold. David's question hung like an executioner's axe above my head, neither man saying a thing. I glanced his direction, waiting for him to tell the pastor this was already settled.

"Yes, there is the book." Pastor cleared his throat

as he looked at me. "Your mother expressed some concerns. Such as what path you were on, or would take, after writing such material."

My heart hammered in the silence. The papers and books on Pastor Reynolds' desk began to swirl. *Love on a Train. Eloise's heart fluttered like she was a teenager all over again, girlish anticipation stirring up in her— there she was, a young woman in love, struck nearly senseless by the face of a handsome man.* My heart raced on. I drew in a breath that sounded more like a gasp. I forced it back out, then inhaled again, urging my heart to slow down, even out as it beat—for Eloise, my character, and also for me, the young woman who thought she'd found love on a train but was now sitting in front of her pastor ready to marry another—the one next to her.

I glanced up at the pastor. "It was fiction, about romantic love, but nothing immoral happened in the story."

"Martha, Pastor Reynolds wants our focus to be on real love, not make-believe." David finally spoke from my side. "He wants to make sure you understand the difference and have set the fabricated one aside before we start our home and our family."

You chose one of my favorite parts to read aloud this afternoon. I heard Gretchen in the silence, what she'd told me in her bookstore the evening of my signing. *The part where your hero, Jacob, saw Eloise's flaw as his instead of hers. He became a true prince at that moment, for me.*

David was looking my way, so I turned his. Toward my prince. The one who was to be my hero. I saw on his face the sort of expression that never wavered or changed, solid characteristics that would make him a good husband and a good provider. In his eyes I saw determination. Enough determination that he left me alone on the chopping block so he could make sure I understood, sure our family was going to be sound.

Real love. Not make-believe. Not what I'd felt, not what I'd written about, maybe not what Raymond had added near the end.

"The book won't cause any more harm or make much of an impact anyway," I heard David say to the pastor as an explanation, maybe an excuse for my silence. "Martha is done with writing for good, and the whole thing barely netted a cent in the end." David stretched a hand across the expanse between him and me, and touched my arm. "I never told you this, Martha, but the money you gave me from your book sales—well, it wasn't enough for the lamp I bought. I had to add to it. But that's okay." He patted my arm. "That's how it should be. I'm the main provider. I'll be the only provider once we're established. Pastor, I chose to move the wedding up when I saw that Martha had put the book and writing behind her. You can trust me that I'll make sure our family stays grounded the way it should."

Heat returned to my face as David spoke. I thought of the lamp money I'd given him. And the money I hadn't. My cheeks warmed as I thought of the rest of my profits, tucked into a sock in my dresser drawer. Mills and Boon had mailed my money to the bookstore, where Gretchen kept it until the day of the book signing. She'd given not only their money to me, but also a bonus from my book's sales. "We don't normally do this," she'd said, "but your book has done so well in our store that John gave me permission to share some of it with you." I thanked her, and before I could carry the money to my satchel, she stopped me. "There's something else," she added. "From Mills and Boon. They want you to write another book. More than just one other, actually." She handed me a stack of official letters and envelopes with their name on each one. "And so do I."

The cadence of her words struck up inside of me. My heartbeat fell in with the rhythm. I'd felt it before, and I could feel it now. *And so. Do I. And so. Do I.* The rhythm of a train, its beat on the tracks.

"That's good," Pastor said to David. He sounded relieved, as if he could breathe a little easier now that he had been assured the book issue was settled. "I mean, it's for the best that you've put it all behind you and will keep it that way, now that you're starting your family." The pastor was watching me. I could feel his stare, so I looked up. I knew I should nod. He waited. This was the moment to confess, to admit to the money I'd hidden away, or to just agree with everything they said, but all I could think of was Eloise. Her heartache and mine as we searched for and tried to understand love. I stared at Pastor Reynolds. I watched him watch me. He glanced down for a second, then cleared his throat. "I know you'd never do anything like this, Martha, but you must realize that any sort of passion not centered toward your husband would be...well, it would be wrong."

"I could never write a book like that about David." The words were out of my mouth before they were even a thought. I could see on Pastor's face this was as good as confessing that what lay behind me was wrong. Wrong, as in tainted, not wrong as in impossible. And impossible was what I realized I meant.

"Good, good," Pastor said. "I would hope not."

David relaxed in his chair while I stared at the pastor, at my husband-to-be, and finally at my lap. At my fingers. At hands that had always loved to write.

"So, any other questions?" Pastor Reynolds asked. "Or thoughts?"

I shook my head. I wound my hands together, laced finger through finger, and held them in a ball that looked like it would never write again. Never expose what pounded in my heart.

"I think we'll be fine," David said. "I think we're ready to tie the knot."

Chapter 9

The cold inside me stung more than the wind outside as David walked me home from our meeting with Pastor Reynolds. I wrapped my arms around my chest and shivered against both as we hurried into the biting fall breeze. David dropped an arm around my shoulders, drawing me close as we continued forward, our steps never altering.

"Everything will be okay," he said, snugging me close to his side. "I know how families and life are to be handled."

We climbed the stairs to my parents' front porch and stepped inside the door. He didn't remove his coat. We stood facing each other, he gazing down and me looking up in the quiet of my parents' living room.

"Well, goodnight," I said at last, glancing at his chest and rubbing my arms, trying to dislodge the chill.

His hand rose. He brushed a strand of hair from my face, layering it back with the rest of my hair, nestling it into the wave where it was supposed to be. The strand fell as he removed his hand. He caught it, jabbed at it this time, but still it refused to stay.

"That's okay," I said, tilting my head away from his third attempt. "The wind has probably created its own style."

He dropped his hand, leaving the strand dangling over my forehead. "You understand Pastor Reynolds' concern over your book, don't you?"

I focused on his chest again. "I understand that what I wrote made women feel good, even if it was just a story."

"It was about infatuation, though. Not love. Not real love, anyway, like the pastor expects in a family." He tucked his coat tighter around him. "I promise you you'll be okay. I'll help you figure things out." He leaned my direction, gave me a gentle kiss on top of my head. "You rest. I'll see you tomorrow."

I stepped from the doorway as he strode down the porch steps, and I closed the door between us. I waited for a feeling, any feeling. Reassurance, hope, a flicker of anything that was an indication of real love. Mama said marriage wasn't made of feelings, it was work and devotion. I glanced toward the dining area. I could hear her and Daddy back there talking about nothing, as they often did, staying out of my and David's way, even though he had gone. I wanted to interrupt them, ask my mother if feelings were always wrong, and if having none was really more right. Their voices labored over what Mama had done today, little details that made her a good wife and our house a good home. I knew what her answer to me would be as I listened to the drone. No feelings was what she would tell me was right. No feelings was what I saw on her face most of the time.

"I'll be back soon," I called. Before my parents could respond, I slipped out the door and ran down the sidewalk. Karen lived only a few blocks away. It was dark and it was cold, but it didn't matter. My coat was open, sailing behind me as I ran, ran to her house with my hair flying loose in whatever style the wind chose, that question thundering in my chest.

Chapter 10

The air didn't chill me the way it had earlier when David and I walked to and from the church. I was warmer, somehow, maybe because Karen was at my side this time and because I was in the company of my best friend. She looped her arm through mine as we sauntered forward, feeling safe in the neighborhoods between hers and mine, feeling alive in that space between girlhood and adulthood.

"I have a question," I said. "The other day when we were looking at tablecloths and napkins, you said Mama and David were the white tablecloth and I was the red napkins. You also said I had to find a good way to keep being red or I'd bleed out on their white." I glanced up. Karen was listening, as I knew she would. "To me, red means passion. Feelings like the ones I had when I wrote *Love on a Train*. I'm not having those feelings about getting married to David, so maybe I really did change. Maybe I've stopped being red. If I have, should I expect some other sort of feeling?"

Karen tugged me forward with her arm, drawing me close while swinging the two of us into more of a sashay than a walk. "Well, I imagine you're still red, but when I went home that day, worried about you, my mother told me not to be. She said you're going to be out of sorts right now, not quite grounded in who you are because you're getting married." Her arm tightened and she pulled me even closer. "So don't worry about how you feel. Or don't feel. You're probably still red. It's just all jumbled up with the hurry of getting married."

"So if my feelings aren't quite right, right now, they will be later? Sometime after I'm married? Manageable ones, not the kind like when I wrote *Love on a Train*?"

Karen glanced my way. I could feel the frown in her thoughts. "*Love on a Train* was a beautiful story."

"But just a story, in the end. And too red for what I'll have with David."

Karen moderated her pace. She was thinking, probably pursing her lips as she always did when she was deep in thought. "I expect my mother was right, and you'll be fine. Getting married is a big change. It will be for David, too, when he sees his white tablecloth all spotted with red. But don't worry. Each of you will adjust. Assuming you want to..."

"Of course I do."

Karen glanced my way, and then looked forward again. "Okay, just checking. A good maid of honor always stands by the bride. And maybe what this bride needs is to forget about the wedding for a little bit and relax. Concentrate on walking silly with me for now, the way we used to, and just forget about everything else."

I let her sashay me in wide swings down the walk, broad sweeps that felt like an eraser wiping out where I'd been. I fell into the momentum. I swung hard with her. I did my best to wipe clean everything behind me so I could make a clear path ahead. Start fresh, like David said.

"I can't." I stopped, and Karen jerked to a stop beside me. "I don't mean the silly walk. I can do that. I mean I can't forget everything else. There's so much to do, and things I'm not supposed to do. And I don't think I can do or not do any of it if I'm not feeling right." I dropped Karen's arm and pressed my palms against the sides of my head. "I hope your mother's right, and this is just the wedding jitters. Because I don't feel like a wife right now, and I want to. I should. Do I look like a Mrs. David Tidwell to you?"

Karen peeled my hands from my temples and lowered my arms. In the dim light the shadowed grooves that stretched across her forehead told me she understood that sashaying wasn't what I needed. "Breathe deep," she said. "Inhale. Then exhale." She drew in a deep breath herself, her chest swelling beneath her coat. I did the same. I drew in a breath so overstated my lungs felt like they'd explode.

I let my breath out in a gush and looked at her. "I've never been this way before."

"That's true, you haven't." She continued to frown. "But my mother said this is normal. I want to believe her, too."

"So do I."

Karen linked her arm through mine. She tugged me forward, took us farther down the sidewalk, this time at a slower pace.

"Do I, though?" I asked, looking over at her. "Do I look like a wife, even if I don't feel like one? Is that normal? Is that what real love and marriage are?" My hands twitched. My heart pounded. It wanted to live. Live peaceably alongside the white tablecloth, live satisfied with commitment and a good man.

"You're going to be a wife." Karen tilted her head to the side, gauging her answer instead of me. That's the way she did things, and why I always trusted her. "And when you are one, you'll probably look like one. And feel like one, too."

I glanced down the street. It was too dark to see anything in what little light there was, but I checked anyway. I saw no one and heard nothing. I turned back to Karen. "Maybe my problem is still tied to my book. Maybe if I'd written my real ending to *Love on a Train*, like you said, this wouldn't be happening. The one that ended unhappily, that no one would have wanted to publish or read. Maybe that would help the old me be finished and the new me begin. Mills and Boon could have published the other real one, if they wanted a book. It's probably better." My eyes were wide; I felt their enormity in the dark.

Karen frowned. "Wait a minute. The other real one? Not the ending you said you're looking for with David and wouldn't bother to write?"

"No. Not that one," I whispered. "Mine isn't the only real ending. There's another one. One not by me."

Karen frowned even more. "What do you mean, not by you?"

I pressed my lips together, thinking of the book in my nightstand's drawer. The one I intended to destroy. But hadn't. Yet. "By him. By Raymond, I mean."

Karen's mouth and eyes took on the same shape. Rounded. Agape at what Raymond had done. Agog that his name was even being spoken by us again.

"He showed up at my signing. He's married, or something, according to David, who talked to him. But Raymond brought a copy of my book for me to sign.

David took it from him outside on the sidewalk and had Gretchen give it to me. Raymond disappeared as soon as Gretchen brought it inside the bookstore. He never even came in or waited for me to sign it. He had added to it. Pictures. Ones he'd drawn…with some words here and there, especially toward the end…" My voice cracked in the night air as Karen looked at me. Words vanished, explanations stopped, and sobs erupted instead. Tears emerged without warning, so many they flowed together in one painful stream. "I…I didn't look at his pictures. I couldn't." My voice broke like a child's. "I didn't sign it, either."

Karen's arms swept up and around me. She pressed my face into the shoulder of her winter coat and held me there. The wool scratched; it hurt as I soaked it with tears, but I burrowed deeper in spite of the pain.

"You have to read it," she said near my head. "You have to see all of his drawings, too. Do it. Now. Before your wedding. Go home and read all of it, so you don't miss a thing. Start at the beginning and read clear to the end." She held me for a moment, let me shake and shudder. "Once you read that book, you'll have your answers. And your feelings, also. You can do it. Even with less than three weeks. Go home and get started. Now."

Chapter 11

Karen stopped walking with me at that point. She stayed where she was and sent me off in the direction of my home. To read. If I had hurried away from my parents' house earlier to meet her, I hurried even more back to my house to meet me. In my book—in Raymond's book—in our book. The night air was even more brisk, invigorating, a friend instead of an obstacle as I ran. I smiled as I went, a smile of relief that in my house, in my room, in my nightstand's drawer was the answer to my feelings. I'd finally know. I could finally face who I was, see who I was going to be, and move on. With real feelings and real love.

"Are you all right?" I heard Mama call from the bottom of the stairs as I fled to the top. "Something happen to David? Is that why you ran out of here the way you did?"

David. I lifted my book from the drawer, held it the way Pastor would a hymnal. Pastor Reynolds. David. And now Raymond. All with a piece of my puzzle, all handling a piece of me, all waiting to put theirs into place.

"Martha, is everything okay?" Mama's voice wasn't made for yelling. It jumped up a half octave mid-sentence, then thinned out like a pitiful yodel.

"Yes, Mama." I stood near my closed bedroom door as I yelled back. "I'm fine. Everything's fine.

Going to bed."

Mama was quiet. Her silence uneasy. I knew she was worried. I touched the edge of my book as I waited. The closer the wedding came, the more frantic Mama grew. My book, the fact that I'd written it, bothered her still. The silly love story she'd warned me about was right here in her house, but she didn't need to know that. I was the one who created it; I was the one who had to bring it to an end.

I could hear my father, his soft tenor, as he tried to dissuade Mama from interrogating me further. My father appreciated David, even admired the way David worked, but I thought he never intended for me to marry David when he first brought him home for supper that night. It was Mama who saw that possibility. It was Mama who cut this trail to the altar for me and was determined to keep it clear. Daddy just kept picking up the rubble she created as she did.

Their voices faded as Daddy led her away. I leaned against the door, my back to the wood, my book clutched against my chest, fat with the extra pages Raymond had added. When their voices were gone, I straightened and walked to my bed. I sat, leaned back against the headboard, and stretched my legs out in front of me. *Love on a Train*. I opened the cover, turned page after page until I saw—

One should always have something sensational to read in the train ~Oscar Wilde

The Beginning—1

"Want to see a picture of the girl I plan to marry?"

From those words and that instant, I fell into my story. I was pulled in with the tenacity of quicksand, surrendering to a force too powerful to resist.

Something hidden, something deep inside, shocked me as it responded. It needed to live, to explode, to sink as low as it could go and then burst upward, gasping for air. I needed to breathe, to drink in all that I'd written. Let my emotions, so dried out and listless, swell and rupture with the wetness and new life of tears.

Chapter 12

Although the train moved forward, Eloise Morgan's heart stopped at Jacob's question. Her thoughts stopped also. Even her future crumbled, and lay somewhere on the tracks behind them. Jacob's face was alight with excitement, the sort of vibrancy a man in love would emanate. Eloise peered into his eyes, wishing it were her she saw amidst the flames that danced there. But they were there for someone else, for the girl, whoever she was, that he planned to marry.

She twisted her right foot in her shoe, repositioning the cloths her mother had layered inside it. He probably knew. He'd probably noticed her gait was slightly abnormal no matter how much her mother tried to disguise the shorter leg. Jacob would want someone perfect, someone not hampered by impediments or flaws, no matter how clever she was at hiding them.

Jacob Lane was a little older than she was. He had that look of a man just back from the war, desperate to begin his life anew, something she'd come to understand about him over time, and something she'd sensed the first moment she saw him on the train. One thing Eloise knew for certain that first time, knew as clearly as if God had written it across the heavens, was that Jacob was the man meant for her. She'd nearly stumbled at that first encounter, and clutched at the rags in the bottom of her shoe the way she'd learned to do as a girl, holding on, managing to stagger down the train's aisle past him and find a seat, wishing he'd turn his head away from the window, and the older gentleman he was conversing with, for just a second and glance her direction.

I paused and looked up from my story. Even though I'd called him Jacob, every inch of my hero was Raymond. I even gave him Raymond's black hair, his coal eyes, his dark complexion, and ruddy skin. His height, his weight, the animation I saw in Raymond's every expression, his love of life. It was all there, everything I'd noticed about Raymond in those first few moments were written into Jacob, and pulsing in my memory now. I blushed. Raymond surely recognized himself and knew I'd written this about him. And yet…he was still bold enough to bring a book for me to sign. Even though it was for her.

I listened to my heart in the quiet. I never knew one could beat so guttural, so deep, so singularly. Resurrecting passion hurt. Resurrecting rejection hurt even more.

I glanced down at my book. Raymond would have recognized me, too, even though I'd called my heroine Eloise Morgan, given her lighter hair and a limp so undetectable with rags stuffed into the right shoe that no one should have known. Except Eloise. And her mother, who had coached Eloise on how to stand, how to walk, whether or not she should run, and how her hem should hang. *No one will ever know,* her mother said nearly every day. *Not until you take off your shoe.* She'd never take her shoe off, then, unless she was alone. That's what my heroine grew up to believe, until she saw Jacob. From that moment on she couldn't fathom being alone, just like she couldn't fathom being in a man's company without her shoes. Until Jacob.

He'd begun to sit near Eloise, with time, time that seemed to drag on forever as she watched him and wondered about him. He was there twice a day, morning and night, both of them commuting into and out of the city for their jobs. He was tall, he stood straight, he took notice of everyone and everything as if each moment of life was a gift he'd never tire of. She guessed at first that his vibrancy was because he'd survived the war, but now she knew better. Now she understood that vibrancy was because he was in love. Love was what made him so alive with a passion similar to one she shared—for him, though, rather than with him. Especially now that he'd asked her that question...

The first time their eyes caught, she saw herself in his gaze. It was as if they'd known each other forever. He looked startled as he looked at her, and then he turned away, back to whatever person sat near him, the one fortunate enough to hear his voice and share his day. His glances continued after that, fleeting senses of puzzled recognition until they evolved into a nod, a hello, and finally into words. Little fragments at first, then eventually his name, her name, where they'd gone to school, what their jobs were. "Jacob Lane," he said, and she told him her name was Eloise Morgan, but to herself she was thinking Eloise Lane, Eloise Lane, Eloise Lane, and admiring how perfect it sounded.

She asked about the war, wondering if her guess was right. He said yes, he'd been there, but then he glanced away, relief swallowed by confusion on his face. After that he never talked about the war again, and Eloise never pressed him.

Whenever they spoke, whenever his eyes shone, she strained at her right shoe. She ground against the cloths, wishing they weren't there—actually, weren't necessary. She adopted exercises in the evening, hoping she could stimulate her right leg, cause even a tiny spurt of growth for that moment when she was finally with him, in his presence, without her shoes.

She began re-stuffing her shoe with new cloths, also, folding them more carefully, putting in an extra layer to compensate until the exercises worked. "You're tilted too far. What's wrong?" Her mother noticed the little changes, made Eloise walk back and forth across the living room to see what the problem was, up and down the stairs, and on the sidewalk in front of the house.

Eloise didn't tell her mother about Jacob. He was too perfect, too impossible, too improbable for a girl like her. That's what her mother would say, and then she, too, would add more cloths, or even take some away if she thought that would help. But if Eloise could encourage her leg to grow, if she could find the right amount of padding, she would never have to tell Jacob about her invisible limp, her one flaw. And he wouldn't have to tell her about the war and whatever confounded his expression that time she'd asked. He could savor his thoughts, she could master her stance, and Mama could stop fretting and worrying, sighing that this was the way it would always be for her only daughter.

I stared at that paragraph, also the ones above it, and blushed, remembering how I'd stumbled past Raymond that first time on the train, overcome with emotions I'd never dreamed possible. Like Eloise, my expectations were low for myself, allowing Mama's definition of love—find a good husband and be a good wife—to pave my course.

"Martha, this is David Tidwell."

I laid my book down and stared at my bedroom ceiling, remembering that introduction, recalling the first time my father had brought David home for dinner. David came months before I first laid eyes on Raymond, my father introducing David to Mama and me as a bright young man full of promise at Daddy's shop. "He's my new intern. I'll need his help with the war orders that keep coming in, so I'll be spending a lot of time with him. Thought inviting him here was a good way for the two of us to get to know each other better, and cover the things we don't get time to cover during the day." My father looked almost apologetic for bringing this stranger into our home, even though he'd asked Mama about it beforehand and she'd happily prepared an elaborate meal for the occasion. I shook David's hand and looked at his face. I saw business there. And numbers. Things I realized later his father had planted until the day he was gone. Things my father, the artisan, needed, giving David a job.

Mama had said David would make someone a perfect husband, after meeting him that first night, one who would be snatched up in a hurry with the low man-to-woman ratio, thanks to the war. She insisted my father invite David over often, and she built him into our lives as my father complied. I didn't pay much attention back then. I didn't make the same association between David and me that Mama had. I really didn't understand about love, whether it was calculated or felt. Not any more than I did now.

I lifted my book off my lap and turned the page. Perhaps it was good to see myself, my story, and the conflict that was about to sprout in my life, from a new vantage point. God's vantage point. One that put Him in a position to have intervened. He should have stopped me. He surely knew there was trouble coming my way over imagining Raymond in love with me when he really wasn't. God could have shown me that a suitable match, a more practical one, was being laid brick by brick in my life and my home, and forced me to realize it. And relish it. And want it.

The next page of my story was covered by a small drawing, one Raymond had inserted. I closed my eyes for a moment, drew in a breath, and lifted the book close. When I opened my eyes, I saw. Saw what I'd never seen on the train. Not that first day, nor any other. Until now.

There Eloise was, the back of her as she staggered past Jacob down the aisle. And there Jacob was, turned in his seat, watching her after she'd passed.

I dropped my hands with the book, letting it fall onto my legs. The breath I'd been holding seeped out. I burned with envy toward Eloise. I wished Raymond had turned to see me that very first day, the way he drew Jacob watching her. Noticed me at least, even if he never let me know.

I laid a finger between the pages where his drawing was, and closed the book over it. His picture had shown the back of Eloise, along with the back of Jacob's head, so I didn't know what expression was on Jacob's face. I couldn't tell what he was thinking as he watched her. What would have been on Raymond's mind, had he looked at me.

I thought back to the stiff suppertime conversations with David that Mama had encouraged during those early days. I thought of Raymond and the way my heart surged after I met him. It soared, in fact, riding somewhere in the clouds far above the train where I'd given it away. I remembered Mama steering me into the kitchen on occasion, away from the table during those suppers with David, always to question me about my moon-eyed looks. She took me from the meal under the pretense of helping her with the dessert or to get more of the main course, but once we were out of Daddy's and David's earshot she would frown at me and insist I pull myself together and make a good impression on Daddy's apprentice. "What for?" I asked, and she sputtered like her engine was about to die. She could tell it wasn't David on my mind. She detected it was someone else lighting up my face. "You've got to get a hold on yourself," she warned, when David and Daddy couldn't hear. "How do you ever expect to be a good wife, asking silly things like that?"

Martha Haynes, Martha Haynes, Martha Haynes. It filled my thoughts as soon as I began speaking with Raymond. I intended to be a good wife. And I imagined I'd be one to Raymond Haynes. Even standing there in Mama's kitchen while she poured her all into directing me, I could smell him, the fragrance of a man who had survived a war, built bridges, and came to work fresh and smelling of aftershave every morning. Just like he boarded the train fresh and smelling of wind and machinery every evening. I drew in a deep breath, wishing he were near so I could smell him for real. "I don't know what you're thinking," Mama whispered close to my face, "but you'd better put it away and get out there and behave like a proper young lady. You do your best to impress David. Make your father and me proud."

I began writing at that point. Every good work of fiction has at its core a conflict, and that was mine. I'd nod at Mama, resist shrugging like I wanted to. I did my best for her and Daddy, wondering all the while if Raymond would prefer a proper young lady over the energy I felt as we'd begun to talk. David barely moved as he spoke, whereas every feature of Raymond's face became alive when he did. Even his eyes danced in accompaniment to the words that poured from his mouth.

I reopened my book to the place my finger held. I drew it close and stared at Raymond's drawing. If only that had been me, his attention on me as he watched me struggle to my seat.

Chapter 13

"Goodnight," my parents said outside my door.

"Turn your light off and get some sleep." Mama's voice was close. "You have so much to do with that new job responsibility of yours on top of your wedding coming up. Try to rest so you look and feel refreshed in the morning."

"Okay, Mama. Goodnight." I turned off my lamp and lay in the dark, listening to their nighttime noises as they went to their room and settled in. I rested my hands on the pages of my book, sensing Raymond's drawing in the dark, tracing around the paper's edge with my finger. I couldn't see any of the words I had written, but I felt them, felt every passion Mama had warned was wrong and vain, a waste of a sensible girl's time. If she came into my room right now and saw what I was doing, she'd snatch this book out of my hands. It would go up in flames after she admonished me that marriages built on emotions didn't last. Neither did infatuations. Unfortunately, Mama was right.

I stared into the darkness, listening to the house grow quiet, wondering why Raymond had Jacob notice Eloise the same moment she'd noticed him. Why he added that to my novel. When there was no more sound from my parents' room, when everything remained still long enough for the two of them to have drifted off to sleep, I reached for my lamp and turned it back on. A cone of soft light illuminated my lap, the book, and Raymond's drawing.

I began reading the page behind the picture, more of Eloise's and Jacob's story, how their relationship began to build on that train. How she longed to expand it beyond their car, their seat, the few hours a week they rode together, but how he never offered or expressed the same idea.

I stared across my room at the opposite wall, ashamed at the number of times I had stared across my parents' table at David but wished it were Raymond sitting there instead. I'd wondered how Raymond would look in something other than his work clothes— in business clothes or casual ones like David wore. Just thinking about him back then, just imagining Raymond across the table from me, had fueled me to more animated conversation, made me prod for something more exciting at home the same way Raymond engaged me on the train. I asked more questions, I probed for David's core, I inched to the edge of my seat hungry to converse the way I did in the morning, in the evening, on the train. I blushed at the memory.

"You ask a lot of questions," David had said one evening. He always answered them, though. He gave concise, well-calculated responses Mama approved of, displaying all the characteristics that made him a good prospect in her mind, a good worker in my father's.

I asked more because David answered less. Less than Raymond did when I quizzed him. I chiseled away at David's exterior, hoping to find and release his fountain of life inside. I wanted it to gush forth like Raymond's did, wash over our evening table and make me laugh and want to dance so Mama would stop worrying I was just being difficult.

"Don't be so fresh," Mama would say in the kitchen. "It's good to show interest in David's day, but keep it to that. What he did, how it turned out. Ask those sorts of questions, not how he felt about them." She frowned, and I saw the silent tsking in her brows. "Sometimes you worry me," she said.

Every taste of who Jacob was made Eloise hunger for more. Each conversation filled her like a banquet, never leaving her starved or sated, only craving more of the delectable flavor. More of him, of what he said, of the way he looked at her when he finished telling her something, that fleeting look that sometimes seemed like he was baffled, but nonetheless made her more and more at home with him.

"Sit here," he'd begun to say. He'd save her a seat in front of him, his long arms dangling over the seat's back, holding it for her until she boarded. Eloise fell into the seat that first time, trying to brush against his hands, wanting to fall into his lap instead, having to struggle to compose herself before she turned and glanced into his handsome face.

She rode sideways in her seat on those days, one of his hands dangling behind her head, the other near her face so she could see his animated gestures as he perched on the edge of the seat behind her and leaned her direction while they talked. She was careful when she sat so that she was turned to the left, her right foot lifted only slightly off the train's floor. She pinched the cloths with her toes, holding everything in place, not ready to be with him without her shoe. Not quite yet. But soon.

"Would you like to go out to dinner sometime?"

David had asked me at last. At last to Mama, a flush of excitement crossing her face as she glanced up from spearing fried potatoes with her fork. I looked from her to my father, then at David, wondering if he meant all of us, but their faces told me he was asking only me.

"There's no need, really," I answered, dabbing at my mouth with my napkin. The toe of Mama's shoe nudged my ankle. I glanced her way. I could see by her face my answer wasn't proper, the way a grateful young lady should respond. "Thank you anyway, though," I added. Her toe bumped my ankle again. I frowned, I wanted to shove Mama's foot away, but I knew better.

"That's fine," David answered. Offense was there in the clipped way he spoke, but not in his expression. David was professional; he could have been telling me thank you for looking at a piece of metal I'd decided not to buy.

"She didn't mean it." Mama jumped in, her expression dissolving from warning to melted butter as she turned from me to him. "She misunderstood, I think, didn't you, dear?" Her buttery look slid my direction.

"I didn't think so." I glanced from her to David.

"The invitation was for a date, if you'd want to call it that. But if you're not interested…" David's expression was the same, constant instead of shifting like my mother's.

"Of course she's interested." Mama jumped in again. The toe of her shoe nicked me, insisting I say the right thing this time.

I glanced at my father. He was watching. Watching me, not what I said.

"Certainly," I replied, dragging my gaze to David.

75

"Dinner would be lovely." The toe of Mama's shoe backed away, taking the threat with it. But the look on Daddy's face stayed with me, set in my mind forever. "Thank you, David." I glanced back at my father, tried to catch that look of watching and studying again, but he was focused on his plate. "I…I would be honored to go."

Mama resumed eating her fried potatoes, a smile on her face. Daddy was quiet, his silverware lying crosswise on his plate like he was done. I could do this, I told myself. I could join David. He and I could eat silently in a restaurant the same way we ate in near silence at my parents' house. I had Raymond for conversation, I had him to make my heart beat wild and hard.

At least that's what I thought at the time. That's what I believed when I lived and wrote about Eloise and Jacob.

Chapter 14

I followed Harvey Wilson and Mr. Arnold down the hall to the main conference room. I'd rarely been in that room, most of my work done in Mr. Arnold's office or sometimes in a courtroom at a hearing. The two men paused at the door, opened it, and stepped aside, allowing me the chance to enter before they did. David would call this the door of opportunity. He'd step through it anticipating great things, ready to offer back even greater. I could imagine his voice, feel his invisible nudge—go on, step through, make the most of this until we're married and start having children.

I paused at the threshold, knowing that going through to the other side might be going backward instead of forward. Back to Raymond, back to bridges, back to a heart made even more raw now that I was reading my book and seeing his illustrations. "No, sir, you go in first, please." I stepped back and to the side. Mr. Wilson and Mr. Arnold frowned, first at me and then at each other. If Mama'd been here, she'd have nudged my ankle with the toe of her shoe again. Not that she cared about my job. She cared about David, getting me married to him, teaching me to do everything right so I didn't ruin this golden opportunity.

"I insist," Mr. Wilson bowed slightly.

I blushed, I nodded, and I plunged through the door. I stopped on the other side, where three sets of eyes stared my direction.

"Over here, please," Mr. Wilson said. His fingers were at my back, guiding me with the slightest of touches. I followed his lead, Mr. Arnold behind us.

Before we took our seats, Mr. Wilson made the introductions—the patent attorney he chose to work with, another engineer, and a young woman who was the attorney's secretary. I made note of their names and faces as well as their rigid postures, while Mr. Wilson went on to explain that once the patent details were worked out, Mr. Arnold's agency would draw up the first contract. Everything about Mr. Wilson's idea was so new, so novel and grandiose, that as he spoke, the overstated pomp around the table began to make sense. They were trying to package something foreign, something almost intangible, and each one felt a little uncertain as to what his or her role would be as this project progressed.

The three of us had seats on the opposite side of the table from the other three. It felt like a standoff, the way we were positioned, but from all evidence, everyone was on the same side. As Mr. Wilson led, and they deliberated, I took notes. I paid attention to the smiles, listened to their tones, and found myself conjuring up a list of adjectives about each one—tiny descriptions as to why this gathering felt less friendly than everyone behaved like it was.

Mr. Arnold produced a copy of the contract Mr. Wilson proposed to use once his patent was completed. The engineer across the table leaned forward, one hand inching in the direction of the papers until his forefinger lit and dragged the stack his way. Tones changed. Even though they softened, the words sounded harder. Every comment sank deep into me, beyond the level of rote dictation to the areas where I thought and felt, where I listened and learned, where Raymond's animated descriptions of his work came to life with what I was hearing now. Most of all, to where I wrote.

"The LaVelle Bridge."

I stopped. I looked up. Raymond had mentioned that bridge. The ground work had begun but had come quickly to a halt. There was a delay. The conversation between the engineer and attorneys at the table quickened. I glanced down at my notes. I'd missed some of what they'd just said. I began to write with a fervor, backtracking in my head to what I had heard but not listened to after someone said "Lavelle."

"We already had this sort of plan in place. At least very similar," the engineer said, pointing at Mr. Wilson's paperwork. "You can look at our blueprints."

Raymond had planned to shift to the LaVelle Bridge project as soon as he was finished at Madison, but LaVelle had stopped. It didn't matter in the end because, soon after that, Raymond had disappeared.

The patent attorney and Mr. Arnold discussed dates, they argued signatures, they debated prototypes and legalities. I took down everything that was said while thinking back to the comments Raymond had made about this bridge, the comparisons he'd made between it and the one he was working on at the time. He probably hadn't known about Mr. Wilson or the battle I witnessed now, but Raymond knew bridges. That became more and more clear as the debate across the table's top continued.

The attorneys and engineer arrived at a deadlock. I glanced at the secretary. She watched her attorney, ignoring me as if I didn't exist. She was engaged in the battle, not just a taker of notes. I had no desire to be in this battle. I would have, months ago. I would have battled alongside Raymond, never imagining my life and skills used any other way. But that was then...

"Onsite inspections. They start tomorrow." Mr. Arnold laid his pen on the table. It stopped the debate, it turned the commotion in the air to ice. Papers disappeared into folders and then into satchels. Chairs scooted back, handshakes took place across the table's top, and people stood.

Onsite? I glanced at Mr. Arnold, then at Mr. Wilson.

The three visitors walked out of the conference room and away from our offices. Mr. Arnold threaded Mr. Wilson and me back to his office, where they remained standing when the door closed behind us.

"Tomorrow." Mr. Wilson looked at Mr. Arnold, and they exchanged a brief nod. "I'll pick you up here." Mr. Wilson turned to me. "At eight in the morning." He returned his attention to Mr. Arnold as my mouth fell open. Bridge projects and their names spilled from Mr. Wilson's mouth. I closed mine. I heard Raymond's job go by, along with other bridges he'd mentioned.

"I...I..." I wouldn't go to those places. I couldn't go where Raymond had been or even talked about. Not yet. I wasn't ready.

Mr. Wilson glanced down at my skirt, my shoes. "Wear comfortable shoes when we go," he suggested. "And make sure your coat is warm enough. It gets breezy out there."

No, I wanted to say. They continued to talk, to discuss how to solidify Mr. Wilson's rights to this design so he could legally cement his patent. I thought of David, of the impossibility of getting him to allow me to step down from this assignment. Everything I could tell him of the meeting, of the debate and the tension, would only energize him, appeal to his business side. Possibly make him envy me for the excitement.

Raymond would be excited also. He would join these men. I could imagine his long arms in broad gestures as he described impossible spans, his eyes alight with the improbable girding and tension that held everything in place. Raymond would have made a good engineer, except he was more alive with his hands on a project than on an idea. He wanted to touch what was to be done, not just plan it. I was glad he was gone, if I had to be at the places he'd talked about, especially the last place he had worked. His absence was enough of a presence.

Mr. Wilson and Mr. Arnold finished. We were done. I left Mr. Arnold's office and hurried to transcribe the notes I'd taken. My book. I needed to read more of it tonight. I would rush through dinner, through our last meeting with the organist before the wedding, then return to that other world. The one where Raymond still lived, so I could finish it. Iron it out and close the last page on that presence. Know where I was going, where he'd gone, and move forward, even if I found myself standing under his bridge.

Chapter 15

Sometimes Jacob drew pictures. Not just with his hands in the air, or with his words in vivid descriptions, but with a pencil. He sketched for Eloise what he saw, plain lines on pieces of paper coming to life as he joined them together. It was there in his drawings that she saw even more of who he was. She saw with his eye, an artist's eye, almost God's eye—the length, the height, the depth, and the time that life really existed in.

"You're quite good," Eloise said. "Your art makes everything so real."

His pencil stopped when she spoke, leaving the bridge he was drawing unfinished. Leaving the old man in the foreground, who'd interrupted Jacob at work by asking for a smoke, stranded in his addiction. Jacob glanced up from the drawing on his lap, making Eloise feel like a naughty girl for interrupting. She drew back into her seat, and stopped stretching to peer over it to admire his art. He was too ruddy to blush, but she knew he had.

"You needn't finish it," she said, glancing back. "You're good enough I'd know that bridge anywhere, and I'd recognize that old man in an instant and offer him a smoke even without him asking." I know you, too, Eloise thought to herself as she watched Jacob's invisible blush. I know every nuance of your world from your drawings, and the stories you share, and from the

occasional queer look you give me as if you'd already told me everything sometime before.

"My mother..." he began. He'd never spoken of his mother. Eloise twisted in her seat again, strained to peer over its back so she wouldn't miss a thing. "She called me an artist." Jacob fidgeted with the corner of his drawing. "I sent her pictures of the war, instead of letters. She said I brought life out of death."

Eloise turned all the way around in her seat. She drew up on her knees, her toes clamping onto her shoe and its padding so it wouldn't drop to the floor. She knew that life. It was in him, it exuded from him, and she shared it. Her shoe slipped off. It clattered to the train's floor, leaving her foot cool and exposed. It dangled there in the air, flat without the cushion of the padding, naked in public for the first time.

"There's no real good in being an artist," Jacob said as Eloise drew back. "Not for a living, anyway."

She eased down onto her haunches, extended her right leg toward the floor, and searched with her foot for the shoe. Her toes bumped against it, scooting it a little farther away.

"I mean, I can't make a living with my drawings, so I'm not really an artist."

"You make life with your drawings," she said. "So I imagine you could make a living with them, also."

He gave her a puzzled look. As if he'd heard those words before.

Her toes scraped along the floor. She tried not to frown as she rummaged for the shoe, its padding. She finally felt the cloths, a soft wad on the vibrating floor. "Your drawings come alive. I find myself in them, even when I'm not." She caught the fabric with her toes and clung to it until she bumped into her shoe again. She balled the cloth beneath her foot as she shoved it in, an uncomfortable mound under her toes. She had to leave it that way. Jacob created life in his art. She created an illusion. The illusion of walking normally. She'd done it for years, and she'd do it again today when it was time to get off. She'd leave the train without a wobble, and she'd walk away from him. He'd never know.

I laid the book on my stomach, propped like a tent, with the pages face down against the sheet I had draped over myself. I drew in a long breath, watching the book rise until I let the air out, then watching the book fall. I did it again, thinking about Eloise's world—my world until Raymond left. A happy world, different from the grownup one I had now. I took another breath and let it out, blowing the stress of my day away. The mechanical stress that came from taking notes for an engineer and two attorneys. The personal stress that came from eating supper in near silence, keeping my part of the discussion to little more than the simple exchange of the day's facts without saying a word as to how I felt about them. Mental stress from organizing music for the wedding to be sure there'd be no awkward silence. And finally, the emotional stress that came from this book. A stress that was much harder to let go.

I had walked in a professional sort of neutral through Harvey Wilson's battle. I'd stated the facts about it at the dinner table when asked. I'd omitted my thoughts, my personal reluctance to continue in a job where Raymond's absence stood far too near. And I'd spent the last of my strength with the organist, calculating the seconds, predicting the incoming crowd so there'd be no lull. Just smooth transitions, one piece blending with the next. Seamless. The illusion of a whole.

The illusion of walking normally, just like Eloise.

Chapter 16

Mama crept in a small circle around me, smoothly, the way a lion moves as it surveys its prey. She glided from one step into another until at last she broke from her circuit and came my direction, shoulders hunched forward, one hand snaking out to give my wedding gown a tug. She drew back after a good solid yank, and studied me with a frown. Shaking her head, she resumed her stalk.

Ida Mae stood back several feet beyond Mama's loop, her arms folded across her chest, straight pins jutting from between her lips. Ida Mae was Mama's friend from church; a seamstress we'd hired to sew my gown, and she'd created exactly what we'd asked for. And she'd done it fast. I glanced from Ida Mae to Karen. She gave a dramatic roll of her head as Mama's back rounded past her. I nodded. We both fought back grins.

I peered down at my dress when Mama looped behind me. I lowered only my eyes, too afraid to bend my head with Mama making her circuit. Gradual slopes of lace over white ran from my chin to the floor, yards of elegance designed to turn me into a bride. It was beautiful. It was lovely. Even though the gown's design was modest and simple, the way Mama said David would prefer, it was still rather expensive. Mama and Daddy had offered to pay for it. I'd argued, but David thought it was right to accept their offer. I knew he was feeling the pinch of the wedding costs, even though the ceremony was unelaborate and the number of guests small. But this gown was worth what Ida Mae asked. It dazzled me. Surely it would him, too.

"Okay, raise your arms," Mama ordered. I looked up. She was standing in front of me.

"But I won't be raising my arms during the wedding."

"We need to see where the hem goes when you do." Mama tucked her chin against her neck, tipping her head down, her eyes focused on my hem. "Come on, go ahead and lift them."

"But, Mama, I won't…"

"Of course you will." She glanced up. "When you toss your bouquet, and when you give David a bite of cake. And who knows when else. You'll surely wave at someone, so we need to make sure. You're the bride, after all, and everything has to be perfect."

I shot my arms into the air like someone had jabbed a gun in my back. I heard Karen snicker from behind, then slap her hand over her mouth.

"See?" Mama said. "See how your skirt pulls up off the floor?" She pointed to my hem, her finger never leaving its target as she walked toward Ida Mae. "You need to let the shoulder seams out just a little, so the skirt doesn't hike up like that. And you have to do it soon. The wedding's in seventeen days, you know." Mama lowered her hand and looked up at me. "Okay, drop your arms."

I let my hands fall to my sides as I watched the straight pins in Ida Mae's lips jerk up and down. Karen stepped in front of me. She pretended to straighten my skirt, her hand still over her mouth.

"It's okay, Mama, really, everything's fine." I kept my face straight as I leaned around Karen.

Ida Mae didn't budge. Neither did the pins as they fell still, angled Mama's direction.

"It is not okay, and Ida Mae won't have a bit of trouble fixing it," Mama insisted. "This is your wedding day, and this dress has to flow with you, no matter what you do or what happens."

Like a holdup, I thought, refusing to say it out loud or look at Karen. If at some point during the ceremony I had to raise my hands for a robbery, I needed to look my best. No matter what.

Ida Mae finally budged. She marched my way and tugged at my shoulder seams, both sides at the same time while she studied my sleeves. She was an excellent seamstress, and I knew she would have planned ahead for any sort of alteration. Her seam allowances would manage Mama's insistence even if her mood didn't. An altercation over an alteration. I smiled and looked at Karen. I wouldn't say it now, but I would later when we could giggle out loud together.

Ida Mae moved to my side, her fingers tracing the seam around my right arm. A flash of white to the right caught my eye. I glanced where I saw it, and there I was—my reflection, in the mirror Ida Mae had been blocking before. I turned and stared at the woman who looked back at me. She was a bride. A real bride. Someone on the verge of becoming a wife. My giggle vanished as I stared at my image.

"Want to see a picture of the girl I plan to marry?"

My skin turned white as Raymond's question popped into my mind. It was as white as my gown, as white as her face had been on his paper. I twisted my head a tiny bit, inching my face to the right while I kept my eyes on me, in the mirror, on my reflection. I'd wanted to be her. I'd wanted to be the girl in his drawing.

"What in the world are you doing?" Mama asked.

My eyes hurt from the strain. I couldn't crane far enough to see my profile the way his picture had been drawn. I wanted to, but it was not only impossible, I knew it was foolish.

"Martha, you know your eyes are going to stick that way if you keep that up. You don't want to march down the aisle on your wedding day with your head twisted to the side so you can see where you're going." Mama stepped between me and the mirror. It was Mama I saw now, her care and her worry that something would go wrong. I wondered how I could tell her, without terrifying her, that I was doing things she'd never understand to make sure this wedding took place.

"Mama…"

Something touched my hand, gently, wrapping my fingers around a handle and pressing them closed.

"Try this," Karen whispered near my ear.

I looked down at my clasped fingers. Karen had placed a hand mirror in them and then backed away.

"Go ahead. Look," she said from the side.

I lifted the mirror, dragged it upward, and inched away from Mama until it was there, to my right, just the right position to see me, all of me, but especially my profile in the large oval glass. I studied what I saw. I superimposed the side view of my face against the one Raymond had drawn, the one I'd seen again last night where he'd placed another copy of that drawing into the story just where it belonged.

Eloise ran her finger along the thin wooden frame, traced the rectangle around the penciled profile Jacob had drawn, the creases still evident where the paper had been folded in his pocket before he showed it to her. It wasn't an exact likeness of her, but it was good—her fair hair, her fine eyebrows, the way her eyes shone above cheekbones that were pronounced and high.

I stared at myself in the mirror, its frame surrounding me like the one around Jacob's drawing. I saw a likeness of her, the girl Raymond planned to marry, but not the real girl. I also saw what I should have seen then—Raymond's amazing talent. He could glance at anything and put a perfect replica of it on paper. I'd told myself at the time that he was young when he'd drawn that profile I thought was me, fairly new at faces, maybe, not practiced enough to draw from memory. I'd forgiven him its minor inaccuracies, my look still plain enough I believed it had to be me.

Raymond had redrawn that profile and inserted it between the pages of my book, right where it belonged. It was identical to the one I'd seen the first time, every nuance in the picture the same, every nuance in her face slightly different from mine. I dropped my hand with the mirror to my side and looked at my reflection straight on.

Jacob sat beside Eloise that day. Her heart nearly burst out of her chest when he did, leaving her melting and freezing all at the same time. His eyes were alight with more excitement than she'd ever seen, a desperate excitement he could barely contain as he grinned down

*at her. The lean strength of his thigh pressed against
hers, her skirt so full and in the way that she gathered
the bunches of its fabric into her lap so she could sense
his leg better. Her mind shouted admonitions all the
while, how wrong she was and how bad, but her heart's
passion beat louder, more powerful, more pure than
anything she'd ever believed or been told.*

*He swiveled in her direction, his knees touching
hers. Eloise's face grew so warm she worried it looked
like it had leapt into flames. That's when he asked
her—asked her if she wanted to see a picture of the girl
he planned to marry.*

*Eloise's heart stopped. She could feel the color
drain from her face. She understood now why he had
never asked her to dinner, never held her hand, never
made an attempt to say he felt the same way about her
that she did about him. He reached into his shirt pocket
and withdrew a folded piece of paper. She pressed back
against the side of the train, its vibrations harsh instead
of soothing as she fought the urge to cry. She would
have yanked to her feet and fled before he could open it,
but her legs had turned to mush. She steeled herself,
cold icy steel, as she forced herself to be brave. She
would look at this girl's picture, be happy for him, even
if his happiness didn't include her.*

*Each fold that he opened and smoothed flat was
like a hammer to her heart, one after another, until the
paper was even. He pressed it on his long thigh, then
held it up for her to see. There she was, this fair-haired
girl, her profile penciled onto a page.*

*Eloise gasped. She looked from her to him and saw
the gleam of anticipation in his eyes. The war was done
for him, he'd survived, and he was ready to live and*

love. And he loved her. And she was Eloise. That was her profile, a likeness of her drawn from his memory. His face was alight with the passion she'd so longed to see—for her—her face alight in the exact same way, but of course for him.

I'd stared at Raymond's second drawing of that profile last night, even long after my tears had obscured its view. There were no creases on the one he'd placed in my book. He'd redrawn it just for me, newly done, a reminder of how foolish I'd been to think it could be me.

An arm draped around my shoulders, and I was drawn into a hug. Karen's scent was there as she held me, my image in the mirror gone, dissolved and drowned with tears.

Ida Mae came near also. "That's what I like to see from my new brides," she said. "Tears of joy. You're going to be a beautiful bride."

Even Mama came close. She placed a hand on one of mine. "Worth every cent," she said, a tremor warbling each word. "Worth every penny."

Chapter 17

"Fourteen more days." I said it out loud, not necessarily to Karen, even though she was right there walking alongside me, the two of us downtown for a bride and maid of honor Saturday lunch. Fourteen days to a new beginning for me, and fourteen days to an ending for Karen and me. I slowed my pace. Karen did too, as if the same thought had occurred to her, both of us delaying the moment we'd no longer be free to do things together this way, as a twosome of girlfriends instead of a threesome, a husband figured into our plans.

"I should have driven us here," Karen said, making change inevitable, reminding me it was already upon us, both of us, not just me. I glanced her way, trying not to look worried or surprised. "I could have. In fact, it would have been good practice."

"Practice? Driving me around? You thinking about driving streetcars next?" I laughed, bumped against her shoulder, waited for her to laugh in return and take all of the adulthood out of these changes. I looked up, her lips were pursed. "You're not, are you?"

She lolled her head, lolling her reply as she did. "Not quite…"

"Not quite thinking about it or not quite driving them yet?"

"We heard from my father. He may be gone longer

than he thought, which means money may be a little, well, scarcer than he'd anticipated. My regular job pays barely enough to cover the basics, so I thought I could maybe put my driving skills to use."

I glanced her direction. "Skills?"

"Well, okay, maybe not skills, but at least I drive. Sort of. Lots of people don't drive, though, and they need ready transportation. I could run errands. Get groceries for people. Things like that."

I moved closer to Karen as we walked on in silence, girlhood slipping farther behind us. "Your mother doesn't care?"

"I'm letting her think about it." Karen grinned.

"Well, before you start your own errand service and I lose you altogether, is your maid of honor dress ready? I mean, it's not too late, maybe, to have Ida Mae work on it if you want her to."

"I thought it was ready…" She frowned at the walk in front of us. "But I haven't raised my arms in the air with it on yet. I might need to catch the bouquet or something. Gosh, I hope I left enough seam allowance in the arms in case I need to let them out a little."

I grinned; then she grinned. In a moment we both laughed. I hadn't laughed in days, maybe weeks. The facial muscles used for giggling felt tight, like they had forgotten how to have fun.

"Mama meant well, but she really was a bit ridiculous at Ida Mae's the other evening," I said. "And covering your mouth didn't hide your grin at all. And did you notice the straight pins in Ida Mae's lips? They were like tiny poisonous darts aimed Mama's way." I laughed harder, tears gathering in my eyes as I bent forward. I pressed a hand against my chest as the laughter rolled.

Karen grabbed my other hand and we laughed together, bumping our shoulders against each other this time as we walked, relieved to be away from everything else and be ourselves, away from cars and jobs, needles and seams, deadlines and gowns. Tears raced down my cheeks. I caught the first few with a swipe of my hand, but there were more. Like my laughter, they gained momentum, a wellspring gushing up, until they washed my laughter away and all I could do was cry.

Karen wrapped an arm around me. She yanked me close as I fell from gaiety into sobs. She held me, and she drew me into a tight embrace as she steered us to the side, away from heads that were turning our way. She sidled us along the stores' fronts, out of the mainstream of people, doing her best to create our own private little sanctuary.

"It wasn't me," I blubbered against her shoulder. "It wasn't me that Raymond drew. I knew that, or at least eventually I thought I did, but now I'm sure. It wasn't me." The last three words sounded more like a wail than a sentence. It was like vomiting a conversation, dry heaving the last thread of hope held onto by my heart.

Karen squeezed me more. She had known also. We'd assumed it was someone else and that he'd gone off to marry her. I was too distraught to even blush at the way I was behaving on a public sidewalk, but humiliation was still there. Humiliation that the whole world would be aware of what had happened to me if they understood my book. I coughed. I choked. I gave birth to a whole new wave of sobs. Raymond knew. Now that he'd read my book, he knew how much I hurt, and yet he dared to draw her again, the woman he loved, the one he'd disappeared for. Another sob, a great ball of agony, erupted from my gut. It emptied me as it gushed upward. I trembled, I cried, I leaned into Karen until the last of my tears filed out. I thought I was empty after Raymond disappeared. But I was emptier now, now that the pain he'd left was exploding so it could vanish also, leaving nothing behind at all.

Fourteen more days. Fourteen days to recover, realign my thinking, awaken and restore my wounded heart. Karen handed me her handkerchief, and I blew my nose. Fourteen more days to appreciate David for what he was—a good provider, a practical man, someone reliable. Fourteen more days to finally pay attention to the things Mama had said, like how steady he was. He tackled life as if he wrote the script and knew every scene of it. No surprises with David. Being with him was the way Mama said marriage would be. Sound. Predictable. Good and right for me.

"Keep reading your book," Karen said. I glanced up. "Finish it."

"I can't." I wiped my face with a corner of her handkerchief, and straightened. "I mean, I don't need to now." I caught my reflection in the window behind her, saw my eyes, how puffy they were, how unlike a girl that someone would plan to marry. "I'm not the person who wrote that book anymore. I can't be. That was then, and this is now. It's time to move on."

"You have fourteen more days," Karen said. "That's plenty of time to finish it. Make sure you do." She took me by the arm, pivoted me on the sidewalk, and marched us onward. She hurried. Fourteen days. Now it wasn't enough time to finish my book.

Chapter 18

Caging a heart—it couldn't be done. Not a heart in full blossom of passion. Stopping a roaring river would be easier, or harnessing a violent hurricane with bare hands. Eloise clenched her teeth until they hurt, clenched her hands into fists hard as stones, clenched her chest muscles until they spasmed into knots. Her heart wailed and thrashed where Jacob couldn't see it, couldn't hear its clamors, even though he sat near, so close, on the train. Her heart refused to be silent, to be held captive. It cried out to touch him—her husband-to-be—to squeeze in next to him and stay, to talk of their future as if it was now. But she didn't. She sat still and listened as he spoke of work, drawing little sketches of what he'd seen.

He drew with less animation than before. She noticed that, and she remained quiet as he paused to glance at her. "There should never be a compromise," he said. Each word was chosen carefully, laid as stones, as if to form a path. He continued to look at her. Then he returned to his drawing and filled in the support beam in his sketch. "No holes, either. Only integrity. Holes make the structure weak." He looked up again, but this time he gazed toward the front of their car, the rumble of the train the only sound as she watched a slight frown spread across his face.

"You draw bridges well," she said. "But I

especially like when you draw people. Like the profile you let me keep." The one he'd drawn of Eloise, the girl he planned to marry. If she could veer his conversation away from work and to the two of them, their upcoming marriage, and their love… "It's hanging on my wall."

He stared at her, his frown and his gaze probing into her privacy, asking questions he wouldn't let her hear. She wanted him in the depths of her, she wanted to know him and to let him know her. She opened her eyes wide, inviting him deeper, begging him with silent shouts through her return gaze.

He shook his head as he looked away, his questions still there.

"Draw something for me," Eloise said. She touched his arm with her fingertips. "Draw me a picture of where you lived as a boy."

He kept a small pad in his lunch pail. He was never without it. He opened the metal pail and extracted the pad, tucked the sketch of the bridge inside it. Setting the pail on the floor, he positioned the pad on his knee, a clean page on the top.

"What are those?" she asked, fingering the edges of other pages torn from the pad and tucked within it.

He shrugged. "Just old drawings."

It was a liberty she'd never taken before, a boldness she'd never exercised. She pinched the corner of one of the sheets and slid it out, two others coming with it and fluttering onto their laps.

She was there again in this drawing that she held. Herself. Eloise. Not in profile, but three quarters of a turn. In front of a business she didn't recognize. She leaned close as he swept up the other two drawings. "Where is this?" She frowned at the name on the building. It was indecipherable.

"Barbour's," he replied.

"Barbour's? Where is that?" She scrunched her face.

He shrugged. "It's just a place." He stared at the drawing.

She looked back at the sketch, at herself this time, seeing again how he saw her. After all, he was an artist. He had the liberty of drawing what was in his heart instead of what was in front of his eyes. In her three-quarter angle in the sketch, she looked posed, her right foot flat on the ground, her left toe extended to the side, pointing in a rather chic manner. Eloise blanched. He had drawn her left leg longer. He knew.

He took the drawing from her hands. She let him. He stacked it with the two others. They also were drawings of her, she caught fleeting images of herself near an airplane and another close up. Just her face. The same face as in his other drawings of her, in his style, the way he saw her.

He tucked the pad with the drawings and his pencil back into his lunch pail. The train wheels wailed, nearing the stop. He glanced at her. The train slowed, but she prayed it would keep going. She could see herself in his eyes, the perfect her, the way she wanted to be and be seen.

He leaned toward her, his face close. Then his mouth. His lips. Until his touched hers, the two of them fitting together as if they were one. She was shocked at the softness, the smoothness, the tender cushion his lips formed as they melded into hers. His hand came behind her head and his fingers threaded through her hair. He drew her face even closer, knitting their mouths *together. She inhaled him. She tasted and drank in every nuance of the texture of his lips as she absorbed them into hers. Soft, firm, hungry, gentle. Her first kiss. It would never leave her. It would last forever. Even long after the train finally ground to a halt.*

I inhaled, just as Eloise had done, drew in a long breath that never seemed to stop, recalling how Raymond's lips had felt on mine. That was the moment Raymond and I had become one, the very fibers of me joining him. I let the breath begin to ease out. No wonder letting go of him had been impossible. That joining, that blending and entwining, could never be merely unraveled. It had to be torn apart, instead. Each fiber ripped from itself, filaments and frayed ends left dangling. Not even able to bleed.

I glanced at the book. I couldn't read on. I flipped the page over to mark my place and saw that the next three pages weren't my words but his drawings. Pictures Raymond had inserted. I closed the book. I couldn't stand to see them. He'd likely drawn more of her, the other woman. Even when he'd drawn Jacob watching Eloise's back on the train, wasn't it only because he was amazed how much I resembled the one he loved?

Reading this book made fourteen days too far away, yet too near. Maybe Karen should read it instead, and give me a book report when she was done. If I kept reading, my head would become more jumbled, and my emotions more raw. Fourteen days weren't enough, if all I did was become more fragmented. I needed them to hurry. When I became Mrs. Tidwell, I would put all of this girlish heartache behind me and focus on David. Not Raymond. Not Jacob. Not Eloise and all of the obstacles between her and her love. Especially if it turned out those relationships weren't real love, after all.

I glanced down at the book, my finger still inside where Raymond's pictures lay. I had to know. I had to hurt one last time to say goodbye. I opened the book, pressed the pages flat where the first drawing lay. It was of her outside the store. Barbour's was written above the store's doorway, and she was standing near the front. Her feet were flat on the ground in this drawing, both toes pointed forward. I frowned. His drawing hadn't been that way when I'd seen it on the train. Raymond drew her without the pose I'd seen the first time, the one I'd used to dramatize the flaw Eloise tried to hide. He drew her more like anyone would stand, instead of like the woman in his first picture.

I glanced at the next two drawings. There she was in front of the airplane. Silly for me to have thought this was me the first time I saw it, since I'd never flown, and had told Raymond more than once I never intended to. This would be his wife again. My face burned with my own foolishness that I hadn't recognized that before. Including these sketches must have been his way of making sure I knew the truth, so I could go on. Have a different happy ending than the one I thought I'd have, or had created in this book. And then the final picture, the third one, was her face. I closed the book. Humiliated. Ashamed. I should never have written it. Never have hung my infatuation and broken heart out there for everyone to see.

I closed my mind like I had the book, sealing away my words, his drawings, the whole fictitious tale and my vain imaginations. I held the book tight, clamped its pages together so the world couldn't see, and Raymond wouldn't know. What I knew, what I'd written about, what I wanted to forget.

But her face remained behind my closed eyes, within my thoughts. The last sketch I'd glanced at was still there, as if etched on my soul. I reopened the book and thumbed through the pages until I came to that third sketch again. I pressed the book flat and looked at it. I saw there the very thing I'd tried to see in the mirror at Ida Mae's. I saw myself this time in the features he'd drawn. Far more than had been there before. I brought the picture closer. The distinction of my eyes showed through, the sharper angle of my nose. I turned back to the woman near the airplane. She was far away, and her face less distinct and harder to decipher. But the way she stood—it was the way anyone stood, but it was the way I stood. And the coat the woman wore—it was like mine.

I was bleeding through, seeping into Raymond's art where I hadn't been before. I closed the book, held it against my pounding heart. It was too late for that. Raymond was married...or nearly...even David had said that. And I was engaged.

But his pictures... If they were speaking, if they were more than just sketches... They were telling a story my prose didn't touch. His pictures were worth a thousand of my words.

Chapter 19

"Thirteen more days," Mama said. Her voice was loud enough it carried over the congregation as people milled together after church services. Ida Mae stiffened from across the large foyer. She was Mama's intended target, and I watched Ida Mae turn her back to Mama and resume her conversation with another lady from the church.

"Mama!" I tugged on her sleeve.

"Thirteen days isn't much time," Mama said again, tossing a glance toward Ida Mae. She touched my arm, leaning close to me. "This is my only daughter's wedding. I want it to be special. We have the church lined out, the reception planned, and someone to take pictures. All we need now is the gown."

I watched Ida Mae say goodbye to the woman she'd been speaking with, then make her way to the door.

"Mama, go tell Ida Mae to stay here and talk to her friends. She has plenty of time to alter my dress."

"No, she doesn't." Mama followed Ida Mae's exit with a narrow-eyed look. "I checked her to-do pile when we were there, and she has gobs of hemming, a stack of patterns cut out but not pieced together yet, and some basting to remove—why, she has enough sewing projects to keep her tied up clear through next year. It's best she go on home and make sure your wedding gown is finished first. After all, thirteen days isn't much time."

Thirteen days. Ida Mae disappeared through the church's main door, and I saw myself leave right along with her. Mama was working hard to hurry my wedding day forward. And I knew Ida Mae would do her part, too, even without Mama's public suggestions. They were both going forward. To the same goal, just at two different speeds. I was going backward. The church door closed behind Ida Mae.

"Your mother's right." David stood at my side. "Ida Mae needs to tend to her duties." David rested his fingers around my elbow. "After all, the bride has to be beautiful."

I looked at David, gave him a tiny but appreciative smile, and then gazed beyond him at the emptying foyer. Karen was still there, chatting with one of our friends. "Excuse me," I said to David and my mother. "I need to speak with my maid of honor."

David relinquished his hold as I turned and walked Karen's way. I could feel Mama watching as I slid into Karen's and our friend's conversation, their laughter over whatever they'd been talking about reminding me of yesterday, when Karen and I had laughed before I cried. They swept me into their discussion, their gaiety, and I laughed along with them until our friend said goodbye. Karen and I watched her hurry to catch up with her family as they headed out the front doors. I stole a quick glance at Mama when they were gone. David was still there, engaged in a discussion with her and her friends. About the upcoming wedding, no doubt, even though Ida Mae was long gone. I turned back to Karen. "I want to ask you something about the book," I whispered.

"You're having trouble reading it," she said. She didn't bother to ask. She knew. That's why Karen was my best friend.

I nodded. "I wish I'd read it sooner." The absurdity of what I'd said was obvious, but not on Karen's face. Once again, she was too good a friend for that. "Another time would have been better. Any time before now. And I certainly can't read it after..." I nodded toward David, but he had moved. He was standing with his hands clutched in front of him, his arms hanging down in a large V as he spoke with the pastor. "Can you take it?" I asked, looking back at Karen.

Her lips puckered, and then she nodded. "Sure, if that's what you want."

I nodded. "Can you come for lunch? I can give it to you then."

She shook her head. "No, sorry. My aunt is coming by. She's spending the rest of the day with us. Maybe tomorrow?"

I saw myself again in Raymond's drawings. I stood the way the woman at Barbour's stood; I wore the coat she'd had on near the airplane; I felt her features as I grimaced at Karen's inability to take the book today. "Okay, I'll call you tomorrow after work. No take-backs," I added, cementing the pact as if we were still girls.

Karen waved as I joined David and my family. I took David's hand. "I'm ready." I gave his hand a slight squeeze. "Sorry to have kept you waiting."

David gave my hand a gentle squeeze in return. He was good; he was stable. I just needed to hold on.

Chapter 20

The train became a tomb. Even the sense of the kiss Jacob had shared waned, the absence of it making the emptiness far worse than if he and Eloise never had touched. It was a vacuum—the train, just like Eloise's heart—full of his presence, full of his absence, drawing life out of her with each passing moment. Jacob hadn't been there in the morning, the day after the kiss. She was disappointed, but not alarmed, for this happened on occasion. She glanced around the car, searched the array of familiar faces before she took her seat. His schedule changed on occasion, or sometimes something unexpected came up. That afternoon it was the same, though. He still wasn't there. She took her seat and stared straight ahead, riding in the rattling quiet. He'd be back in the morning. He never missed two days in a row.

She replayed their conversations in her mind the next day to fill the silence and help her pretend he was there. She dug for memories in which he'd spoken of the future, their future, and she held onto those conversations as her rock. Like when he'd spoken of his house. He'd drawn it for her once. She'd taken it from his hands, and when he saw how much it pleased her, he took it back. The surprise she felt must have shown on her face, for he laid it on her lap, but then took it again. "What are you doing?" She tried to tease, and snatched the drawing from his fingers. "That's mine," she'd told him, but she was thinking, "That's ours."

He'd bought the house for the future, for the family he planned to have, and she'd begged him to show her. He showed her on paper. That was his way, and she accepted that. Seeing anything he drew was seeing his heart—far better than seeing the actual object—and what was in Jacob's heart was also in hers.

She boarded again, eager, praying she'd see his face. It had been days, so surely he would be there. She nearly stumbled in her haste, her right shoe slipping, and she shoved her toes in as far as they'd go. She glanced up, feeling the flush of anticipation mingling with the humiliation on her cheeks. She scanned the other passengers, took a tally of their faces, their hair, their hats. He wasn't there. She looked again, faltering along the aisle as she did. He was sick, maybe. Very sick. She'd visit him if she knew where he lived.

Every morning and every evening she searched the passengers, hoping. Until at last the fear that she'd never see him again overcame the hope that she would. She sat alone in the vibrating tomb. Alone, but crowded by thoughts of him. The diminishing sensation of the kiss they'd shared, the suffocating ubiquity of his absence—all added to the emptiness he left behind.

She couldn't go on this way. She'd go to his worksite. She had to do something. She couldn't lie dead in this traveling tomb. She glanced out the side window as a blur of nameless faces and buildings rushed by. She would find him, or at least find out what happened to him. She'd take a streetcar farther into the city than she ever had before. She would go there, and she would find out.

I closed the book over one finger, holding my place. This was my last night with my story, since Karen would take it tomorrow. I'd eaten lunch with David and my family after church, spent the afternoon with Mama, poring over last-minute details about the cake and other snacks we'd have at the reception. I cooked our supper, cleaned up afterwards, telling Mama to go relax with Daddy. I was cooperative, I was generous, but I was afraid. The book had followed me all day, tiny resemblances of me in Raymond's drawings cropping up in my mind. I shoved them back continually, tried to cut loose so I could go free, but everything stayed there, creeping back in again and again.

When I came to my room at the end of the day and prepared for bed, I didn't even glance at my nightstand, other than to turn on my small lamp. I crawled into bed, shut the light off, and lay there. My eyes were wide in the black of the room, and I willed the book away. But its invisible presence was as powerful as Jacob's absence. I'd turned the lamp back on, withdrawn my novel, and read.

I sighed. I reopened the book to where I'd left off a few minutes ago, to the next drawing that was there. It was a sketch of Raymond's house, a new drawing of it, since I still had his original one. The house looked the same as it had in the first picture. So did the shrubbery he'd sketched around it. I peered at the windows, wondering if he'd added a face—his or mine. Or hers. The windows were blank. I burrowed deeper into my pillow and lifted my knees so the book rested against them. I saw it then. The thing that made this picture the perfect illustration for my book. There was a suitcase on the front walk, halfway between the house and the street. It was black, he'd penciled it in, and it looked fairly large. I didn't know whose it was, or whether its owner was coming or going. All I knew was that it was his house, the one he'd bought for the family he intended to have. The family he hadn't meant to be me.

Chapter 21

"You're early," Mr. Arnold said. He looked pleased, an expression I saw more and more as I worked with Mr. Wilson. "Harvey's not...I mean, Mr. Wilson isn't here yet, so relax a few minutes. I perked some coffee, if you want some."

I didn't wonder that he'd suggested coffee. Dark circles hung beneath my eyes like ugly drapes. I'd tried to hide them—and the puffiness that grew from staying up late and reading—with powder, but it hadn't worked.

"Thank you," I said. I rarely drank coffee. Karen had suggested I take it up when I wrote my book. She said authors always smoked and drank coffee, it was part of their image. She'd laughed when she said it, and so had I. We wouldn't have laughed if we'd known that reading my book would eventually drive me to caffeine far more than writing it had.

Harvey whisked into the office just before eight, bringing with him an apprehensive energy. I looked up from the half-drunk cup of coffee my hands were wrapped around, its artificial restless energy beginning to course through my veins.

"Good morning," we both said at the same time. We smiled, and he gave the cup in my hands an appreciative nod.

"Might do the same myself while we gather up

what we'll need for the day." He hurried off to Mr. Arnold's office at the pace of a man already fueled with coffee.

I finished my cup as the two men charted the course for the day. I had everything I'd need in a satchel. I'd also worn comfortable shoes and an extra warm jacket. I'd been to a bridge site once— Raymond's—the time he was missing. I'd learned that time about comfortable shoes and the wind that whistled through a construction site. Somehow the air picked up the chill from gray metal and hammered it against any exposed skin it could find. That's probably why Raymond's face and hands had that rugged look. It was handsome on him, but I had been frozen to the core, chilled deep inside, where I already felt hollowed out and alone.

"Let's go." Mr. Wilson breezed back through the open office area where my desk was. Other girls were starting to come in and get settled. I felt their envy at the special opportunity I was being given, but I would gladly have offered any one of them my place. Going out there where Raymond had been wouldn't affect them—brisk winds stirring up memories that, for me, needed to go away.

"We're going to the Sinclair site," Mr. Wilson said. "It's an older bridge construction, a relic from before the war, and I'm going there for comparison. The engineer and the foreman who know the most about that one are meeting us there." He glanced down at my shoes, looked up, and grinned. "Good girl," he added.

Caffeine, previously a surge of liquid power, exploded into tiny sparks all through me. Sinclair. Raymond had never talked about that bridge. Nothing of him would be there. No presence, no absence, only the distant knowledge that he built bridges, but that was enough.

Mr. Wilson drove us to the Sinclair Bridge. He chatted the whole time, his excitement for his vision, with his deep-down worry it would never be seen, trickling up to the surface and spilling out in one steady stream. My caffeine nerves fed off his tension, my own fears percolating to the surface—what if Raymond happened to be at one of these sites? I stared out the passenger window as Mr. Wilson rambled on. I knew he wouldn't be. Raymond was surely long gone. Showing up at my signing with a book he'd illustrated was... Well, maybe he hadn't meant for me to sign it at all. No matter what his sketches insinuated, he hadn't come back for the book. It was most likely the fond goodbye he'd never given me, a way of saying thank you and farewell at the same time.

"Here we are." Mr. Wilson maneuvered his large car into a parking space. The Sinclair Bridge loomed above, a monstrosity that seemed close even though it was still a slight walk from where he'd parked. It was built to be a transport over railroad tracks for cars and trucks that were barely visible as they inched their way high above us, back and forth across its span. "We're meeting the two men over there"—Mr. Wilson pointed beneath the bridge—"where we can discuss the undergirding and structure. I chose this bridge because there's no water for us to deal with. Everything will be right out there in the open on this one. Good place to start."

I trailed Mr. Wilson from the paved parking area to a grassy expanse, and then over dirt and gravel until we were standing beneath the bridge, joining the two older men already there waiting for us. Trains idled not far away, and tires rattled over wooden planks above. I removed a pad and pencil from my satchel and drew near the men for introductions, ready to decipher and record everything they said.

After the men nodded their greetings and made a few preparatory remarks, they turned away. I watched as they waved their arms at the expanse above, fingers pointing to beams and rivets over our heads along the supports. The noise cocooned them, bundled them together just as the train's noises had bundled Raymond and me together long ago. I scooted closer and listened as they described how this bridge had been built, beam after beam, rivet after rivet, steel, wood, and cement coming together. As I took notes, the chill and the rigidity of each section came close. The coldness felt the same as the time I'd visited Raymond's bridge. I hadn't belonged there then, but I was a part of this now. I was a tool. Not as valuable as the hammers or drills, but still a tool—chilled and icy—but of use. I listened. I wrote. Other people's words. Emotionless, without feeling. My own words and my feelings held back, muddled, having no place here and now.

The men moved deeper beneath the bridge. I followed, pressing close enough to catch their conversation and maybe capture some warmth, taking their words down one at a time, my jots and tittles bringing structure to their knowledge, the same way this bridge had been put together.

One of the men tugged a fob from his pocket and glanced at the time. There was a general sigh as they took a breather, glanced around, and surveyed the undergirding surrounding us.

A picture is worth a thousand words. In their quiet I drew a few lines in the upper corner of the page where I'd taken notes—vertical and horizontal lines, after which I added some angles. A bridge appeared as my lines fell into place. It took on life, the way Raymond's bridges had. My heart began to pound, bringing warmth and a smile. The sound of the traffic above me dimmed; the rumble of trains nearby became soothing. Love on a train. My heartbeat steadied, it leveled out, and everything in and around me warmed and softened. I looked up. Mr. Wilson and the other two men were shaking hands. They were done. So was I. We said our goodbyes, and I followed Mr. Wilson back to the car.

"Thank you," he said as he looked over the top of his car at me before we climbed inside.

I gazed across the wide roof and smiled. "No. Thank you," I said.

We settled into the car. He rested one hand on the steering wheel and stared straight ahead before pulling away. "We finished early. How about some lunch? There's a little diner not far from here. We can eat and still have enough time to check one more site. The Madison Bridge. We'll look it over on our own, then meet with those fellows tomorrow."

Raymond's last job. I pressed my satchel against my lap and stared ahead. My heart hammered against fragments of girding I hadn't realized were still there but that needed to give way. Raymond wouldn't be there, yet he would. He would be everywhere. I couldn't escape him. I glanced out the side window as Mr. Wilson drove us to the diner. That was why Karen wanted me to read my novel. Excavation. Construction.

Clearing away the rubble that remained.

"There it is," Mr. Wilson pointed through the front window. I scanned the buildings along the street, searching for a diner. I craned to the side, peering at names above the storefronts. "Not the diner," he laughed. He pointed up into the air. "The Madison. That's where we're heading after we eat. It's a real beauty."

I followed where his finger pointed. My heart clanged against the erected steel. The bridge was beautiful now that it was done. A work of art. And no wonder…an artist had a hand in its creation.

Chapter 22

The train's vibrations were like tiny fingers tickling the soles of my feet and massaging my tired back. I rested my head against the window, letting the small pulsation soothe my thoughts and ease my aches from the day. It had been a long day, but not the kind of long my father enjoyed. This one was long of bridges. This one had brought time too near to and yet too far from Raymond.

The train's engine waned and the brakes squealed as we slowed to a stop. I stood with the other passengers, tugged my satchel's strap over my shoulder, and wrapped my coat tighter around me. I filed off with the others, dropped down onto the station's platform, and lowered my head against the evening chill for the walk home.

"Martha?"

A hand touched my elbow. I looked up. David. He was there, his work clothing showing beneath the front opening of his long coat.

"I thought we could go out this evening. Just the two of us." He tightened his hand on my elbow. "You've been looking tired lately. I thought I would take you to eat and help you relax. We'll talk about anything but the wedding, since I'm sure it's why you're so worn out. I'll tell you about my day. Then you can tell me about yours." David was struggling, working hard to say the right things to me, almost as if he were reciting lines someone else had written for him. I listened for Mama in what he said, but it wasn't her. Her input was generally more direct. This was gentle. More gentle than David usually was, and more tender than Mama understood.

"I was supposed to call Karen…"

"Call her later?"

He looked so disconcerted and uncertain, I had to smile. Being alone with me this way was a challenge for him. Understanding how to be a couple was baffling. He was a facts and figures man, one cut out to be a good provider.

"Sure." I nodded. "I can do that."

He relaxed, and steered me to the main sidewalk by my elbow. I would get the book to Karen later tonight.

David fumbled through topics foreign to him as we walked to a restaurant and even as we ate, struggling with the nuts and bolts of what created a marriage instead of objects of metal. His halted approach made me feel more like a project than a work of art, but that was okay. He was trying; this wasn't David's way.

"Twelve more days," he said as we finished our dinners. "Oops. I'm sorry. We weren't going to talk about the wedding."

"That's okay," I said. I stretched my hand across the table and touched his. His skin felt warm beneath my fingertips. In twelve days I'd see and feel more of that skin. I withdrew my hand and folded the napkin in my lap. "Maybe we should do this again tomorrow night," I suggested, looking up. "Just you and me, I mean. Go out. Talk. Get more used to being with just each other." I unfolded my napkin and wound it around my hand. I pulled it tight and held it in place while I waited for his answer.

"That's kind of expensive." I could see the calculations of a responsible husband running through his mind. "Maybe we could go for a walk after dinner instead. Your mother already invited me to eat with you tomorrow evening. We could walk while we talk about our days, after supper."

Wear comfortable shoes. It ran through my mind. Mr. Wilson's admonishment. I felt, even now, the lesson I'd learned when I'd visited Raymond's worksite the first time, and which had been repeated today. I'd stumbled there earlier, at the bridge sites. Mr. Wilson had saved me from falling by latching onto my elbow. He'd glanced down at my shoes, as if they were to blame.

"Sure," I said to David. "A walk would be nice." I checked the time. It was late. Too late for Karen to get the book by the time I got home. Tomorrow, I told myself. I'd call her later and promise to get it to her tomorrow.

"You'll be short an hour's pay." Eloise's boss frowned when she asked to leave an hour early.

"One of the other girls offered to finish my work for me," she assured him. *"And I understand about the cut in pay."*

"Very well, then. We'll see you tomorrow."

Eloise knew she should have felt guilty leaving her post that way, but she didn't. She couldn't. She would resign someday, anyway, as soon as she and Jacob were married. If he was all right...

She boarded a streetcar near the same place she did her train every evening, but this time she went the other direction, farther into the city, fairly certain she could find Jacob's workplace. She took a seat near the front of the car, sitting where there was something to hold onto, as if she could steer and have control of where she was going. The streetcar lurched forward, a different group of faces surrounding her, none of them familiar like the ones she was used to when she traveled on the train the other way, to her home.

She watched the stops, watched people board and get off, gauging those that looked like construction workers to see who was dressed like Jacob. At last they approached a stop where a smattering of men with lunch pails stood waiting. The streetcar slowed, and she held on until it stopped. People entered, the men that reminded her of Jacob sauntered past in heavy clothing with smudges, weathered skin on their faces. She stood, made her way down the steps, and was on the street. When the car moved away, she stayed there. She listened. She inhaled. Jacob worked heavy equipment; he smelled of oil and grease. She turned, listened again, and breathed.

"Can I help you, young lady?"

She jumped and whirled around.

"Are you lost?" The man standing near looked kindly enough, an older gentleman, with brows furrowed the same way her father's would if he knew she was here.

"I was looking for the Macon Bridge. They are nearly finished with it, I think, but it's near here, isn't it?"

His frown stayed. She saw her father in his expression again, wondering why a young woman was in the city on her own like this.

"My fiancé is there. I'm looking for him." She *blushed, hoping he would think it was from the cold.*

"Well, it's near the river. It's the new overpass, a big project, and you're right, it's nearly finished." He *pointed, and she followed the stretch of his arm. Tall buildings blocked most of her view. High. Jacob always spoke with animation and excitement when he spoke of high.*

"Thank you." She *turned and walked in the direction he pointed. Listening and breathing as she went. She'd find him. She'd find out what was wrong with Jacob.*

Stepping through the row of buildings into the bridge site was like bursting from one world into another. Tall buildings and pavement gave way at her sides and fell behind her, while rough ground, muddied water, and different noises took their places. She felt Jacob in this chaos, felt his enthusiasm, appreciated the daring and the strength that overcame natural elements to do something enormous and frightening. She stood at the edge, the precipice between her world and his, this unexplored cavern as frightening as the one that had grown inside her ever since he had disappeared.

She watched the operators of the nearest machines. She saw men with tools, with clipboards, with cigarettes, and with buckets in their hands. She watched for Jacob amongst them—black hair, tall and lean, a smile that warmed her whenever she saw it.

Two men passed nearby. They were intent on the project, deep into a discussion as if nothing else existed.

"Excuse me."

They continued past.

"Excuse me." She said it louder.

They stopped and frowned. She saw in their faces that she was wrong to be here. There were no other women around. She felt as foolish as she saw she looked in their eyes.

"I was...I was looking..."

And then she saw him. Coming up the rise behind the two men, each step measured, and heavy, and slow. His head down, he was watching the ground as if to be careful of each place he put his foot.

"Nothing. I wasn't looking for anything," she apologized. "Just looking."

She turned away, embarrassed and ashamed, not only for herself but especially for Jacob. What would the men say to him if they knew she was looking for him? She glanced around for a place to hide, the quickest way to get out of sight to save him the humiliation. A truck was not far away, parked at the edge of the site.

She started toward it, praying he wouldn't see her. Her right foot staggered on the uneven ground as she hurried, rocks tearing at her shoe, causing her to slide on the padding beneath her foot. She paused, steadied herself, and straightened her foot and the shoe. "Please don't see me," she whispered. "Go on with your work. Don't notice me."

She listened behind her as she tackled the rough ground ahead. She hoped the two men had walked on, and she wanted Jacob to walk on also. He was okay, that was all she needed to know. It was late. Clearly his hours had changed and that was why she hadn't seen him on the train.

"Ma'am?"

She stopped.

"Ma'am?"

Eloise made a slow turn and glanced behind. The man she'd seen, the one she'd thought was Jacob, stood not far from where the other men had stopped, but they had gone on. His face was twisted into a question. It wasn't Jacob's face after all but another man's that only looked similar to his. "You looking for someone?"

She nodded, then shook her head, turning the rest of the way around to face him. She felt foolish. She was out of place. The ground was clunky and the rocks obstacles beneath her feet.

The man stepped her direction. The question on his face dug a series of tiny grooves in his forehead, turning it into a frown. If she could run, she would. He stopped in front of her. "You lost or something?" Cold air whipped between and around them, flapping her skirt against her legs. Eloise gathered her skirt in a fist and held on, her face warm in spite of the chill.

"I'm fine. Just admiring the bridge." The wind whisked at her lie. She lined up the toes of her shoes and watched his face.

"Don't see too many women down here. Don't allow them, really, so be careful and don't get too close." The man walked away.

The chill of the wind was balmy compared to the chill that filled her inside. A chill unaffected by her flaming humiliation. She'd never come here again. This was Jacob's world, a man's world. She'd leave it to him and wait until they built their own world.

She glanced across the construction site. The two men were long gone, and so was the one who had spoken to her. She turned, then walked away, stopping once to look back. Eloise Lane. She looked down at her feet as she went on, watching where she stepped as she headed back toward the streetcar stop. Eloise Lane. Eloise Lane. Eloise Lane. Somehow. Someday. Surely.

Chapter 23

Eleven days. Eleven more days until the wedding. The list of everything left to do ran through my mind as I filed yesterday's notes on the Sinclair Bridge. Mr. Wilson told me to spend the morning turning my notes into a format he could use and to give him a copy. I did. Between each phrase and clause I transcribed, another task to be done before my upcoming wedding cropped up. The shower. Making sure the church was spotless. All of it sprouted in between girders and rivets, cement and steel. Work to be done, mechanical work instead of works of art.

"Ready?" Mr. Wilson showed up at my desk after I'd eaten the half sandwich I'd brought. I tossed my wrapper into the wastebasket and wiped my mouth with a cloth napkin. "Madison Bridge is waiting."

"Yes, sir." I left my apple behind, filled my satchel with pencils and paper, and followed him out of the building, feeling again the envious stares of the other girls in the office.

I sat low in Mr. Wilson's car seat as we passed through downtown, and sank even lower when Raymond's bridge appeared. I made myself invisible. I didn't belong here as Martha Cole, not as the woman, the writer, not as someone who'd known one of the men who'd help build this bridge. I faded, blended into the background, the noise, and the ground as much as I could. I faded and blended even more after Mr. Wilson parked and we walked toward two men, two different men this time, who were waiting for us near the edge of what was left of the construction site. This bridge was big and beautiful, majestic, and nearly one hundred percent functional. I felt its pulse as clearly as I felt my own, a beat and rhythm I couldn't stop as I followed the men, taking down everything they said.

I could hear Raymond in the descriptions they used. I remembered the terms, the language of a bridge's birth, except I heard everything in Raymond's voice instead of theirs. Little lines fell into place in the upper corner of my notes again. Up and sideways, angled and thick. Everything Raymond had taught me appeared on the page during the lulls of their discussion.

"This is an amazing opportunity," David had said the night before, at dinner, when I'd described my day at the Sinclair Bridge and how this one had looked when Mr. Wilson drove the two of us here after lunch. I'd spoken the way those men and these did—a precision of steel here, supports there. Ground, engines, and vibrations. But my drawings, the ones evolving in the corners of my pages, were different. They were worth a thousand words, full of the passion Raymond saw, full of the vitality his artist's eye brought to the structures, and to me.

"Like that." Mr. Wilson's finger appeared on top of my drawing. I slapped my hand over what showed of my sketch, my cheeks bursting into flames. "No, let them see it." He placed his large hand over mine and drew my smaller one away, leaving my little drawing exposed. "See how she drew it?"

The men stood back and stared at me as if they'd noticed me for the first time. They didn't come forward and look, they just stared. I blushed. I prayed these weren't the men who had been here ages ago when I'd come searching for Raymond.

"Come on," Mr. Wilson insisted. He waved them forward, but he didn't wait. He took my pad and carried it to them, instead. He held it up, pointed to my drawing, and forced them to look. "See that? See the height? This beam right here?"

The men shuffled, then leaned closer. I couldn't jot down what they said without the pad, but a discussion began, one word at a time, until momentum built. I stepped nearer so I could hear. I'd memorize what they were saying and write it down when they gave my pad back to me.

Phrases stood out, and I caught words. They were arguing more than discussing, Mr. Wilson deliberating whether this bridge hedged on the design he was patenting, going on to explain why his idea would work better than older bridges built before the war. The other two men debated what he said, the conversation picking up steam, a rush of words so thick I couldn't keep up, until like a fast-moving train on a collision course, it stopped. The whole discussion exploded at one word. Haynes. As soon as one of the men said the name, my heart exploded also, along with my thoughts. The ground became unsteady, and the air around me too thick to breathe. Haynes.

"Here," Mr. Wilson extended the pad my direction. "Sorry. I guess it's hard for you to keep up when I have your pad."

The pad touched my hand. I couldn't force my

fingers to clamp around it. Mr. Wilson pressed it against my palm. "Thank you," I whispered. I knew I said it, but I couldn't hear it. All I could hear was Haynes. Martha Haynes, Martha Haynes, Martha Haynes.

"I never met him," Mr. Wilson was saying. "I thought I knew everyone."

"He does groundbreaking," one of the men said. "Gone now, but he had definite ideas that sound kind of like yours. Kind of like that picture she drew."

All three men turned and stared at me. I stared back.

What else had David said last night? Pay attention, do a good job, don't talk. They don't want your thoughts, just their own and for you to do your very best to record them. David would be horrified I'd drawn a sketch, but he'd be proud of my dictation skills. I poised my pencil over my pad, picturing David, and how he'd looked last night.

Gone now. What the man had said about Raymond crowded David's image aside.

No matter how hard I focused, it rang in my mind. Gone now. Raymond was gone now. David's face flitted away. Raymond had gone away, was gone forever. Except around me. Here he lingered, here he continued to survive.

"Wish I'd met him," Harvey Wilson said. "Anyway…" The men trailed deeper beneath the bridge, near the water's edge. I followed, pencil on pad, a new page on top, one without a sketch.

Tonight, after I did one last tally of the guests, and after I met with the women who were to help with the reception food, and after dinner at my parents' house,

David and I would go for our walk. We'd hold hands. I'd wear these shoes.

Karen may have to wait.

Chapter 24

"Miss?"

Eloise glanced from watching the scenery outside the train's window, across the empty seat beside her. The regular passengers had fallen into a rhythm, just like the hum and rattle of their daily ride. Jacob had always sat beside her, once they began to sit nearer and then together. No one else ever tried to take his place and sit beside her now; that seat was forever his, even when he wasn't there anymore. She looked up, expecting a stranger to be standing there, someone who didn't know she was paired with an invisible other, and who maybe wanted to sit in Jacob's seat.

The porter stood in the aisle, one hand holding onto the back of the seat, the other clutching Jacob's lunch pail. He leaned close, his face fleshy and kind.

"Yes?" she asked.

"I've been waiting for your friend to come back, but he hasn't. I was saving this for him." The porter lifted the familiar black pail. "He left it behind, and since I haven't seen him for a while, I wondered if you could give it to him." He extended the pail her way.

The black lunchbox felt like a lifeline when she grasped it, a tie to her fiancé, a thread that connected her with him again. "Yes," she said, and she clamped both hands around it. She hugged the black pail to her chest. "Yes, I can do that," she promised.

129

"Good." The man straightened. His eyes crinkled into a smile. "I figure he'll be happy to get it back. You have a good day, now." He bowed slightly and strode toward the front of the car.

The pail warmed as she held it against her, the black metal losing its tinny coldness. She hugged it, breathed against it, using her heart and her love to bring it warmth.

She smiled out the window, seeing nothing of the scenery, only seeing him. The surprise he'd have when she approached him with his pail. He was all right somewhere. The lunchbox was proof. It was a sign. She liked signs, and she breathed against this one as she remembered his kiss.

Before the train came to the station where she would get off to walk home, she eased his lunchbox from her chest and settled it onto her lap. She ran her hands over its top, feeling the change, the warmth it had absorbed. She caressed its sides, fingered its handle, lifted the pail, and heard its contents slide to the edge. She set it down again on her lap and undid the front clasps. She'd clean it for him, throw out the old wrappers and pieces of food but save anything else.

As the lid opened, she saw just what she expected— food crumbs, lunch wrappings, his pad, and his pencil. Then she saw an envelope. It was long and brown, neatly tucked against the side. She pried it away with her fingertips and removed it. Closing the lid to the pail, she lifted the envelope's flap and peered inside. Pictures. Some he'd drawn, some actual photos. She set his lunch pail aside on the seat and removed the sketches and photographs. One by one she looked through them and studied them—drawings of people and places, photos of the same. She flipped through each one quickly, thrilled to have this unexpected part of him again.

As Eloise neared the last one, she saw her. It was a photo this time, instead of a drawing. Not of her, Eloise, but another her. She lifted the picture and held it close. This was the profile of the girl Jacob planned to marry. This was the actual photo he'd drawn it from, the sketch that Eloise had thought was of herself. Her hand trembled. The likeness was so similar to herself. Similar, yet not. Jacob's drawing hadn't had minor inaccuracies after all, he hadn't been careless or inexact, nor had he seen Eloise with an artist's eye. He'd drawn her, this woman in the photo, and he'd drawn her exactly as she was, and he'd truly drawn the woman he planned to marry.

Eloise's fingers fumbled back through the pictures and drawings. She pawed through them, awkwardly at first, then furiously. She, that woman, was there in every sketch, every photo. Not Eloise, but her. She'd been there the whole time. It never had been Eloise.

"You getting off, ma'am?"

The train had stopped. She looked up and out the window. They were at the station and the porter was leaning over the seat again. "This is where you get off, I thought maybe you didn't notice." He held onto a bar overhead.

Eloise shook her head.

"You sure?" the porter frowned. "You'll just sit here for a bit until we take off again."

She nodded.

"Okay," he said. "If you're sure."

She sat, time standing still like the pictures Jacob

131

had drawn, like the photos he'd carried in his lunchbox.
When the train finally lunged forward, she didn't care
where it was going. Pictures and drawings slid from
her hands and across her lap with its jolt, a few
slipping onto the seat beside her. Jacob hadn't planned
to marry her at all. It had been another woman all
along. She closed her eyes, and dropped back against
the seat. The train rushed on. Somewhere. Just a train,
now. No love. Just a train.

I closed my book but left the lamp beside my bed
lit. I couldn't stand to be in the dark right now, I
couldn't bear the emptiness that had haunted me since
the day I'd found her photo in Raymond's belongings
and realized I wasn't the one. Not the one he'd planned
to marry all along.

I'd tried to call Karen this evening after everyone
and everything else was taken care of, to give the book
to her, but she wasn't home. Her mother said Karen
claimed she had some last-minute wedding shower
details to take care of and had driven off. I listened as
her mother droned on about how she wished Karen
didn't have to drive, especially at night, and how she'd
advised Karen to take care of the shower much sooner
than this. I let her ramble, glad she was filling my head
with wedding talk, taking up all of the room she could
in my mind so my novel and the fact I'd have it for one
more night would be shoved to the background. "Have
her call me, please," I said when Karen's mother
finished. She promised she would, but once it reached
ten o'clock, I knew Karen wouldn't call. I'd come
upstairs to my room and settled in bed with my book,
just as I did every night, filling and emptying myself,
old hopes and old passions resurrected, then put to

death. Something I should have done long before now.

My bookmark lay beside me. It had slid off my lap as I closed my book. I picked it up and thumbed through the pages, looking for the place I'd stopped reading. I found it at last. The place where the train rushed on without love, where it became just a train. I slid the bookmark in at the next page. Karen would see how far I had read when I gave it to her tomorrow. Surely she'd be satisfied. It was nearly half the book. Enough to know I'd been wrong to read this now and had to move on as best I could.

As I closed the book, the page slipped. It slid loose from the binding, most likely because of all of the pictures Raymond had stuffed inside. I tucked the page back, and as I did I saw several drawings the next page over. There were five altogether, each one similar except for the last one. Raymond had drawn a train, our train, in these sketches, first going one direction, then the other. I could see Eloise's head through the window, her hair color off, more like mine, Raymond's drawing resembling me. Outside the train, amongst the people on the station's platform, the crowd varied with each drawing, but one person stayed the same. It was Jacob, but it could have been Raymond, since I'd written Jacob that way. He was near the train's door, and the door was always closed. The train sped by, and he always watched. In sketch number five, the last one, the train sped by, Eloise—or me—in the seat, the crowd milling on the platform, but Jacob wasn't there. He was gone. Gone. Gone to be with her, I presumed, and he'd left Eloise behind on the train.

Chapter 25

"Martha!" Mama's voice sailed from the kitchen, overpowering the supper noises that were amplified in her flurry.

How does she know I'm here? I asked my father without saying a word. My eyebrows, raised and furrowed at the same time, met his gaze as he peered over his newspaper at me from his favorite chair. I undid the scarf around my neck and hung my coat on the rack. Pans clattered and clanged, something was boiling and something else sizzling, yet somehow Mama still knew I'd come through the front door. "What's wrong now?" I mouthed as Mama called my name again. He gave a slow wag of his head, a sympathetic look I interpreted as a warning.

"Coming, Mama," I called. Daddy mouthed something to me. He looked like a fish as his lips formed a neat circle, framing a nearly perfect O. I smiled. O could be anything, even a silent whistle. I straightened and walked to the kitchen.

Mama's commotion was so frenzied I'd have guessed she was preparing to feed the queen. Pans steamed; bowls dripped; chaos roiled around her. "Mama?"

She turned, a pot in one hand, a ladle in the other, her eyes fiery enough to fry everything in sight. She slapped the pot down on the countertop and tossed the ladle into the sink. I watched it bounce and clatter before it settled at the bottom, where it finally lay still. I looked at her. I'd never seen my mother so incensed as she rubbed her hands on her apron, knotting it into fistfuls of cloth as she did so.

She jerked her head toward one of the two chairs she kept at a tiny table in the kitchen. I pulled one out and perched on its edge. She took the other and stared across the table at me. She had that look, the one that said this argument was already done, and she was the winner. "I'm telling you right now," she began. She propped one elbow on the table and aimed her forefinger my way. "Not Karen, not nobody, is going to have a single copy of that book of yours at the shower."

I drew my head back and frowned. "My book?"

"Yes, your book." The blaze in her eyes grew even hotter. "One of the women coming asked if she could get you to sign a copy of your book at the shower. Karen was thoughtless enough to not only say she could, but the two of them put their heads together and decided a tribute to the success of your pre-married days was in order. A full-blown display of your book is what they're planning. It's an insult to your husband-to-be. I tried to put a stop to it, but they won't listen to me. You're the only one that can do that, so get on the phone and do it right now." Her finger arched in the air.

"A tribute to my pre-married days?"

Mama's palm slapped the tabletop. "Pre-married days that are going to last the rest of your life if you let them make a tribute to that book at your shower. David won't go through with the wedding if he hears about this, and hear about it he will, since his mother and grandmother will be there. Lord help us. After all I've gone through to keep his mother from finding out, too." Mama wagged her head as she patted her chest with one hand. She looked tired, and frightened, even in her fury. She'd look even more tired and frightened if she knew *Love on a Train* was my true story, at least to the point I'd read to last night. "You remember when you almost lost him, don't you? You remember that?" Mama regained a little steam and leaned one elbow on the table again as she stretched my way.

"Mama, please calm down. I wasn't sure yet, back then. I had to be sure, didn't I?"

She drew back, not in the least fooled or consoled. She felt the lie. It wasn't David I wasn't sure of, it was Raymond. Allowing David to take me to the occasional dinner in those days meant nothing to me. There was no commitment on my part at all, but to her it had been a near engagement, one I'd almost ruined.

"He let go. When you just disappeared, leaving him nothing to hold on to, he let go."

Barbour's. That's all I'd had to go on after I found the other woman's photo, the real woman Raymond planned to marry. I stayed on that train instead of getting off after I found it. I rode to another part of the city before the train looped and made its way back to the station and beyond. By the time I got off it was night, dark, and I was somewhere different than my usual stop. I collected Raymond's things and put them back into the lunchbox and got off the train, a different porter on shift by then. He gave me a smile. I was a stranger to him, just another passenger taking a ride.

"Goodnight, ma'am," he said as I exited.

Barbour's. It had occurred to me as I put the sketches and photos back in Raymond's pail. I walked to a nearby diner, went inside, and sat at a small table by myself. I ordered a lemonade and stayed there long enough for the diner's customers to change two or three times.

"Do you know where Barbour's is?" I asked the man at the register when I was ready to leave.

He frowned as he made change for me, his lips working as he tried to recall. "No, not sure as I've ever heard of it. Is it a store? A town? Or one of those countries we fought overseas?"

I shook my head. "Not sure myself."

When I called home from the diner, Mama wailed, but I could hear it was in relief. She reprimanded me for being late, for terrifying her and my father, and for not being at the supper table across from David like I was supposed to have been.

"He just ate and left." The fluster went out of her once she knew I was all right, but her voice was still strained. "You stay put. Don't you dare move. Your father will come get you, and don't you ever do this again. You scared us half to death."

Daddy came. It took him long enough to get to me that we both had time to recover from Mama's flurry. "You know what Barbour's is?" I asked him.

He didn't look at me as he threaded our car through dark streets dotted with occasional globes of light. He shook his head. "If you're looking for something, little girl, now's the time to find it." That was all he said. But it was enough.

I'd spent the next evening at the library, the next at a cinema watching a documentary on our soldiers, how they were trained, and the war. Barbour's had something to do with them or it. The name sounded foreign, but I wasn't sure if it was, and it was a place Raymond's heart had gone. Or stayed. And I had to find it.

"So," Mama said from across the kitchen table, jarring me from my memory of how I'd come to disappoint David. "You get on over to the phone and call Karen right this second. That book of yours can never be a part of your marriage."

Barbour's was most likely where Raymond was now. I'd found it eventually. Far away, on the coast, near the camp where he'd learned to fight and love all at the same time.

"I'll go over to Karen's, Mama. I'll be back before supper." I stood, glanced around the kitchen at Mama's cacophony of cooking, wondering if I dared to leave her alone in this chaos. "You go sit down, and I'll help finish cooking our supper when I get back."

She shook her head, and I could see the tired apprehension on her face again. "No, you get on. Get this straightened out and be back in time to eat. I don't want David to go through that again. You either. You'll lose him for sure, next time. No more books and no more disappearing all of a sudden and running off to do whatever you please."

I hugged her, felt the weary worry in her grasp. Then I slipped upstairs, grabbed my novel from my nightstand, and took it with me. I couldn't live with two different worlds in the same house. It was past time to leave my old one with Karen. I couldn't destroy it, like I'd once thought. I just had to get it out of my head and out of my nightstand's drawer. Not out of existence.

"Karen's been expecting you," her mother told me when she answered the door. I gave her mother an apologetic look. She and Karen both had borne scars for me when I'd supposedly left David before, suffered probing accusations from my mother's tongue. Judging by the return smile on Karen's mother's face, I knew I was right—they'd suffered some more.

"Come on upstairs," Karen called from above us. I smiled at her mother and followed Karen's voice.

"Come on in," she said, using an arm to usher me into her room. "Sorry I wasn't here last night when you called."

"Your mom was worried, and I'm sorry you were out driving so late. Especially since it was for my shower."

Karen shrugged, and pursed her lips.

"It was, wasn't it? For my shower, I mean."

"Let's talk about why you're here."

"Okay…" I frowned at her as I laid my book in her hands. "You want to talk about why I'm here? Well, I didn't finish this."

Karen stared at the novel before she took it.

"I left off almost exactly where I am now, where I was then. I have to leave that old heartache behind right where it is, and get on with my new happy ending." I dropped into her desk chair. "Mama's onto me, but besides that, this is the route I have to take. It's the one that's real, at least. David's here, and Raymond's gone."

Karen left her bedroom door open. I rarely did that at home, but her mother was different from mine. Karen's was like a companion, whereas Mama stayed a mother. I envied the free flow between the two of them and was grateful when they swept me into their circle.

Karen took a seat at the edge of her bed. She turned

my book over in her hands, opened the cover, and stared at the place where Raymond had written his name below mine.

"Heartache doesn't disappear just because you're not looking at it," she said.

"I'll need lots more time than I have if I continue to read that," I said. I watched her thumb lightly through the book's pages and stop where my bookmark was. I pinched my lips together in a straight line as she looked at Raymond's drawings of me on the train and him standing outside it. She frowned, perused the words on the page before them, then closed it.

"Last time you went after this happy ending," she said, looking up at me.

"That's what has Mama in a tizzy." I tried to laugh. "I just heard a rendition of how near I came to losing David when I pursued that happy ending." My laugh fell flat.

Karen set the book on her bed and came and knelt beside me. "I remember that time, the days you were gone. My mother was barely enough of a dam to stand against your mother's determination to figure out where you were and what was going on."

"I never thought I'd get on an airplane," I said, looking down at her. "Never in a thousand years."

"But you did. As frightening and as painful as it turned out to be, you did it."

"I had to. I had to find that happy ending and bring it home."

Barbour's turned out to be a restaurant on the west coast near the fort where Raymond had trained. It hadn't been easy to identify. The library hadn't solved the mystery for me, but another veteran from the war did. And when he recognized the name and described it for me, I knew that was where Raymond had been, probably where he had gone, and understood it was probably where he was today.

"Your mother wasn't easy to fool." Karen shook her head. "If you'd been gone even one more day, she probably would have figured out you weren't off visiting my sick relatives with me at all."

I smiled. I'd told Mama I'd be gone and that if she needed to find me, she could ask Karen's mother how to locate me. I'd called from work, my suitcase with me, told Mama I'd return in a couple of days, and then I hung up. I disappeared, Karen's mother making excuse after excuse for me, why I couldn't be reached, that Karen and I were just fine as we visited a couple of elderly ailing aunts of hers.

I'd flown into San Diego, knew approximately where Barbour's was, and went there. "Have you seen this woman?" I asked as I showed the waiters there the photo of the woman.

They nodded and smiled. They were Greek, and in broken English they told me about her, about the American soldier she was to wed, that even a night ago the two of them had been there, in the restaurant, the woman's father, a very good friend of theirs, giving a toast to the upcoming wedding. Then they marveled how similar I looked to her, wondered if I was related and had come for the ceremony.

I nodded. I lied. "Yes, for the wedding." Tears exploded in my chest as I smiled.

The waiters waved and pointed the direction she lived. I stood stupidly, nodding at information I didn't want.

"Thank you," I muttered. I stumbled with feet of stone for the door. I stood on the walk outside Barbour's, the same place she'd stood in the picture, far too heavy to be able to fly back home. I staggered forward, roved aimlessly along streets with names I didn't bother to read. I fell into a seat at an outdoor café, slumped with my elbows propped on the table's surface, and stared. I'd hoped to find him when I flew to California, prayed it wouldn't turn out the way it had. I'd left my return flight open, wanting a pair of seats together instead of just one. It was to be love on a plane—the happy ending for my own life story, and eventually for Eloise. I could still hear the noise, the sunny beaches sort of noise, as it rolled around me, none of it distracting me from my sorrow, none of it mattering at all. A young waiter brought me a menu, and I asked only for water. He'd frowned and snatched the menu away.

"That was the last time I saw him," I said out loud, staring at the rug on Karen's floor. "In that hum of voices around me, a flood of words I didn't care about, I heard him. His voice. And when I looked up, I saw the two of them, strolling along storefronts. She was laughing and gay; she had my heart for him. She even had my smile, almost my face. She touched him the way I'd wanted to, the way I was supposed to but never had. She did it with finery and elegance. She was sure of herself, where I never had been. He nodded at everything she said. He accepted her fondness, and they strolled on."

I looked at Karen beside my chair. I nodded toward the bed where my book lay. "Mama doesn't know, yet she does. She's terrified of that book, and now so am I.

She said there was talk of having it at the shower, and she wants to put a stop to that. For David's sake. And I guess ultimately for mine."

Karen laid a hand on my knee. She kept it there for a moment before she stood. I didn't watch. I felt her go back to her bed and pick up the book. She opened it to my bookmark, and began to read.

Chapter 26

Eloise rode the train late into the night. She rode until her fare ran out, and then she rode more. The train made a pass through the city, eventually returning to her original stop, the one she should have gotten off at much earlier, the one where she would have gotten off if she'd never seen Jacob's pictures.

It was dark when she stepped onto the station's platform, early morning dark, and she clutched the handle of his pail in her fingers. The metal was cold again, her warmth long since gone. It was too early to go to work, so she walked. Walked streets she'd never ventured onto before, too heartbroken to care about unfamiliar street names or the few unfamiliar people she passed.

"Miss..." A hand touched her arm, the weight of the voice, the stench of it, startled her. She lost her footing, the pail flying from her fingers as she grappled for the nearby wall. Her right foot buckled as the shoe slid off, leaving her clawing at rough bricks as she crashed to the side.

Darkness struck as her head hit the walkway. The black was inside her now, not just in the predawn of the city. Hands fumbled over her, odiferous grunts filled the air as everything she owned was stripped from her pockets. Tin scraped along the sidewalk, and she heard Jacob's pail, the memories of him, being carried away with heavy footsteps. Then the darkness engulfed her until everything was gone. She was alone, inside and out.

Chapter 27

"There's another drawing," Karen said, looking up. "Want to see it?"

I didn't answer. I couldn't. I stared straight ahead, and in my silence I was aware of her tilting my book. She turned it to one side, then the other, then righted it again.

"I really don't understand the point of this…"

I glanced at her. She was frowning at the page and tipping her head as if that might help. "You mean it's abstract?"

"No, silly." She tilted her head again. "I'd say Raymond's artwork was never abstract. It was dead-on accurate, if anything. Maybe that's the problem. Maybe this picture is exactly what it is, and I'm looking for something more." Her frown deepened until slowly the furrows relaxed and her face became her own again. Then it broke into a smile. "I get it, now." She looked at me. "That was it. He drew what was right."

I stood. I came to my feet in one slow, exaggerated motion, walked to Karen's bed, and sat beside her. I stared at Raymond's drawing as she held it up for both of us to see. He'd shaded the scene, creating darkness, a night image with a cone of light from a lantern in the center. Nothing in the light. It was empty, the lantern barely seen at the top.

"I don't understand," I said, frowning like Karen

had before.

"See the hand?" She moved the book nearer to me.

I frowned more and peered closely until I spotted it. A hand holding the lantern, barely visible in the dark. I looked at her. "So?"

"That's a man's hand," she said.

I leaned close again and squinted. I shrugged, and shook my head.

"He's a tall man," she said. "You can tell by what little we can see. You can tell by the angle of his wrist, the marks on the ground where the light hits."

"Tall like Jacob? Or Raymond?"

She nodded. "I assume Raymond, actually. In your story, Jacob wasn't there at the time."

"What would he have been looking for? The pictures that were lost?" I watched Karen as I asked. "Or for me?" We both glanced down at the drawing. "Was he looking for me?"

"He was looking, but I'm not sure for what." She set my bookmark there at that page and closed the book. "You have to read on to know for sure. But he was looking, or he found something you don't know about but you need to know." She extended the book my direction.

My heart pounded. Pounded foolishly, since I already knew the answer. He'd found her. The real her. Far away on the west coast. I'd seen them with my own eyes, and nothing could change that. I shook my head. "No, I can't. Some of his pictures, they resemble me. But I think he was just trying to be nice. That's behind me now. I have to move forward. I'm running out of time."

Karen settled the book onto her lap. I heard the

sigh she probably didn't want me to hear as she stared straight ahead. I glanced around her room, recalling how much it had been a part of me, growing up. I hated the thought of leaving this behind after I was married. David probably wouldn't understand my need to run here now and then, re-center, and get Karen's perspective on life.

"David!" I leapt to my feet. I glanced at her window; it was dark outside. "I'm late! Mama will be livid!"

"Wait, I'll drive you."

I bolted for Karen's door but stopped when I heard the sound of car keys behind me. "Really? You're good enough to just jump in the car and give me a ride now?"

Karen grinned. "Let's just say I can promise you won't be late."

Chapter 28

The noises Mama had made earlier were gone. The house was quiet when I flew in through the front door, Karen's car rumbling away outside. I made my way to the kitchen and gave Mama a nod, even though I wasn't positive I'd accomplished her mission. I didn't know if I'd made the impact Mama wanted on Karen about banning my books from the shower.

"Let's eat," Mama said. It was her way of nodding back, of saying "thank goodness" and "thank you" at the same time. I tried to smile. Mama's tired announcement brought everyone to the table, and in silence we sat down and ate.

"Good roast." My father took a stab at the quiet. Mama nodded. She glanced at all of us, then returned to her eating. "Had another large order at work today," he tried again. "Also had a difficult customer, but David handled him."

I expected David to step in at that point and pick up with the story of the difficult customer. Even Mama should have said or asked something, but neither did. They looked up, but returned to their food and eating as if my father had said nothing of significance. I did the same, wishing one of them had said something. Anything that would fill the air, erase Raymond's picture from my thoughts. I looked at the roast on my plate and took another bite. The wedding was coming at all of us too soon, and yet not soon enough.

"So, how's the bridge work coming?" Daddy looked my way.

Bridges. I nearly dropped my fork. The word struck like a hammer, and the bite of roast in my mouth wanted out. I lifted my napkin and pressed it against my lips, holding the roast in while I tried to chew. My father's smile, his good intent, faltered as he looked my way. The hammer struck again as the bridge question lingered in his eyes. I choked the meat down, turned away from his look, and studied the food on my plate. Everything blurred. The roast swirled with the potatoes, a teary blend of food I could no longer eat.

"Which bridge did you see today?" David added.

I shook my head. I kept my face down, wishing no one would see what I knew they saw anyway—tears, as they splashed onto my hands and soaked into my napkin. I stood. I turned and darted from the table.

I ran for my room, a place David had never been. He could follow me anywhere else, inside or outside of this house, but the threshold to my room was one he had never crossed, never even asked to. I closed the door behind me and fell face down on my bed. I tried to stop the tears, but I couldn't. I was powerless against the deluge that burst upward, from deep inside, and then out.

If anyone dared to come to my door, I didn't hear them. The only sounds were my muffled wails as I bled agony into my pillow, pouring out my pain, hoping to suffocate the fictional me out of my soul for good.

I cried, upheaving misery into the dark for hours. I cried until my sobs were gone and nothing was left behind. Darkness from the room crept inside me and filled the emptiness, the void where pain had been. My last few gulps echoed like whispers in the vacancy. I was alone, inside and out, and there was no light.

Chapter 29

"Nine more days—are you excited?"

I glanced up from the notes I'd taken for Harvey, data about bridges I'd merely been staring at, and turned to the side to the young woman who worked next to me. There was excitement in her eyes, a girlish anticipation that slapped me with the harsh realization her enthusiasm should have been mine. I shoved the bridge notes aside, shifted in my seat, and forced a smile.

"I'm sort of tired," I said. It was an excuse I was giving her, but for me, I needed it as a reason. "It keeps me from being as excited as I want to be." I fell back into my chair, letting my hands drop from the desk to my lap. I'd slept hard after last night's cry. I'd slept late this morning until Mama finally pried me out of bed, gasping when she saw how awful I looked. Her motherly side took over, claiming I should have stayed at the table and eaten like I was supposed to, to keep my energy up, should have kept myself thinking straight so I wouldn't be as apt to fall apart the way I had.

The girl laughed. "Bet you won't get much rest through your honeymoon, either. Think of all the material you'll have to write about after that!" She giggled. Another girl working nearby joined her. "You'll need a vacation after that, so you can sleep and catch up." The giggling increased.

I glanced around at the other girl and forced another smile. Honeymoon. Vacation after that. Mama'd said as much, also, when she rolled me out of bed this morning. "You have David worried now about your job, the way you broke down last night at the mere mention of it. He's thinking about having you quit early, maybe before the wedding, even, so you can keep up your strength." Mama stopped then, standing in front of me as I sat on the edge of my bed, blankets and sheets in knots behind me. She squeezed in beside me, and even though it was morning, I could see the tiredness still in her eyes. "I want what's best for you," she said. Her closeness felt good. For all her veneer of determination, she was still my mama inside. "There's a lot to be said for stability. It isn't fanciful, like what you wrote about, but it's real. David will make a good husband. Everything will turn out fine as long as you don't let yourself get all confused."

I batted some of the sleep from my eyes and looked at her. Confusion was exactly what I was fighting; I just couldn't tell her.

"So you did get Karen all straightened out about no books at your shower, right?"

I nodded, promising myself I would call Karen and be clearer with her about the books. For Mama's sake. Mama had nodded in return and tsked in a way that had made me sigh when she stood and left my room.

"I only write fiction," I said to my coworkers around me. "Nothing that really happens."

"Honey, sometimes all we got is fiction."

I swiveled in my chair and looked back at the woman who was talking. It was one of the few married women in our office. Some married women who'd had to work during the war still worked after it. But most of them returned home when their husbands came back, leaving behind the jobs they'd learned and done well when times were harder and their husbands were overseas. Our gazes met around the girl whose desk sat between us.

"Oh, don't say that." The girl next to me turned also. "I read Martha's book, and I'm planning on every word of it being true."

The married woman lit up a cigarette. She'd never done that before, and we stared, watching her light it, the flame igniting in the air, power emanating from the cloud of smoke she blew in front of her. When she finished the ceremony, her eyes squinted through the haze and fixed on us. She took the cigarette from between her lips, dangled it in her fingers as she propped her elbow on the desk and leaned into the smoke. "Don't say I didn't warn you." She took another draw on the cigarette.

Her smoke swarmed our direction. I inhaled, taking in everything she'd said, feeling the power with which she'd said it.

"When did you start smoking?" one of the girls asked.

"Yesterday," the married woman answered in another cloud. "After I came home from work, tended the kids, fixed supper, cleaned up, and put the kids to bed. I told my husband I was going out for a loaf of bread. He didn't even say anything, just sat there behind the paper, reading and puffing on his pipe. I never bought the loaf of bread. Just these." She lifted a small pack of cigarettes for us to see. "And this." Then she held up the lighter.

I looked at the other girls. Their eyes were wide, either with fright at this woman's picture of marriage, or envy for having a husband. I stood up and walked to the coffeepot. I poured myself a cup and returned to my desk. Writers smoke and drink coffee. I inhaled the woman's smoke and took a sip, letting the writer in me bubble up, surprised how much I missed her.

Chapter 30

Mama had a plate of sandwiches on the table when I came home. Meatloaf sandwiches, with a bowl of potato salad nearby.

I hung my coat on the rack and came into the kitchen. "Mama?" She never made sandwiches for supper, only for dinner.

"There you are." She turned from the sink, every dirty dish already washed except for the ones on the table. "Hurry on upstairs and get dressed for your wedding shower. Your father gave me money, and I bought you a brand-new outfit for tonight. You can use it on your honeymoon, also. Try it on, and then we'll eat and be on our way. We need to get a move on."

"A new outfit?" I hoped she saw the gratitude in my look while I saw the question in hers. The need for reassurance about my book, the divorce between it and me, my shady past nowhere near my promising future. "Everything's okay, Mama. Please don't worry yourself so much. And thank you, and thanks to Daddy, too." I nodded and went upstairs. I'd called Karen from work, told her no displays of my book could be there. She'd laughed and promised. Nine days. And now my wedding shower. I shook my head and chose the fresh new outfit from my closet.

****

Karen had decorated the church's annex in rose

and dark blue, colors that blended and contrasted well together, creating a warm clash of day and night, spring and winter. I smiled. What she'd done relaxed me. I entered the annex and immersed myself in the welcomes of my friends.

A table towering with gifts stood at one end of the room, rows of chairs bowed in an arc around the front of it like happy smiles, rainbows, half-moons of anticipation. I couldn't believe it was for me...mine...and I glanced at it over and over as I mingled with friends, sipped rose-colored punch, and nibbled on dark blue cookies I wondered how Karen had made.

"You haven't spoken with Mrs. Tidwell yet," Mama said near my ear. Her fingers squeezed my elbow as I glanced around the room. "She's sitting in the front row, right over there. You need to go sit with her and chat for a bit." *Please make sure she knows nothing of your book.* That's what Mama was really saying.

I eyed David's mother from where I stood, took in her perfect posture, her tailored outfit, and her overall staid composure. She had come to our house for Sunday dinners a couple of times. The first time was early on, when Mama was the only one entertaining notions of David being my future husband, far too early for me to have registered any more about David than his first and last names. "Just stay still," Mama'd insisted before Mrs. Tidwell arrived that first time. "Be real polite. Nothing more than yes, no, or thank you is needed if she speaks to you." I shrugged when Mama turned away. She'd wasted an admonishment, since my intentions toward our Sunday dinner with Mrs. Tidwell were exactly like Mama's—say nothing, just eat and be polite.

The second Sunday dinner was different. By that time Mama had watched my eyes and behavior light up with a new passion. She'd seen my writing, too, and feared the worst. Not long after, she'd watched my fire go out, the wind disappear from my sails, as I began to drift. She helped me drift into David, saying over and over that it was right and good. When that second Sunday dinner had neared, Mama's tactics to impress David's mother had narrowed, been honed to a fine skill. "Don't mention anything about writing. Keep that to yourself. David and his mother don't need to be frightened away, and hearing about such things would surely do it."

I didn't budge as I looked at Mrs. Tidwell sitting primly in the front row of chairs nearest the gift table, the stranger I'd never tried to know, the one Mama had pretty much prevented from knowing me. Mama's grip tightened on my elbow, and I twisted my arm to get loose. Mrs. Tidwell didn't see our skirmish. She was engaged in a civil conversation with her own mother, at her side.

"You can learn a lot about a man by his relationship with his mother," one of my friends stepped close and whispered as Mama's fingers tightened around my arm.

I noted the erectness in the way Mrs. Tidwell sat. I wondered if I could learn more about David from her behavior than from their relationship. Mama nudged me her way.

After church, that day of our second dinner with Mrs. Tidwell, David had gone to pick his mother up. In the hour he was gone, when it was just Mama, Daddy, and me preparing for that meal, I discovered my writing was gone. Pages and pages of *Love on a Train*, the pages I'd written until I'd stopped after finding her photo, had vanished. I panicked, I ranted, I raved, I accused Mama of taking them. "Please, Martha, you have to understand," she stated firmly but quietly. "It was necessary to clear our house before our guest arrives." I said nothing to Mama. I said nothing throughout our lunch with Mrs. Tidwell. After David and his mother left that afternoon, I helped clear the dishes, then went to my room. On my pillow the rumpled pages lay, pieces of garbage staining their wrinkles, a note on their top. "You need to finish this, little girl, in more ways than one. You're not done. And until you're done, you're not ready." It was Daddy's writing, and I'd cried.

Mrs. Tidwell looked our way as Mama nudged me again. David's mother held her head high, every bit like David in her pose. I wanted to stop. I wanted to run. I wanted to bypass the woman who would never be able to really know me, or me her.

"Mrs. Tidwell," I said, as Mama maneuvered us in front of her. "I'm so glad you were able to come. And you too," I included her mother.

"I wouldn't miss it," David's mother replied, his grandmother nodding in agreement. "Please sit down." She patted the empty seat on her other side. "My sister is coming, also, and she's bringing her daughter. They should be here soon, but please sit and talk with me while we have a chance."

Mama tugged me down toward the seat. I wanted to glare her way, but I smiled instead, keeping my eyes on Mrs. Tidwell. My mother-in-law-to-be in nine days. I dropped into the seat her hand had patted, Mama taking the one next to it. I leaned back, letting the two mothers see each other. I knew at least one of them wanted it to be that way, even if the other looked slightly surprised.

"We're so glad you could make it," Mama reiterated. I knew she'd fill time and space with niceties, kind little comments that really said nothing about what was on her mind. Mrs. Tidwell smiled, leaned forward a bit more as Mama did the same, their good manners volleying back and forth across my front.

I spotted Karen on the other side of the room. She was watching us, and her lips pursed when she noticed I was looking at her. I wanted to excuse myself and go ask her how all of this had happened. How we had suddenly grown up and found ourselves on these complicated adult paths.

"David says you're…"

"A marvelous secretary," my mother finished for Mrs. Tidwell. I saw the surprised look on David's mother's face as she leaned farther forward. "She's very good at her job," my mother continued, "but will be resigning soon, after she's a homemaker."

"I gathered all of that," Mrs. Tidwell said. She looked at me, one of her hands finding and covering mine. "I understand from David that your work is very important and you're quite good at it."

I nodded. I was startled by the warmth of her hand.

"Mrs. Cole."

I glanced up, and both mothers glanced up with me. Karen stood in front of us, her hands clasped as she bent my mother's way. "Excuse me, but we have a question about arranging the snacks. Could you come and help us, please?"

I'd never seen Karen so demure. Even I was convinced she needed my mother's help as she went on to welcome David's mother and grandmother, and apologized for the interruption.

Mama cast a panicked look in my direction, worried my marriage would be in jeopardy if she left me here alone. I could see her thoughts—an imaginary woman could saunter by, one who would stop and mention my book in front of Mrs. Tidwell while Mama wasn't there to deny its existence.

"We really need your advice," Karen cajoled, to get Mama up and out of her seat.

Mrs. Tidwell and I watched Mama finally rise to her feet. As Mama and Karen walked away, I suddenly wished Mama would come back. The silence was already thick without her pointless niceties. They had their place, and the things on my mind, the things important to my upcoming marriage to Mrs. Tidwell's son, were inappropriate to discuss.

David's mother squeezed my hand. I looked away from Mama's back and down to Mrs. Tidwell's nails. They were manicured to perfection, clean to a fault. I prayed that when I looked up Mama would be scurrying back across the room our direction.

"Well, my dear," Mrs. Tidwell said. "There's one thing you need to know. My son, David, is nothing like me." She leaned close as she said it, her sweet fragrance filling the air. "He's like his father, God rest his soul. I was their wife and mother, and I learned to do a good job."

Her sweet delivery, the private confidence she

shared…neither revealed if she was asking me if I was equal to the task, or warning me to flee if I wasn't. Secretaries, especially those who excelled at dictation, didn't flee. They followed the rules, took precise notes of everything everyone else said, and set it in stone forever. But authors were different. They had the ability to create and destroy worlds, write a character in and write another one out. The writer in me felt the panic of being unsuited for the environment I was headed toward. I wanted to erase myself and run.

"Excuse me," I said as I stood, her hand sliding away as I did. Mrs. Tidwell's rigidity returned as I glanced down at her. She stiffened in her seat, the pleasantness I had not expected and did not understand vanishing into the smile she now had on her face. It was the right kind of smile. Mama had it, too. I returned one myself. "I need to greet some of the others who've just arrived. I'm so glad you could come. And I'm glad we had this chance to talk."

She and her mother nodded as I turned to walk toward Karen. I fought the urge to run, but I measured each step instead, placing one foot in front of the other without faltering. Mrs. Tidwell must have been fishing for the writer in me, and she'd found it. I'd thought that part of me was pretty well gone, but there it was, barely a nick beneath the surface.

One foot, and then the other. Just like Eloise. I walked away, trying to hide my limp.

Chapter 31

I began to write again. I didn't mean to, but I couldn't stop it now that this part of me had been unearthed—by David's mother, even if she didn't know. I wasn't writing on paper, as Mama most feared. I was writing in my mind and my heart, capturing stories that were springing up, encouraging characters who emerged from deep within, so deep I thought they no longer existed.

Each face watching me open my gifts, in the arc around my shower table, erupted into a character. No matter that I knew them, had interacted with these women throughout my whole life. As I smiled and thanked each one, their stories rolled out on their faces. I saw them. I read them, and I felt mine rise up and join them. Women whose hearts secreted different lives than they were experiencing chatted and flattered me while sitting primly on their seats, their compliments promising me fiction—promising me a lie. The sort of lie no one dared to reveal. Except an author.

"I'm exhausted." I sank back in my chair after the last gift had been opened, the giver thanked, and smiles exchanged. I watched as ladies stood and headed toward the refreshment table. There were still plates of dark blue cookies and plenty of rose-colored punch left over to satisfy them, not to mention the number of snacks Karen had lured my mother away to arrange earlier. "My face hurts from smiling so much," I whispered to Karen as I rubbed my cheeks. Gifts for my new home with David were stacked in front of and around me, the wrapping paper neatly folded on the floor nearby.

"Keeps the divorce rate low," Karen whispered back, bundling all the cards together. "No one wants to go through this twice."

I didn't have a character for Karen. She was honest and real to the core, no crafty surprises behind tinsel smiles. Only honest surprises, ones that amazed her also, like learning to drive. Mama said being too real was why Karen wasn't married yet. Karen was too clear, too direct, and men didn't like that.

I didn't have a character for Mama, either. Or for David's mother. They were icons instead of people, standard setters for brides-to-be as they fitted young women into scripts where every page was already written. And the same.

I pried myself out of my chair to help Karen gather the gifts. We stacked them at the far end of the table, ready to be driven to David's house as soon as the crowd thinned. Each shiny new appliance I touched, each soft colored linen, each glass dish or metal pan felt like hope in my hands. The promise I was going to be a real bride. Soon. Someone who knew her role and how to act it without being told.

"Well, that went well," Mama said from behind me. Karen and I both stopped. We glanced at each other and then at Mama. We knew she didn't mean the accumulation of fine items lined up and ready to go. It was my book she was talking about, and we gave each other invisible nods.

Mama glanced aside and drew in a breath. We turned and followed her gaze. She was staring across the room where David's mother, aunt, cousin, and grandmother were standing. They milled near the exit, chatting with a few of our friends. Mama was silent, that breath clamped inside until David's family finally disappeared through the door. We watched it close. When we heard it latch, Mama's breath eked out.

"There," she said with more vigor. "That went well."

I'd never seen my mother look so worn. Maybe there was a character in her after all. If there was, this was the moment it would finally surface. I set the toaster I was holding back on the table and walked to her side. I hugged her and held onto that character who resisted being born. "Everything went just fine, Mama. There was nothing to worry about." I let go of her and looked her in the eye. "Right?"

Mama checked the door again, making sure Mrs. Tidwell hadn't slipped back in.

"Right?" I asked Karen, instead. She started to shrug, but she looked at my mother and nodded instead.

"You go on home and rest," Karen said. "Martha and I will finish up here. Several of the girls are staying behind to help us load everything in the car, and then I'll drive it all to David's."

Mama's brows shot up.

"It's okay, Mama," I said. "Karen drives just fine."

Mama glanced at the door again. Nearly everyone was gone; only Karen's mother and a few of our friends lagged behind. Mama gave Karen a look, then patted my arm and ambled away.

"I know Mama didn't do a lot for this shower,

165

since you handled it so well, but in her own way she did more than anyone else. I mean she wore herself out worrying something would go wrong..."

"She didn't worry enough," Karen said, coming alongside me. We watched Mama retrieve her bag, and limp, more than walk, to the door.

I waited until the door closed before I turned to Karen. "What do you mean she didn't worry enough?"

Karen grinned. She went to the small kitchenette attached to the annex and returned with a bag. "You're not finished here," she said.

"More gifts?"

Karen set the bag on the table and reached inside. Her hand came out with three books, my books, each with a slip of paper sticking out of its top. She set them on the table. "Sit down and start signing," she said.

My eyes widened. I stole a quick glance at the door Mama and Mrs. Tidwell had just gone through.

"Come on." Karen dragged a chair my way and made me sit. She handed me a pen and some ink. "I put the name of the person who wants you to sign it on that piece of paper sticking out." She nodded at the stack.

I stared. My heart raced and swelled at the same time. I didn't know if it was for fear Mama'd walk back in and catch me with my first characters—Eloise and Jacob—or catch me with the myriad of others that had sprung to life in my mind all throughout the shower. I laid my fingers on the top book...on my words, on my experience, on her picture...and opened its cover.

"That one's for Linda," Karen leaned close. "Linda Pierce."

I nodded, removed the slip of paper, and began to write. I was amazed at how it flowed, how good the pen felt in my hand, how much of a relief it was to write my own words instead of someone else's. I finished signing Linda's book, then took the second. Barb. I smiled. Mama'd just die if she knew her friend Barb had my book. I signed it with a flourish, a genuine smile stretching my tired cheeks.

"And last but not least," Karen said, sliding the third book in front of me. I opened its cover, enjoyed the wafting scent of paper, ink, and pages feeling like the very essence of me. I removed the slip and read the name. Maude. I glanced up and frowned. "Who's Maude?"

Karen grinned. "You don't know?"

I shook my head.

"You're going to be as familiar with that name as you are your own before long," she said.

Maude. Maude. I shook my head again.

"Sign it," Karen said. "And make it nice. To Mrs. Maude Tidwell, your soon-to-be mother-in-law."

Chapter 32

I held Mrs. Tidwell's book on my lap as Karen drove us to David's house, her family's car overloaded with shower gifts. "I don't know if she really wants me to sign it or just admit that I wrote it." I tapped the book's cover with a finger, looking at Karen across the pile of gifts in the front seat between us. "Mama knew she'd find out," I moaned aloud. "Mama tried so hard to keep her from hearing about the book."

"David probably told her, dear," Karen's mother said from the back, where she'd insisted she ride, pinched against the door by another mountain of gifts stacked beside her.

I shook my head. "He wouldn't. He was as embarrassed about it as Mama was. I don't know how she found out. Someone must have told her, though, since I can't see a woman like her browsing through romance stories at the five-and-dime."

A soft glow shone from David's living room window as we came into his drive. The rest of the house was dark. He was frugal that way—responsible, according to Mama—as careful with his money as he was with everything else he owned. He must have been watching for us, even though I hadn't seen him near the window. He came out the front door and down the steps before we stopped. He carried himself poised and erect, just like his mother had at the shower. *He's like his father*. She said she wasn't like them, but there he was, posturing the same way she had. *I learned to do a good job.* Mrs. Tidwell—Maude—must have learned to be just like them.

I leaned forward to tuck Maude's book under the seat as David approached the car. It bumped over something long and hard. David reached for the handle of my door and I shoved at both, securing them well out of sight as I straightened. Almost as erect as Maude.

"Did you have a nice time?" David asked. He held my door and Karen's mother's door open at the same time. Both of us slid out of the car, and he looked down at me and smiled.

"We did have a nice time," I answered.

After he closed our doors, he came around to Karen's. "You should have let me come and drive the gifts here in my car," he said as she climbed out. "It wouldn't have been any trouble," he added. He offered everyone something to drink before Karen could respond or we could begin to unload. David was polite; he was doing and saying what was proper, even though I knew he didn't approve of Karen driving. Maybe I shouldn't sign his mother's copy of my book unless it was with an apology for writing it in the first place and a promise I'd never do something so bold as that to her or her son again.

David insisted on carrying the heaviest items, and he also found a way to hold the front door for each of us as we came and went. He was efficient; he was orderly. He had a space cleared out in his home—our home—ready for the gifts to sit until we put them away.

I listened to the small talk he made as we worked, scrutinized what he said to Karen and her mother, and then what he said to me, wondering if there was a difference in the way he treated us. There was none. I received the same "Here, I'll get that" as they did. The same "You're welcome," the same "That's too heavy for you," and the same nod every time he held a door.

"Over there," he said to me just as he'd said to them. I set the mixer where David pointed, then stood and watched him show Karen where to put a stack of towels. Surely it was a trap his mother had laid. Surely he knew she'd brought the book to trick me, part of a plan to save him from a humiliating marriage. His impersonal way of talking to me proved it. "Here, let me move those dishes." David hurried to Karen's mother's side. I watched as he took great pains with the gifts. Surely he was planning to return them.

"Thank you," I said the next time he held the door for me. I timed it so he and I were alone on the porch, Karen and her mother back at the car. "David," I said. I placed the tips of my fingers on his arm. "Your mother was there. I spoke with her..."

He placed a hand over mine. It was warm, and I waited for him to remove my fingers from his arm so we could hurry and help unload the gifts. "I'm glad," he said, leaving his hand where it was. "She said she wanted to get to know you better."

"She did?"

"Of course. She's an upstanding woman, and you'll be her daughter-in-law. It's only natural." He leaned close. "Just be careful, you know. Be careful what you say."

...in the book she handed you. I finished his sentence in my mind. "I won't say anything," I promised.

"Why would you do that?" He leaned back and studied me. "Of course you should talk. She wants to get to know you, like I said."

My face burned in the low light. I was glad he couldn't see it. Evidently he didn't know about the book. Evidently there was no trap, and her little comment about not being like David or his father was her attempt at being friendly. "She said you're a lot like your father."

I couldn't miss his glow as we stood together near the door. "She did?" He turned his head, stared off another direction, basking in his thoughts. "We were all like him," he said at last. "Or at least tried to be. He was perfection. Like a machine. Well-oiled, and precise."

I heard footsteps coming our way as David became lost in thought again, striking the pose that was so much like his mother's. Like his father's, in the end.

David turned at just the right moment to open the door for Karen's mother. I watched his precision, the same I'd seen in Mrs. Tidwell, the woman who wanted me to address my book to Maude. David's father would surely never approve. David wouldn't. If only they weren't so precise, I could sign it for her. Sign it for the real her, not the one that was like her husband and like her son.

I walked back to the car and helped carry in the rest. David hugged me goodbye before I slid into the front seat alongside Karen.

"Is it okay if I just come to your house for a while?" I asked as we drove away. I reached under the seat as Karen and her mother both said, "Of course," my hand bumping against my book and whatever lay with it. I wrapped my fingers around the long, hard object and drew it out near my feet. I glanced at Karen. *A cane?* I asked with my eyes. She frowned, gave her head a tiny wag. I tucked it back under the seat and pulled my book out instead.

I settled back and watched lit windows of houses pass by as Karen drove to her home. I tapped a finger on Maude's book. There was so much I needed to know. About Maude, about the next chapter I'd written, the next illustration Raymond had added. I needed to hear my fictitious happy ending again and see what Raymond thought about it, what *Love on a Train*'s true hero had to say about that sort of love, the sort that ended and began with a kiss—but not a kiss with another.

Chapter 33

Karen sat on the floor in her bedroom and I sat across the room in the same chair I always sat in. She leaned against her nightstand with my book on her lap.

"I did read some of this," she said. "I read where you left off, after glancing back at all of the earlier pictures Raymond drew."

"You don't need to re-read all of that to me. I wrote it. I know Eloise woke up in darkness in a hospital. I know they told her the slight blow to the head caused her to temporarily be unable to see, but that sight should return."

"But it didn't," Karen continued for me, flipping back through the pages we were talking about. "At least not yet. Her head healed, but she still couldn't see. At least where I stopped reading. And there weren't any of Raymond's pictures there. Or anything else he might have added."

I'd written darkness into Eloise's world because I felt it so keenly in mine. I knew what it was like to be without light, my light and hers being the one we loved. Or at least believed we loved. I glanced across the room at Karen.

"What is love, really?" I asked, to neither one of us in particular. Eloise regained a shadowy world. The darkness ebbed away a little at a time until she could maneuver enough to make her way amidst the shadows, but it was a world of form only, no color, no distinction. Just images of dull gray. I lived and moved in those shadows. Mine never went away, but with a pencil and the love I'd once felt, I wrote Eloise's shadows away. I brought life and light and color back to her world the way I wanted them in mine.

Karen stared at me. I frowned at a faint blush on her cheeks.

"You okay? I know it's late. I could go if you're tired."

"No, don't go. I was just pondering your question."

I gave her a moment, hoping she'd reach a conclusion and share it with me. She continued to sit. And stare. Warmth remaining on her face.

"So, is love what Mama says?" I asked. "Commitment, hard work, building something solid with no frills? Or is it something different? Something you feel in your heart?"

Karen looked down at my book. I watched her flip forward several pages, then hold the book so I could see. She pressed it open, another of Raymond's drawings there in front of me. "This is the next picture he drew. He put it right before Eloise's sight began to return."

I leaned close and studied what he'd drawn. There she was, on a street, dark glasses, a cane in her hand as she felt her way along the sidewalk. She was blind. Alone in that darkness. On the other side of the sidewalk was a man, a tall slender man with dark hair. He had his back to her in the drawing. He too had a cane and was feeling his way along the sidewalk. I could tell by the way his step was drawn that he was blind. Alone. In the dark. So near Eloise, yet each still blind and alone.

I frowned as I looked at the rest of the picture. Just a sidewalk and buildings. Other persons in the sketch were vague, unimportant, the subject of the whole drawing was the woman and the man, both blind, both alone, both the same. Near, yet far.

I sat back. Karen returned the book to her lap and held her finger where his picture was. "They were both blind," I said.

Karen nodded, her lips pursing in and out. Like a fish.

"But he left," I continued. "Went to marry another. That's not Jacob in the drawing."

"It's Raymond," Karen said. "I don't fully understand it, but I agree he drew himself. Best I can tell is that he understood you, how you felt, and what you were going through."

"Not that he was going through it himself." I heard the ring of hope in my voice even though I stated it as a fact.

Karen shrugged. "We don't know that. He's on the other side of the walkway. Might mean the other side of the country, so I just don't know. But maybe."

I rubbed my face with both hands. Did it matter if he was going through the same thing himself? Feeling alone and lost? He was gone, and I would be married in nine days. Married to David, the sort of man Mama said everyone should marry. "Please read what's next," I said through my hands. I dropped them into my lap. I was tired. Exhausted. Empty and full at the same time. "Please."

Karen opened my book, and turned the page. Her voice, one I had known and trusted more than any other my whole life, filled the room. I leaned back in her chair and let her voice and my words flow around me.

It was the scent of him that brought her head full circle, caused her to stop along the sidewalk and turn. Not the sound. The city was full of sounds—vehicles, conversations, store doors opening and closing. But that scent... She wanted to call his name, to say, "Jacob?" but without the question in her tone. The scent was true, but her heart couldn't believe. Not after losing him...

"What is it?" her mother asked.

Eloise turned back the direction she and her mother had been heading. "Nothing, Mama. It's nothing." Maybe he was with her—the woman he'd planned to marry. Maybe he didn't want Eloise to know he was near, didn't want his wife to know of Eloise at all. Of course. That was it. She was blind, now. Eloise straightened and steadied herself. She would at least try to walk without a limp.

"Like in his picture," I interrupted. Karen looked up from the book. "Sorry, I didn't mean to stop you. But do you think that's what the drawing was about? They were near each other, but he blinded himself to her on purpose?"

"Well, let's see what Eloise thinks," Karen said. She lifted the book and left my question unanswered. I knew what Eloise thought. I wanted to know what *he* thought.

Eloise's senses grew keener, keen enough she would know if he was ever near. She could at least partake of him in that small way, even if it was only his scent. She listened, she felt, she breathed deeply, and she even watched for the tallest of human shadows passing her by. She returned to that same spot day after day, traversed her familiar path, exercising every faculty she had. With hope.

"I found a new position for you," her father told her one evening. "To replace your old one."

Eloise had lost everything following her accident. She'd lost her love, lost her job, lost even her ability to ride the train where love had been. All that had been old and valuable was gone. She'd lacked the courage to imagine new. She thought that, with the old, the future went also, that this was where she would be and what she would do...forever.

Her father stood before her. She could see his gray form even in the dull living room light. "It's in a store near downtown. They need a reliable girl to stock shelves. And once you learn the shelves well, maybe you could even begin to help customers find what they want." His voice sounded excited, he drew near and crouched at her chair. "I'll take you there tomorrow," he said. "We'll ride the train together, and then the streetcar. We'll count the stops, count the steps. You can do this. I know you can."

Eloise heard her mother, something under her mother's breath was said, and her father stood. They moved away, and she could hear both of their voices in another room.

"Foot...fall...danger...embarrassment..." Those were the important words, ones that defined who Eloise was. She sank back in her chair. New was impossible. Even the old had been. Those words had been true with the old, but she just hadn't admitted it, especially after her heart sang.

Eloise stood. She felt and counted her way to the

stairway. She counted her way to the top and entered her room, closing the door behind her. No old. No new. All she had was herself. Whoever that was.

My mouth dropped open. I'd written myself so clearly. How had I not seen it before? I shook my head, my mouth still agape.

"There you have it," Karen said. "And you can close your mouth. You look like a blowfish."

It didn't want to close, but I forced it. And I didn't have to explain the revelation blooming inside. Karen understood. Evidently, even before I did. "That's why you told me to read my book. So I'd understand the old, the new, and what really mattered."

Karen sat without saying a word, just listening to me answer my own questions.

"Is there a picture?" I held my breath.

She shook her head, and I let my breath out.

"Read on, then, if you don't mind." I settled back into the chair.

"It's getting late," Karen said. "Are you sure?"

I glanced at the clock on her desk. It was nearing midnight. It was late. "Nine days late," I said. "Well, eight days in a few minutes. I only have eight days to do this. You'd best read on."

I saw the half smile on her face as she lifted the book and continued.

For the first week of Eloise's new job, her father walked her to the station, rode the train with her, paced the steps to the streetcar and counted its stops, then walked her to the store. They always left under her mother's worries, stopped one block from the house and pried out half of the extra padding her mother had stuffed in the shoe as a further guard, and carried on.

Her father returned to the store at closing time, made the trek back home with her, stopping again one block from the house and re-stuffing the shoe before entering under her mother's scrutiny, her conviction of the impossibility of this new thing.

"It's not really new," Eloise heard her father say one evening. "She's the same girl with the same abilities, they're just stronger now. She's doing fine."

Eloise pondered what he'd said. Her father evidently knew her, understood her, saw how she, the Eloise he'd always known, was improving in these changed circumstances. Then the words "foot... padding...stumble" filled the air. That was how her mother saw her. Those things, too, were true, except she hadn't stumbled but twice. And each time her father had been there and caught her. The past three days she hadn't stumbled at all, and if she did when he stopped escorting her back and forth, she'd catch herself. She would be ready this time.

Their voices became a hum in the background. She sat, settled deep into the sofa, and no longer listened to their words. The hum was like the train, a cocoon of vibration where she'd once fallen in love. She had a different sort of love now. It was the love of her father. A steady, constant sort of love. The kind families are made of. And friendships. Different from the romantic type.

As her parents' voices continued in a hushed drone, Eloise began to understand their love and hers. It was foundational—her father always cementing parts together where her mother spotted flaws and weak spots. Eloise relied on them both and that foundation. It was a work, and solid—and someday she wanted to build upon it, but not just with more of the same structure. She wanted a work of art then. She wanted romantic love. The type she'd had with Jacob. That work of art on a solid foundation.

"Okay, stop." I rose to my feet and walked across the room. I settled onto the floor next to Karen and looked at the page. "Did I actually write that, or are you ad-libbing?"

Karen laughed. "You wrote it, and it makes every woman's heart sing." She closed the book, her finger holding our place, and she turned to me. "Even mine. Is your heart singing?"

I glanced at her, and she smiled. I sat back, hunched where I was, letting the wind seep out of my lungs. "I've lost my work of art," I said, no longer looking at Karen. "I'm just plastering the same old foundation I began with, making it higher and higher." I no longer saw Karen's room, her furnishings, the familiarity I'd grown up with and found safe. I saw me, my solid foundation, pieces of David blending into it, indistinct because he was so much the same. The same as what Mama gave me to start with, what my father had been as our provider. David was my childhood continued, he was safe, he was sure, he was everything Mama said.

"A picture?" I glanced at Karen. She shook her head. "I gotta go, then."

"I'll drive you."

I stood and lifted my coat from the chair I'd been sitting on. "No need. I'll just borrow the cane I found under your car seat."

"No…" Karen opened her mouth, then blushed.

"Someday I'm going to call you Streetcar Karen."

"It's not quite like that..." Her face colored even more.

I smiled, hugged her, and left. Cool darkness pressed against me as I made my way home. But each step was sure and safe. I'd counted them my whole life. I knew the way.

Chapter 34

"I called Ida Mae this morning," Mama said as she scurried to put breakfast in front of me. "It's eight days until your wedding, and she's still not finished with your dress, so I gave her a deadline. Tonight. She argued with me and said she'll have it done day after tomorrow, but I told her that's too late." Mama dropped a pancake on my plate and scooted butter and syrup my direction. "You'd better hurry. And maybe put more powder on your face. Those circles under your eyes are getting darker, you poor thing."

"Did Daddy leave any coffee behind?" I asked.

Mama's eyebrows arched toward her hairline. "Coffee? You don't drink coffee." Her voice arched like her brows.

I didn't dare say writers did or I'd have to peel her eyebrows off the ceiling. "I've had a cup or two at work," I said.

"Well, I'll be." She went to the kitchen and made noises I recognized as coffee noises. I ran my hands over my face. I knew I looked hideous. But it had been one a.m. when I walked home from Karen's, and then I'd lain awake until four. Two hours of sleep. I looked down toward my cheeks. I thought I could see big purple bruises bulging beneath my eyes, like a fighter who had lost.

Mama returned to the dining room and set a

lukewarm cup of coffee in front of me. "There," she said. "It's all that's left, but I daresay you need it." She settled her hands on her hips and studied my face. "Maybe you could catch a quick nap after you get home from work this evening. I'll make a nice pot of chicken-and-noodle soup, homemade rolls, and peach cobbler for dessert for all of us. That ought to perk you up some. After that we'll go try on your gown for the last time."

I took a long drink of the coffee, praying it infused enough life into me I could stay awake for Mr. Wilson's meetings today. His project was becoming complicated. More attorneys and construction companies were getting involved, and I needed to look and act the part of a good secretary. The coffee was good; it would help. But Mama was right. I knew I'd need more powder on my face to make up for the lack of rest.

I set the half-empty cup back on the table and looked up. "Mama, is it okay if I just spend this evening alone?" I braced myself for her reaction. She didn't disappoint me, her eyes rounding out like two full moons. "Now, before you get all worried about it, I just need some time. To rest, to kind of gather my wits, if that's okay. And Ida Mae can have an extra day to work on my gown this way. Let her have the leeway and give me a little break." I felt Mama sifting through my reasoning, searching for lies. Lies that to her meant landmines, snares that threatened the future she considered right and safe.

"Maybe after David leaves and that gown is fitted," she said. "Then you can have all the time you want."

"No, Mama. I mean really alone. For more than an

Colleen L. Donnelly

hour or two. Just me."

Panic lit like fire around her moon-shaped eyes. "Absolutely not! Why, David is a part of our evenings now. He's expected here at his usual time, and he'll eat with us, and so will you. And you'll go to Ida Mae's right after that."

I drank the rest of the coffee and left the naked and cold pancake where it lay. I wiped my mouth with a napkin and stood. I stepped to Mama and planted a small kiss on her cheek. "I know you mean well, Mama, and I understand you do everything for my good. You've taught me well, so you're going to have to trust you've done your work right by trusting me. I need this evening to myself. I'll stay downtown. Go ahead and feed David like usual. Tell him I'll see him tomorrow."

I left the house hungry, rained upon by Mama's frets. They followed me down the sidewalk and stayed with me as I hurried to the train. Once I stepped through the train's door, I left them behind. I washed myself of Mama. Of my father. Even of David. I chose a seat in a new place, next to a person I didn't know, washing myself of Raymond, also. This was my train ride. Eloise's train ride. The one I'd written about, without ever understanding why.

Chapter 35

I lived on coffee all day. I found it pleasantly euphoric as I took notes for Mr. Wilson. The heated discussion around the table didn't make a dent on my elated body chemistry. I wrote their words but thought of some of my own, character comments and stick figure sketches filling the borders of my pages.

Every time Harvey said, "Miss Cole, could you please read that back to us?" I was able to do so. I felt perfectly dichotomous, the staid and predictable secretary alongside the colorful and creative writer. No matter how urgent the command, no matter how thick the deliberation, I followed their words, took them down, and read them back precisely, all the while spinning more eloquent phrases of my own in the background.

I took another sip of coffee, swallowing the last of the rich, black flavor as Mr. Wilson announced a break for lunch. Everyone shuffled papers, focused on what their own hands were doing in order to avoid eye contact with each other. I stood. I wanted to stretch and yawn, but I didn't. I drew in a deep breath instead, smiled at Mr. Wilson, then went to my desk, my sandwich, and my typewriter so I could transcribe the morning's notes.

Mr. Wilson stopped in front of my desk on his way to Mr. Arnold's office. He thrummed long fingers on its wooden top as I glanced up. "I hate to do this to you, Martha," he said. His eyes looked tired, almost as exhausted as mine. "But could you come in and work tomorrow? I know your wedding is coming up and you need your Saturdays, but if you could spare the time, it would be fantastic. I'll pay you extra, if that would help."

I thought of my gown, the most important thing on Mama's list, but it would have to wait until Sunday. I wouldn't ask Mama or David what they thought, I'd just do it. After all, the extra money would mean something to David. "Of course. I'd be happy to help you tomorrow."

My answer brought crinkles to Mr. Wilson's eyes, relieved ones that deepened the tired and strained lines that were already there. He thanked me and slipped into Mr. Arnold's office. I could hear the terse buzz of their voices, detect the unpleasant effects the morning had had on my new supervisor. While their verbal buzz droned on, my coffee buzz wore off. I turned to my typing, my fingers moving much more slowly than they had all morning. Characters that had cropped up with excitement now plummeted like lifeless puppets, dropping through gaps between what I was typing and what I could hear from Mr. Arnold's office.

"Your mother called while you were in the meeting." My coworker who sat next to me was removing her coat, just back from lunch. "Twice," she said as she hung the coat on the rack several of us shared.

I stopped typing. My coffee-lacking characters dissolved into oblivion. "Did she leave a message?" I asked.

My coworker shook her head as she took her seat. "Well, not verbally." She peered at me from the corners of her eyes as she grinned. "But I heard a message in her tone, if you know what I mean."

I nodded, shook my head, returned to a nod, then gave another shake, until I found my head going in circles. "I need more coffee," I said, rising to my feet. "Want some?" I lifted my cup her direction, and she scrunched up her face. "If she calls again, just tell her I'm sorry I can't talk, but I'm tied up in meetings. I'll see her later tonight, and everything will be fine."

My coworker nodded as I went in search of more coffee. Mama needed a night off as much as I did, but she didn't realize it and never would. My hand shook as I emptied the percolator into my cup. It could have been the amount of caffeine I'd consumed—or the amount of audacity I'd dared. I'd written a book. Now I was reading that book. And, worst of all, I was finally ready to sign one for Maude.

"To Maude—Not to the beautiful woman I see on the outside, but to the beauty on the inside that I hope to see, and to be. Love, Martha."

Chapter 36

I knew the trains and streetcars ran until late in the night as I veered from the station where I usually got on after work. I walked the other direction, away from my home, down streets and sidewalks where I could stroll without thinking.

I wove in and out of shops, touching things the way Mama had never let me as a girl, handling glass figurines and running my fingers over fabric. I let my senses guide me, let them experience everything the way Eloise learned to. The way they used to. Before. Before being an adult, before becoming engaged, and before turning into a woman. I lifted a small bowl and looked at my distorted reflection in the glass before I set it back down with a smile and walked back outside.

I inhaled, I saw, I felt. Last of all, when my other senses were sated, I planned to taste. I'd treat myself to the sort of dinner my mother would never cook and David would never spend money on. It was my fling, my last evening of being Martha. The Martha I'd been when I was a writer, the pieces of me that kept emerging as my tale of Raymond and me unfolded.

A bell above the door of a department store tinkled as I entered. I enjoyed its sound, paused, and listened to it again as the door closed behind me.

"May I help you?" An elderly woman appeared, her hands clasped together, a smile mounding her soft features.

"I'm just looking around," I said. "Thank you."

As she ambled away to help another customer, I gazed at the shelves and displays. This was more than just dry goods or knick-knacks; this was an anything-a-person-could-ever-imagine sort of store. I began touring the perimeter, then worked to the center, covering all the aisles and counters, shelves and displays. The bell tinkled over and over in the background as I meandered through nameless customers who came and went. I absorbed all the store had to offer, studied and learned its shelves without restraint.

The elderly woman made her rounds and returned to me. "Anything at all you are interested in, please let me know."

I smiled and nodded, a tiny glass deer resting in my hands. When the woman moved on again, I peered around the store through the deer's clear glass belly. Lights and colors took on unusual dimensions, the same way a story distorted, but enhanced, the truth. I set the deer down and glanced at the front windows. Even though the outdoors was dark, people still continued to pour into and out of the store. I'd never realized how alive downtown was compared to the area I grew up in. Downtown had its own energy. The sort I felt when I wrote.

I walked through the department store's doorway, listening to the tinkle one last time. When it closed and was behind me, I stepped to the middle of the sidewalk, letting people pass me in both directions and on both sides. I breathed. I inhaled the city's energy, absorbed its lights, its sounds, its vibrations. I tossed my head back, closed my eyes, and turned in a circle, breathing in its life from every direction.

I stretched my arms down and back like a bird soaring upward and drew in everything I could. The city's sounds, its flavor, its...

My head stayed back, my arms splayed down, but my circling stopped. I inhaled. Held my breath and tasted it, then released it. I did it again. And when I tasted it, I knew it was him. He was there. I could smell him, taste him, somewhere near. I opened my eyes and lifted my head. I drew in another breath, and then another, searching for the aroma of the man I'd been so sure I loved. I turned both directions. I darted amongst the passersby, seeking out the tallest, the thinnest, the one with the darkest hair. And that smell. I inhaled as I traversed the walkway. I inhaled as I moved up and down, but the odor was distant; his scent had waned. I threw my nose into the air and tried to find it again, sift it out from amongst all of the other odors, but it was faint. It thinned. It slowly vanished, until it was gone.

I made a circle, excusing myself to people who needed to get by me. I crossed the street and inhaled again. I looked up and down the sidewalk.

He was gone.

Just like before.

Music caught my ear. A clarinet, a piano, a soft-spoken crowd spilling out of a restaurant's front door. He was gone. I fell into the sway of people entering through the ornate door. Once inside, I paused—sights, smells, sounds. And new things to taste.

"Table for two, miss?" a gentleman asked as the door closed behind me.

Gone. I glanced around at the couples, distinctive pairs, decked out in elegance, tightly knit and bound together as if they were one. I didn't want to know. I couldn't look for black hair, dark eyes, a smile that laughed with her, the woman he planned to marry.

"No." I shook my head. "A telephone, please?"

"Right this way."

He led me to a dark corner and tipped his head toward a phone on the wall.

"Thank you." I dialed Karen's number and waited until I heard her voice. "Can you meet me for supper? I know it's late...Good. The diner near your house?... I'll be there soon. I'm still downtown, so give me a little bit....And Karen, would you bring the book?... Okay. Thank you." I hung up.

I exited the restaurant's door without glancing back at the couples. Their fairy tale world that looked real. Flesh and blood, men touching women, women enjoying it and wooing them on. Close, romantic. Everything I'd wanted, everything I'd written. Maybe even him.

I couldn't look back.

****

Karen waved from our favorite booth in the back of the diner. We'd been coming here for years, first with our mothers and then on our own. Nothing exotic. I'd eat my usual chicken meal instead of something new and unfamiliar as I'd intended earlier in the evening. Being downtown had hurt, but inhaling it, feeling it, experiencing it taught me one thing—everything it offered was already in me. I wouldn't have recognized and drunk in its distinctive nuances unless that was true. We were one. I'd learned that much about myself, and I didn't need to taste an expensive meal to tell me what I already knew: I was red napkins.

I slid in across from Karen. The smile on her face was like a mirror. Not that I was smiling. It was the satisfaction she had upon seeing me that reflected the relief I felt.

Her smile turned to a grin. "You'd better wipe that glow off your face before you go home."

"Mama call you looking for me?"

She nodded, small at first, but it grew until her whole head was bobbing like a horse's at a trough.

"I had to get away," I said. "I thought it would help me get some clarity. And in some ways, it did."

Karen's nod slowed. She did that thing where her lips puckered out. "You were downtown…"

"I stayed there after work. It was…it was revelational. We should go there sometime. At night, I mean." I paused. "Sometime soon, I guess, since…"

"Eight more days," she finished for me.

A waitress handed us menus, which we took, even though we always ordered the same thing. We each stared at the columns of offerings as if eight days weren't looming over us, as if we really did have all the time in the world.

"I smelled him," I said, without looking up. Karen's menu didn't budge. We held them between us as if I'd said, "Bread and butter sounds good," instead. We sat in silence. I knew what she was thinking. I knew she understood exactly who "him" was.

"You ready to order?" The waitress reappeared.

"The small fried chicken dinner," I said. "Mashed potatoes and white gravy. Green beans."

"Same for me," Karen said. We handed our menus to the waitress and sat exposed to each other, Raymond the only thing between us.

"It was there, the aroma of him, in the downtown air. As strong as I smelled it on the train when he was right there beside me. It was him. It had to be." I fiddled with the glass of water the waitress had brought. "But of course he's gone, so maybe it wasn't him. He's back at Barbour's, most likely, far, far away." I slumped against the padded seat and grasped my head in my hands. "Eight days! In eight days I'm getting married, and I'm imagining the scent of someone who doesn't even love me. What's wrong with me?"

Karen was quick to stretch her arm across the table, her hand reaching to its edge. She didn't touch me, I was too far back in my seat for that, but it was enough to have her come my way and let me know she was there. "All right. Nothing's wrong. You took a much-needed night away, no matter how much it made your mother squirm. You say it helped some, so let's get everything else that's bothering you settled. I'm your maid of honor. That's what I'm for, to help keep things straight for the bride."

I stared at her fingers on the table in front of me, slightly bent but directed my way. I gave a slow nod, dragged my hands down the sides of my face, and slumped farther. "Okay," I said. "Okay," I said again.

Karen straightened and stared at me. "So you have eight days before you become Mrs. David Tidwell."

I nodded.

"You want to do that, I assume. I mean, you do want to become Mrs. David Tidwell…"

"Yes, of course I do. That's what every young woman wants. To be a wife, and someday a mother. Keep a house and be provided for."

"Good. Okay. Good lecture. I asked what do *you*

want?"

I stared at her. My friend who had learned to drive and carried a mysterious cane. She'd gone over the boundaries and was giving me permission to do the same. I ran my hands over my face. Karen had a way of broadening the right path in life without offending anyone except my mother, always staying to the course but allowing in a little extra scenery the rest of us sometimes missed. "Mama would die on the spot if she walked in here and heard you ask me that," I whispered.

Karen leaned my direction. "When your Mama got married, times were hard. People got married more like a business arrangement. They had to survive. Marriage doesn't have to be that way so much these days."

"But what about the shortage of men since the war—"

"Here you go," the waitress interrupted. She slid two identical suppers in front of us. "Anything else?" We shook our heads, and she disappeared.

"Even that doesn't change things for you. You're not competing for a job vacancy, you're becoming a wife. The woman who wrote about love is becoming David's wife," Karen said as she rearranged the food on her plate. She glanced up, one eyebrow raised. "That's a good thing for him. He should be excited." She grinned, and resumed working her gravy into her mashed potatoes.

A good thing. I picked up my fork, then set it back on my plate. I heard the clink over all the other sounds in the restaurant. *Love on a Train* was fiction. The me that wrote all of that was wrong. If it hadn't been fiction, Raymond would still be with me and I would be living my book instead of writing it. With a real happy ending, like he must be doing, not just making one up."

Karen leaned my direction, close enough to spot the tears I was sick of. "Okay, I'm sorry. Please relax. As your maid of honor, I'm here for you. I'll stand with you as Mrs. David Tidwell the same way I stood with you as Martha Cole the writer, the secretary, the woman in love, and my friend. And…I'll shut up if you want."

The tears had their way. They ran down my cheeks and splattered onto the napkin on my lap. I picked it up and dabbed its corner on my face, arresting the streams before anyone else had a chance to notice. "I was such a fool," I whispered. "I just need to admit that and move on. Raymond wasn't in love with me, so I've wasted my time. Even if I am too red-napkins for David, he's the one who is promising to be there with me, take care of me, raise a family with me. That's the kind of love Mama says is real and lasts. That's not what Raymond had for me; he wasn't like David at all. Mrs. David Tidwell will be taken care of by a steady husband, if I can just get the red part of her under control."

Karen said nothing. And neither did she eat. Both of us sat while I cried, both of our dinners chilling, turning pasty with grease. My tears flowed. I couldn't stop them, so I collected them with my napkin. Tears of love spilling out when I'd thought there couldn't possibly be more, darkening the plain white cloth, bleeding it red. I choked out a final sob when I was done, a slight hiccup of pain that drained away. My face felt warm, and I knew it was puffy, my eyes feeling tight and swollen. Again.

"I'm sorry." I held the napkin across the lower part of my face with both hands. I looked at Karen. "I'm sorry I ruined our supper."

She shook her head. "It doesn't matter whether we had supper or not. Eight days is what matters." Whereas eight days had looked like an eternity on her face before, an expanse of time we didn't have to deal with yet, it looked like yesterday now. She glanced down at her side as if consulting with the seat.

"What?" I asked. "What are you thinking?"

She glanced up, then back down at her side again. "Maybe the red will take care of itself later, after you're married." She picked up her fork and bounced it on the cold mound of potatoes and gelled gravy. "You still hungry?"

I shook my head and scrunched my nose. I wiped the napkin over my eyes once again before I laid it beside my plate. "You know, I asked you to bring my book…"

"You did? Oh, careless me. Guess you won't be getting it tonight. Sorry." Karen laid her fork aside and flattened her napkin on the table.

I stared at her. She didn't look up. "That's okay," I said. "I just thought we could read the next part together. I was going to take it home after that, and finish it. Now I…"

"I didn't realize how short eight days could be," Karen interrupted, glancing across the restaurant. "You really don't have much time." She spotted the waitress and waved her over. "Can we have our tab? I'm paying, just put both on one."

"You want to take those meals with you?" The waitress frowned at our untouched plates. "I can bag them, if you want."

We both shook our heads. She filled out a ticket and laid it on the table. Karen took it and the waitress carried our plates away. I started to stand, but Karen stretched across the table and stopped me.

"One question," she said. "I have to know, as your maid of honor and your best friend. Is this what you really want to do? Marry David?"

I stared at her. I couldn't go back, not to what was before. There was nothing there for me. I had to move forward, first as a secretary, then as a wife and mother. I could never be a wife and a writer, David wouldn't stand for that. I could be a wife with tales in my head, maybe. Or tell bedtime stories to our children. And if I didn't marry him, I couldn't be a writer only. Mama said I could never make a decent living at that, even though I'd never told her of Mills and Boon's requests for another book. I would get married. I'd be a wife and a mother. My heart would catch up; my red would mellow. Eventually.

I straightened and looked Karen in the eye. "I'll marry David," I said. "That's what I will do."

That wasn't what she asked. I saw it on her face. "I'm behind you, then." She nodded. "All the way."

We stood. She dragged her bag from the seat beside her and slung it over her shoulder. It slapped against her side. She glanced at me and moved the bag to the other shoulder, the one away from me, and she took my hand.

"Thank you," I said. "I'll be okay now. These eight days will go fast."

Chapter 37

Eloise was aware of him again, of his scent, and as she turned, gray shadows moved around the store. Some tall, some short, but none calling out her name and saying they were him.

"Thank you for coming in to work today. It's such a busy time for you, for both of us, so let's get started. You ready to go to a meeting?" Mr. Wilson stood in front of my desk. I jumped to my feet, floundered for a pencil, for a pad, and reached for the back of my chair to grab my satchel.

"I'm sorry, I was thinking about something else." I wiped Eloise from my mind. I'd given Karen my book for a reason. I couldn't let it keep running through my head. "There," I said, stuffing everything into my bag and grabbing my jacket. "All ready, sir."

He grinned down at me. "You can slow down a little bit. It's going to be a long day, and we want to save all the energy we can." Harvey led me outside to his car, held my door for me, then climbed into the driver's seat. "New bridge on the other side of downtown. Construction hasn't begun yet, so we're just meeting the engineers and architects. I hope to get them to be my first official contract, even with some of the legalities still pending."

Mr. Wilson took us into downtown. I watched from my window, seeing it in the daylight this time, seeing it with its morning energy and trying to figure out where I'd been the night before. I spotted the train station and followed the nearby streets with my eyes, looking for landmarks and store names, wondering where the department store was…and the restaurant.

She left the stack of cups on the counter and made her way into the customer-filled floor, listening for his voice, searching for the aroma of him again. She followed the scent to the door. He must have gone. Had he seen her? Was he avoiding her? Was it even him?

"Did you?" Mr. Wilson asked.

I whirled in Mr. Wilson's direction. "I beg your pardon." I felt my face heat up. "I'm sorry. I guess I have a lot on my mind. Forgive me."

He laughed. "Of course you have a lot on your mind. You're getting married soon. I'm the one who should be sorry. Weddings are full-time jobs. When is it? I've forgotten."

"Seven days."

He took his eyes off the road and stared at me. "Seven days? And you're still working?"

"Well, I wasn't planning to resign yet, just…"

"I mean, I'm thrilled you are, but when I got married I didn't even see my wife for at least a month before the wedding, with everything she had to do, which was unusual for us. We were together every day before that. No one could keep us apart." He chuckled. "My goodness, that was a long time ago."

I tried imagining Mr. Wilson as a younger man, with a young woman, the two of them unable to keep apart. It wasn't an image I'd ever considered, but somehow it was easier to imagine him with whoever his wife was, holding onto each other, than it was to envision me and David the same way.

"You were in love?"

He glanced at me, his brows raised. "Of course we were in love. Still are. But back then, those months we were engaged...whew! We couldn't wait, if you know what I mean. Couldn't get married fast enough. Probably the same for you and your fiancé, I assume."

I looked straight ahead. I tried to smile, but my brows pinched together, making it feel like a grimace instead.

"So maybe it was a good thing my wife...well, fiancée at the time...was totally submerged in the plans. Like I said, planning that wedding took all of her time. How are you managing to get everything done and still work at the same time?"

"My mother helps a lot." I glanced his way.

"My wife's did, too. Even mine pitched in. I guess women like that sort of thing more than we men do, but I have to say, they did a marvelous job. If it had been left up to me, we would have gone to a justice of the peace. My wife probably would have cried her eyes out the whole honeymoon over the disappointment at what I would have considered an adequate ceremony." Harvey laughed. "I've learned to appreciate those things about women, over time. You know, the nice little things like flowers, frills, candy, and candles now and then. Maybe more so now that I'm back from the war. War changes a man. Makes him see love and life with a new fervor. And gratitude."

I stared at him. I didn't realize I was, until he glanced over at me and frowned. One side of his mouth kicked up in a grin. "Having a hard time figuring me for a softie? Well, don't spread it around. Bad for my image. No one would build a bridge designed by a guy who enjoys holding his wife's hand after a candlelight dinner."

It wasn't just imagining him as a softie, it was also pondering my father. He never sat and held Mama's hand, but I saw him doing it often in his eyes. And Raymond. Raymond who took the time to draw the love of his life, the woman he planned to marry, not long after he returned from the war, the war that changes a man and makes him appreciate love and life. "Do you draw?" I asked.

Harvey snorted. "Now that's one thing I don't do." He laughed and turned to me again. "So tell me about your lucky man. He must be proud to get someone like you. You're very talented at your job, talented enough I hope he lets me keep you for a while."

I smiled. "Well, for a while. Same plan we've always had. When we start a family, I'll be home full time after that."

Harvey nodded. "That makes sense. So tell me, how did he ask you to marry him? Anything special?"

My thoughts ran back to the days David was supposedly courting me, the weeks I'd spent focused on writing my book and riding the train beside Raymond, planning and plotting my life with him instead of the one I was ending up with.

Mama's voice rang in my memory, a warning from when things changed, to never do again what I'd done to David. The time I'd disappeared to find Raymond, hoping to cement us as one and bring him back to where we'd begun.

The plane ride home from the west coast where I'd gone to find Raymond had been long. And lonely.

Karen's family picked me up at the airport and brought me home, pretending our lies of me traveling with Karen to visit ailing aunts were true. It was easy to look tired when Mama eyed me upon my return, and the deep-gutted sorrow was unnecessary to pretend.

"Karen's aunt is so ill," I lied as Mama scrutinized me. "It was so sad."

"Not as sad as David has been," she shot back. She caught herself as Karen's mother gave her a startled look. "I mean a different sort of sad," she backpedaled. I left her apologizing to Karen's mom while I disappeared to my room.

David came that evening. We all ate in stony silence, stonier than usual because I said nothing about my absence, made no apologies to ease their misgivings, kept my broken heart to myself, thankful for the quiet. David still came every evening after that. Like a moving statue I dragged myself through the motions. I walked where I should walk, I spoke when spoken to, I went where he or my parents suggested, and before I realized what had happened, I'd slipped into the understanding that I was to become David's wife.

I glanced over at Harvey and watched him drive. I pinched my lips together, tempted to invent a story about how I'd come to be David's fiancée. I thought of my novel, of how I'd wrongly believed Raymond had asked me to marry him when he hadn't. That moment, when I thought he did, was romantic, just like it had been for Eloise. And special. But nothing about my becoming engaged to David was special. Nothing at all. I wasn't even sure if or when it had actually happened.

"He...my parents...it was a rather quiet affair," I

finally said.

"Well, not every man is up front with his feelings. Tell me more about him. Name? Tall? Short? Handsome?" He looked at me. "Draws?" And he winked.

My face heated up. I felt the crimson radiate from my cheeks. "His name is David, and no, he doesn't draw." I wanted to press my face against the cool window to dowse the flames. I glanced at its glass, tempted. "He's a very good businessman," I said, still looking at the window. "He's neat and orderly. Very practical. Blond. Kind of tall, but not overly so." I was running out of things to say. I saw the front of the restaurant I'd called Karen from go by. It looked different in the daylight. Its doors were closed, and people were passing it by, waiting for evening again, when the time was right, and when they were with the right person, the one they loved.

"He sounds…" Mr. Wilson thought for a moment. "Solid. Sounds like he'll make a good family man."

"Thank you. I think he will."

It was no use to stand on the sidewalk and stare up and down the street. Eloise couldn't tell one person from the other. She needed to be near him to know for sure. She needed to hear his voice, touch him, share his laughter the way they used to do. The sidewalk seemed cold and lonely in spite of the hurrying crowd. Individuals, clusters, families, business partners… If he was there, he'd be part of a couple, not alone. She shied back toward the store, felt her way to the door, and returned inside. She prayed he didn't see her if he was there. He'd only be more glad he loved another, and not her.

Chapter 38

I rode home on a later train than usual. Mr. Wilson was right: the day was long, the bridge meeting farther away. It was dusk when we drove back through downtown. I'd watched in the evening light and saw again the restaurant, the sidewalks, even the department store. Somehow they were all there and lit up and alive in the encroaching darkness, even though invisible and quieter during the day. Night was a time for lovers to emerge and find their way onto the streets, bringing life to them the same way a writer brings life to the characters in her mind.

Harvey had offered to drive me all the way to my house. I wasn't sure which would be worse—to be late, like I was, or to be driven home by a man. Mama'd said nothing to me in the morning about not coming home like I was supposed to the night before. She was as cool as the breakfast left out for me, barely managing to give me a look when I said I'd be working all day.

When the train came to a stop at my station, I stepped down onto the platform in poorly lit darkness and turned toward my home. I bundled my coat tighter around my neck and pressed my hands into its pockets to hurry that way.

"Martha?"

I stopped and looked through the poor lighting into the obscured face of a man.

"David?"

He didn't answer. He only stood there, his hands, like mine, shoved deep into his pockets.

"Why are you here?"

"Why are you?" he asked.

"I'm always here in the evening."

"Always?"

The cold air burnt as I breathed in. I wanted to cough, but I let my breath seep out quiet and slow. "Almost always. Pretty always."

"I've been waiting over an hour," he said. He stood so that the light was blocked by the brim of his hat, his features falling beneath a dark shadow.

"Was I supposed to meet you?"

"You're supposed to be on time. Reliable. Home every evening. Especially on the weekend." It was David's voice but Mama's rules, the ones she'd tutored me with all of my life. Actually, probably his rules also. His father's. I didn't know. He and I never spoke enough for me to know.

"I worked extra today. And late," I said. "We worked on the other side of the city, and we had to drive…"

"That won't do when we're married."

The Martha Cole who wrote *Love on a Train* will still be Martha Cole when she becomes Mrs. David Tidwell. Red napkins. White tablecloth… I could see and hear Karen. I could feel my heart beating so hard it threatened to bleed.

"And last night? Where were you?" David continued. "What were you doing? Isn't there enough to do for our wedding? How can you afford to just…disappear?"

I'd never heard sharpness in David's tone before, not even the first time I'd disappeared. Our lives traveled a level continuum—no sudden turns, no rises, no falls. "Didn't Mama tell you I needed a night to relax?"

"Husbands and wives don't get nights to relax. We have responsibilities. Others are counting on us. Will you do this when we have children?" He paused. "If we have children?"

"David, that's…"

"I had plans for us last night. My best man and his wife were taking us out, as a surprise. When I came to your house to get you, and your mother said you probably wouldn't be home…" He glanced to the side. There were no tears in his voice, and his face was still hidden in the darkness. I removed one hand from its pocket and touched the front of his coat. He glanced back at me. "I need to know, Martha, if you want to be my wife or not. If you don't, you need to let your parents know, also. They are counting on us to be a couple."

I slid my hand down the front of his coat and returned it to my own pocket. "And you?" I asked. My voice was loud, too loud, and with too much of an edge for the private conversation we were holding in a public place. I lowered it, and asked again. "Are you counting on us?"

"I counted on you being there last night. I've counted on you being where you were supposed to be in the past, but you weren't. I counted on you getting off an earlier train tonight, and you didn't."

"David, it's easier to count on people if they talk. I don't know what you're thinking, since we never…"

"What I'm thinking? Don't my actions tell you what I'm thinking? Aren't I there every night like I'm supposed to be? And don't I tolerate a lot?" He tightened. I could feel his tension from where I stood. It was as if all the conversations we'd never had were there, exploding out of him all at once. "Your book, for one thing. It humiliated me. It was something I hid from my mother and was glad my father would never have to know about, but I didn't stop you from doing it, or having that book signing. My actions were clear that I chose to stand by you until the writing experience was done. Which it is. For good. I have also allowed you to spend time with Karen because she's your friend. By my actions I supported that friendship, but after we're married I expect Karen to become less important. In other words, I've done my part. Your own parents can testify to that. I want to know if you are going to start doing yours."

Stories didn't end this way. Love stories never had conversations that went like this. Was it my fault my first real conversation with David felt ugly? If I had done the work like Mama said, been committed, been where I was supposed to be, been more reliable and more attentive, would this conversation have sounded more like a conversation between Eloise and Jacob? Been more like what Harvey talked about earlier today? More along the line of a drawing, a sketch of my face, and David asking someone if they wanted to see a picture of the girl he planned to marry?

I touched his coat again, ran my finger around the button nearest my face. "David…" I looked up into the black, wishing I could see his expression. His head was bent over mine. If only he would bend farther, come closer, kiss me, wrap his arms around me and make me feel like a bride. I strained upward, my chest heaving close to his, each breath measured to draw us nearer. I could hear him breathe—light, pensive, controlled. "David, I'm trying. But what I want…what I really need is…" I pressed closer to him, searched for his scent, offered him mine.

He tipped his head to the side and gazed down at me. "I'm glad you're trying. You're not doing it the way I'd expect, but at least you say you're trying." He took a half step backward, the light finally catching his face, exposing the features I'd longed to see. There they were. Unexpressive. The same as always. David was staid, he was reliable, he was there. That's how he told me everything I needed to know. This was the way he would always say he cared.

"Would your best man and his wife like to have dinner another time?" I asked.

"No," he said. "We went ahead and had it. Just the three of us."

"Oh." It was all I could think to say. *I'm sorry* wouldn't come. Neither would *I'll make it up to you somehow.*

He clasped my elbow with his hand and turned us toward my house. "One thing you need to understand about why your punctuality is so important to everyone else," he said as he steered me through the brisk evening. "There will likely be some changes in your father's business. I'll no longer be just an apprentice, but his partner." He glanced down. "As a partner, I plan to grow that business by entertaining, serving potential clients in our home, making your reliability of utmost importance. It's the way my father did things, and my mother never failed to do her part. I'm sure you can do the same, once you take your role seriously." I felt a squeeze through the thickness of my coat. It was an action. It was his way of saying this conversation was settled and all would be well.

"We'll pack more padding in your shoe," Eloise's mother said. "That way you won't walk or do things like something's wrong with you. No one will know. I'll pack it, and you practice walking and doing things right."

Chapter 39

"Now, be sure to apologize to Ida Mae when we get in there," Mama said for the hundredth time. "I told her to have your gown done two days ago, and because you took a night off and worked late the next, I had to call her and tell her we wouldn't be coming by until this evening. I should have mentioned it again at church this morning, but I was too embarrassed to face her."

I walked down the sidewalk between David and Mama. Six more days. Six more days until the wedding, and this was to be the last time I'd try my dress on before the actual day. "I know, Mama. I'll tell Ida Mae." I listened in the quiet for David to tell Mama everything was okay. That I'd apologized enough, I was trying. I needed support instead of pressure. I didn't need to do more.

"Good. As soon as we get in there, make sure you do it." Mama gave her head a sharp nod, and we all marched forward. I stared straight ahead, the same way Mama and David did, watching the last block go by as we neared Ida Mae's house.

We turned in at her front walk and climbed the few steps to the porch. I saw Karen's car off to the side in the drive as David stepped to the door and knocked.

"Well, about time..." Karen swung the door open, her face going from laughing to surprise to quiet as she gazed from me to David then Mama.

"May we come in?" Mama asked.

"Of course, of course." Karen stepped aside as Mama brushed past. I followed, with David behind, Karen's eyes singling me out. *Why is he here?* I saw the question in her expression.

"There you are at last." Ida Mae came into the room. She stopped also, her eyes fixed on David.

Mama poked me with an elbow.

"Ida Mae, I'm sorry we've delayed getting this final fitting done. I've been, well…busy…"

Karen frowned while Ida Mae continued to stare at David.

"We're fitting Martha for her wedding gown…" Ida Mae said to him. "It's rather unusual for the groom to be around for that."

"That's okay, Ida Mae," Mama stepped forward. "He knows that. He's just sorry, too, that you've been held up."

Karen stepped to the side, out of Mama's range and out of David's, also. She made exaggerated motions with her brows and mouth as I watched from the corner of my eye. She didn't have to actually speak. I knew she was asking me the same question I'd seen on her face when we came in. *Why is David here? Really why?*

"Ida Mae." David stepped forward. "Seems we've had some scheduling issues lately. Martha, here, has had some trouble staying on top of things, so I'm here to help her. Doing my part to make sure everything goes smoothly and according to plan."

Karen closed her mouth. Her brows returned to their normal place. She looked away from me, to David, then back to me.

"I suppose that's okay." Ida Mae's brows

furrowed. "I mean, it's out of the ordinary, and a risk for the groom to be anywhere near the bride in her gown before the wedding…"

"I promise I won't look," David said. "Do you have a room I could go to that would be away from the fitting?"

Ida Mae glanced at me. I blushed, even though I tried not to.

"Is your husband here?" David asked.

Ida Mae nodded. If she had been annoyed with me for causing us to put this off, she was extra annoyed now that my fiancé had come with me to help. She motioned for David to follow her.

He glanced at me before he left the room. "Try it on, make sure it's right, and then we'll go. You can get some rest when we get back."

I nodded, the humiliation lingering as I watched him step through the door to where Ida Mae's husband apparently was.

"Is that really why he's here?" Karen whispered at my side.

"Okay, let's get this taken care of," Mama said. I felt her hand at my back as she steered me toward the sewing room.

"You go in there," Ida Mae said as she appeared behind us. She pointed to a door within the sewing room. "Behind that door is another little room I use for the final fitting. Your gown's in there, so go on in with Karen. Your mother and I will wait out here."

"She'll need…" Mama latched onto my elbow.

"Maid of honor's duty," Ida Mae said. She was in command here, and Mama let go.

"Okay, just you and me," Karen said as she closed

the door between us and them. I avoided her gaze as I began slipping out of my clothes. She helped slide my gown over my head when I was ready. It fell over my body with a satiny smoothness that was more like gentle foam flowing over me than cloth. When Karen hooked it from behind, it felt as if I'd slid into a glove instead of a dress. I turned toward the small mirror in the fitting room. I wanted to see me, or as much of me as I could without Mama's or Ida Mae's eyes on me also.

Karen was there behind me. I saw part of her in our reflection, the same question still on her face.

"He really is trying to help," I said.

There was no answer behind me. I looked from the reflection of the wedding dress to her face.

"I've been pondering the red-and-white thing, and why my feelings haven't been quite right regarding David. I paid more attention to my book than to him. Maybe he'll be more red, like what I wrote about...and I'll be more white as I come to understand him and how he thinks...if I do things differently from now on. Maybe we'll be more...or I'll feel more...you know, romantic."

I watched Karen's face, waiting for her to answer. Agree with me, especially, assure me I was right. I waited for a sound, any noise at all, but there was nothing. I felt her hands on the back of my dress, tugging at it, repositioning it, even though what I could see of it in the small mirror looked perfect.

"How's it going in there?" Mama's voice was near the door.

"Just about ready," I called. I turned. I faced Karen. "Do you understand what I'm saying?"

She nodded. "I do," she said. "I understand your logic. Now, step back just a hair, and let me see the front of you."

"Karen!" I took hold of her wrists to keep her from fussing with the gown. "I think this could have been my problem. This may solve everything."

She stared. "I suppose it's like driving. Some I do because I have to, but there's other driving that's…well, different."

I gave her a second to explain. She didn't. I stepped around her and opened the door, marched into other gazes I'd thought I dreaded more. But now, no matter what Mama said, no matter what Ida Mae suggested, either one would be easier than looking at Karen's face.

"Yes, David will like this," Mama said, surprising me. "Why, Martha, you'll be a bride to be proud of."

I saw myself in the much larger mirror Ida Mae kept in that room. Mama and Ida Mae circled me, making comments as they went, comments I ignored. I was a bride to be proud of, that's all I heard. I lifted the sides of the skirt with my hands. I imagined myself walking down the aisle, taking my vows, kissing my husband… I tried to imagine David's face as he watched me, tried to picture the pride I wanted to see, the love I knew he'd someday show.

"Well, I think the dress is as ready as it's ever going to be," Ida Mae finally decreed. She stepped back, hands on her hips, as she looked me up and down.

"Pretty much," Mama agreed. "Just lift your arms once so we can be sure."

Ida Mae tightened as I raised my arms. She relaxed when I lowered them again. She and Mama stood back, and then they came close. Pretty soon their faces were in the mirror with mine, smiling.

"Why, Martha, you're as white as the gown. Are you okay?" Ida Mae's reflection frowned.

Then Karen was there. She parted Mama and Ida Mae like the Red Sea. I felt her usher me away. I heard her assure them I was just fine, nothing more the matter than new-bride jitters.

She closed the door to the small fitting room behind us and stared at me. Mama's and Ida Mae's voices continued on the other side, the two of them cooing and ahhing over the dress and the marvelous work Ida Mae had done. I listened to them, listened to Mama go on about the wedding plans, compliment Ida Mae's work again, rave about David. I looked at Karen, her back still against the door.

"I'm sorry," she said.

My head jerked in what I meant to be a nod to tell her it was okay. I shook it off and tried again.

She straightened and came toward me. When she was close, she took my hand. "You are a bride to be proud of. You're beautiful. You're a beautiful woman, and you're kind. You're good. You should glow."

I turned to the small mirror. Glow? I touched my face, ran my fingers over the white paleness that did indeed match the gown.

Karen stepped between me and the mirror, taking both my hands and holding them down between us. "I want you to be okay and glow."

I gave a short nod.

"I want you to be so okay that even if David always stayed white, you'd be happy." Her hands tightened around mine. "Be so okay that nothing I could

215

say would dissuade you or move you from being sure."

I bit my lips and pressed them together between my teeth. I began a slow nod. This had to be right. My nod grew.

"Not even a thousand words, if I could come up with them, could topple you."

My lips stayed the same, my head nodded more.

"Or a picture, instead."

My head stopped. My heart stopped. I looked at her.

"Could I show you one picture, one worth a thousand words, that would maybe make you wonder…"

Chapter 40

Karen undid the back of my gown and slid it upward over my head. She was careful how she hung it on the hanger as I changed to my regular clothes. In the silence of the fitting room, I heard the satiny fabric glide through the air. I put my clothes back on without watching her. I slipped into my skirt and sweater, stockings and shoes.

We joined Mama and Ida Mae in the sewing room, their compliments and excitement effervescing, bouncing and echoing throughout the room. David joined us when he heard us near the front door, leaving the living room and Ida Mae's husband behind. He listened to Mama's hints and teases about what a beautiful bride I'd be. He looked at me approvingly, more assured than he'd been before. I followed him and Mama to the door.

We said our goodbyes, we expressed our thanks, but it was Karen's face that caught me as I thanked Ida Mae, a whole conversation in that one glance when Karen's and my gazes met.

David took my elbow and walked with me down the front steps. I glanced at Karen's car as we passed, the top of a pair of crutches showing in the passenger window. *Some driving I do because I have to, but there's other driving that's...well, different.*

David steered me forward, the crisp night air, the

successful fitting, energizing him. He talked more than he had on the way to Ida Mae's. He spoke of the temperature, the sidewalk that needed repair, what he planned to do tomorrow at work. I noted the change, and combed through it for red. I listened to what he said and tried to visualize every facet, create pictures and images from his facts. But it was just words. His words, not mine. White words that lined my eternity, without any red or pictures to bring them to life. Yet.

Surely this would change.

Chapter 41

We hadn't done such things since we were girls. Karen and I had created secret ways to communicate back then, never with much to say, just thrilled we could sneak messages to each other that no one else ever knew of.

She'd done it again tonight. I didn't realize it until I was alone in my room, Mama effusing to my father in their room about my wedding gown, how pleased David seemed with the successful fitting, and how wonderful I'd look in six more days. I removed my sweater, my skirt. My shoes and my stockings. I hadn't noticed before, not when I'd been as white as my gown in the fitting room, not even when Karen had asked me if a thousand words or one picture could daunt how sure I was.

But there it was. Like the padding in Eloise's shoe—a picture folded and tucked in—just small enough that my foot wouldn't feel it through my stockings.

I took the paper from the toe of my shoe and sat on my bed near the lamplight. I knew the paper; I'd seen it over and over in Raymond's illustrations. It was his. This must be the next one in the book. Karen must have continued reading without me, and whatever she'd read or seen was important enough she thought I should know.

I opened this drawing the same way Raymond had opened the picture of the girl he planned to marry. Every fold felt like a hammer to my heart, every crease like a dagger in my soul. When at last the picture was open, I pressed it flat and smoothed it against my thigh, the same way he had long ago on that train. I turned it over and looked at it.

I stood, redressed in everything I'd had on before, and slipped downstairs. Karen would still be up. She'd be waiting for me. I lifted my coat off the rack and went back out into the night.

Chapter 42

The front door opened as I climbed Karen's steps. She stood there holding it, ready for me, a look of relief on her face.

She waved me inside with one hand while with the other she placed a finger at her lips to warn me to be quiet. She latched the door without making a sound, and we tiptoed up the stairs. I smiled in the quiet that we hadn't lost our skill. Even with age, being larger, with the convenience of telephones, we still had our childhood stealth and the appreciation that even when there were things to say, silent means were available. In this case, Raymond's picture had said it all. His picture was indeed worth a thousand words, and we knew it as we stole up the stairs.

We stood and looked at each other after Karen closed her bedroom door behind us. The house was still, her mother long since in bed. I pulled the drawing from my pocket and held it out. She took it, turned to a drawer in her dresser, and retrieved my book. She slid the drawer closed with one knee, then crossed to the head of her bed, where she sat. She patted the long empty space beside her, and I took my seat there.

This time it was Karen who unfolded the drawing. She did it with great care, as if it would go away and the illusion that had brought me here so late would vanish. My heart pounded with each fold, just as before.

It kept time for the ceremony, marched me toward what might be a fork in my road.

When the drawing was at last fully opened, she pressed it flat, and we both stared at it. There he was. A self-portrait, an exact likeness of him as he walked away from a statue, a statue of a bride, a church in the background. The base of the statue was square and solid, a good foundation for a figure of stone. The bride's gown was full, as full as the base, a slight teepee upwards to her waist, plain, without frills. Her arms were close to her, bound in front, her hands clasped together. Her bodice was of the same block formation, strong, not beautiful, just plain and built for strength. Her face, a featureless cement with a veil covering her head, had his rendition of a face drawn over its front. Around the base of the statue, a bouquet of flowers lay strewn, a few dangling from his hand and falling to the ground as he walked away. Raymond's back was to her. The statue behind him, his face flushed, his eyes sad but alive. A new kind of alive. One I hadn't seen before.

"That's not you," Karen whispered. "My guess is you didn't even look close enough to see that." She held the drawing near me, one finger pointing to the features he'd drawn on the bride.

She was right. I hadn't looked at her face. I had reacted, rather than known. This picture, one I didn't even look at closely, undid me. I stared at the features Raymond had drawn on the bride and saw again—her. So like me, yet not. The faint differences between us were there—the nose, the chin, tiny distinctions that set her apart from me. I looked for the refinement I'd seen on her in California when I'd gone to look for him, and it was there, even in her disappointment. I felt for her. I felt for the heartache I imagined she must have but that he hadn't drawn onto her face.

I looked again at the foundation the statue was built on, the firmness that should have transitioned into a work of art but didn't. It merely continued upward as a shapeless and faceless extension of stone. Nothing about it would make the heart of an artist or a groom beat with passion. Or make an author with the heart of a bride create with passion, either.

"He didn't marry her…" Tears of elation, of joy and sorrow, of pain and excitement swirled in my breast. My heart sang, it trilled, it did everything Mama had warned me against. It cried out in even greater thrill than Eloise's had in my contrived happy ending. "What do I do?" I whispered to Karen.

We both glanced at the clock. It was late. It was actually tomorrow. Five more days. We glanced at each other. I jumped to my feet, but her hand caught mine and held me.

"Sit," she said. "What you do right now is listen while I read."

I stood for a moment, then dropped back to her bed. I sank into her mattress, and she let go of my hand. I didn't budge. I listened.

My words filled the air, the darkness Eloise walked in, the futile sense of Jacob always being near—yet not. But somehow his absence was more real than those who really were around her, the scent of him, the memory of him, the pictures he'd drawn still vivid in her memory.

"Don't come for me this afternoon," Eloise told *her father as he walked her to the store where she worked.*

"Don't come for you? But it will be dark when you're ready to come home."

She glanced to her side at him. She couldn't distinguish the look on his face, but she felt it, and she knew he understood. Day and night were the same to her, dark and light equal shadows of gray.

"And don't come and follow me," she admonished. "You have trained me for this. You've made me strong. You built a foundation, you've shown me the way, and Mama has done her part, too." They both knew Mama had built a crutch for her while her father had taught her to walk. She squeezed his arm, grateful for both, now that she understood.

He left her at the door to the store. She waited to go in until she was certain he was gone. When she could no longer sense his presence, she entered and began her day, began to test the foundation they'd laid.

"Funny how this all ties together," I interrupted. "It's like I wrote a self-portrait instead of drawing one. Self-portraits for both of us, it seems. Raymond found his in there, also. At least maybe…"

"Well, you wrote what you were discovering, when it came to you. Turns out, he was the same."

My cheeks warmed, and my breathing sounded labored. Had everyone who'd read my book known? Had they seen me there in the pages like he did? Stripped bare and naked? I glanced at Karen, thinking of Maude. Would she assume I was that in love with her son? Or could love him that way? Did she just hope? Vicariously?

Karen smiled, and my questions slowed. "You're in every page of this book," she confirmed. "But so is he. And he recognized himself."

"Is that why he left the garden where the statue was? Did he leave the bride behind because he knew how I felt?"

Karen shook her head. "No, you didn't write that script for him. He wrote his own, and he's relaying it to you in his pictures."

The train was a daily reminder, the surviving fragment of a love that was lost. Eloise replayed her memories as she rode to and fro, able to live in the images now that she was alone and her father no longer rode with her. She took the remembrances out one by one, the same way Jacob used to display his artwork for her when they rode together.

"Miss?"

Eloise looked to the side, hearing the porter's voice.

"This was left for you." He lifted one of her hands and placed something there. It was hard and heavy, and he closed her fingers around it and wished her a good day. She heard him shuffle down the aisle, a soft walk she could barely hear above the hum of the wheels on the tracks.

She held the object in her hands, staring straight ahead and squeezing her fingers to discern what it was. Hard. Long. Pointed at one end.

She carried it off the train with her, gripping it tight as she walked toward home. When she reached her house she let herself in, the scent of her father's pipe filling the living room. Only then did she lay the object down. She heard the metallic clank as it clattered on the table near the front door.

Her father's evening newspaper rattled. "Did the train wreck?"

She could hear the laughter in his voice. "No, of course not. Why do you ask?"

"You have a pin there, one of the spikes that holds the tracks together. Someone somewhere might be having a train wreck."

She fumbled with her hands over the table's top until her fingers bumped the cold hard metal. This time when she touched it and felt it, she recognized what it was. The spike that held the track together so the train could stay on its course. So love on a train could continue and never be thrown off its tracks.

"Hmmm," Karen said. She lifted my book and turned it sideways, tilting her head as she studied the page.

"Another picture?" I was afraid to look.

"Umm-hmm," she said, concentrating on the drawing. "It's drawn on the horizontal this time. It's a long track with a train on one end, heading toward unfinished rails. Not very imaginative this time."

I looked at Raymond's picture. Karen was right. A train on the left, facing unfinished track to the right, men standing around the track, tools in hand to get the track laid. We both stared at the sketch. She held the book farther away, then brought it near. We tilted our heads one way and then the other, frowning and either pursing or biting our lips.

"There's a bird in the sky, there on the left." she said. "A mountain range in the distance…"

I leaned closer. "That's not a bird, that's an airplane. It's coming from the west." We both leaned even closer and she nodded beside me.

"And look," she said, pointing at the men working on the tracks. "Two of the men where the track is most undone are watching the plane. One is pointing at it."

I studied the men again, each with a tool, piles of ties behind them, rails lying undone ahead of the waiting train. "They don't have the spikes," I said. "They're waiting for them. Must be a bundle of them coming on that plane."

We looked at each other, both of us seeing what he'd drawn at the same time.

"The train was waiting for him to come. Maybe to come back. *Love on a Train* couldn't be finished without him." We said the same thing in different ways, but we said it together. My jaw fell open, my book fell closed. We stared at each other again.

"Is it fiction or real?" I asked at last, terrified of the answer. "Is he here? Or was it just about Jacob returning for Eloise, and this is Raymond's contribution to my story and nothing more?"

Karen placed a hand on one of my shoulders, her expression pointed. Like a spike. "It doesn't matter."

My jaw dropped. "It does matter. It really matters. It makes all the difference in the world."

She shook her head. "No, it doesn't. What matters is you. Where you are. How you feel. He could be in Timbuktu or next door, and it doesn't matter. It's where your heart is—that's what matters."

My heart. It surged up from the depths, ready to beat and create on my foundation. It wasn't happy with bricks and stones, hard work, reliability. It wanted the spike, just like every woman did. With spikes it could build a work of art, not just more of the same solid structure.

I thought of Eloise and the countless times she'd believed Jacob was near, and the equal number of times she'd been wrong. I could be doing the same thing—wishing, dreaming, missing Raymond so much that his absence was as powerful as his presence, making me think he was there, when he really wasn't. But David was. Could my heart build a work of art with him? Hammer something into place so it could eventually turn into a thing of beauty? Or did my heart only want to build with Raymond?

I took the book from Karen's hands and turned the page, looked at what was behind Raymond's drawing. "He's here," I said. "He has to be."

"He *was* here," she corrected me. "He came back to deliver this book to you. He never made it inside the bookstore that day. Remember? He made it as far as David, and then he left."

My mind raced back to that afternoon when Raymond had been so close. So close I should have known, but I didn't. I hadn't felt him while he was outside the bookstore, talking to David. I should have, yet I didn't. Or couldn't.

"I don't remember what David said." I replayed those minutes, the ones when I saw Raymond's name, when David came into the store, when I stared out the front door's glass, wondering where and why Raymond had gone.

"David told Raymond he could get your signature easier, didn't he?"

"Yes, and David said he explained why he was there, but I'm not sure exactly what he said. Plus Raymond was married. Or would be sometime soon. Or at least that's what David said and I've believed. Until now." I'd stayed until the bookstore closed, waiting for Raymond to return so I could see him again. Bring closure to his absence. See him with her, or at least know he was with her. But he hadn't come, not even to get my signature. "He came back that one time, though," I said. I looked at Karen. "He at least came back from wherever he'd been to give me this book. Do you think he came back *for* me when he did that?"

Karen looked from me to the book. "Well, let's think of all his pictures, at least what we know so far. It seems he's writing your story, yours and his, more than Eloise's and Jacob's. And it seems he's heading toward a happy ending. But then, when he ran into David…maybe everything changed…"

I grabbed her arm. "Do you think he's still here, then? Do you think I've been near him? On those countless bridge projects has he been right there, and I just never saw him?" My eyes felt enormously wide, wider than they'd ever been. I could feel the cold around their edges where they rounded like saucers. I lifted the book and thumbed through pages and pages that we'd already read. "It's here somewhere. I know it is. He has that answer in here somewhere, I just have to find it."

Karen slapped a hand over the book. She pressed it flat to my lap and held it there while she looked at me. "Stop," she said. "And breathe. You have a wedding gown hanging a few blocks away. You have a fiancé who lives several blocks farther. You have a mother who will stop at nothing to wed you to him. In fact, I wouldn't be surprised to find a drawing of her destroying train tracks, if Raymond knew what he should about her."

I stopped. I breathed. Karen was right. She lifted her hand off the book, and I let the book stay where it was. I could never live any sort of happily-ever-after if I suddenly ditched everyone and everything that relied on the next five days. I'd made promises to them, as well as to myself. I'd begun building on that foundation, for better or for worse. I couldn't be frantic. I had to know what mattered to me, just like Karen said.

I toyed with the corners of the pages of my book. "I have five more days," I said. "You've got to help me."

Karen nodded. "Take the book. Finish reading it this time, or at least see what he drew for the end."

I wanted to tear it open now. I knew what I'd written, I wanted to see what he drew, scan the little word changes he'd made. I nodded. I put my coat back on, holding the book inside it against my chest. I'd hold it there all the way home. My heart would pound against it at every step, ready to build. Build something. Something that needed to look like art.

"You were right," I said before I left her room. "Even if he's not here, even if he's gone back to marry her after all, I have to face this. I have to know what I want for myself before I offer something to David. You're a good maid of honor."

She nodded. She stood and hugged me.

I paused in her doorway. "Is driving different with crutches? You know what kind of different I mean…"

She blushed, and I left. Holding the book tight against my chest, every step taking me either nearer to or farther from the place I'd fallen in love. And hopefully to a new place of being in the right kind of love.

Chapter 43

My eyes, exhausted and dried out, never stopped moving. Five days. I'd stayed awake after sneaking back into my house last night and skimmed what I'd written in my book until I came to Raymond's next drawing, one of Jacob walking behind Eloise—or Raymond behind me—tools in hand, ready to secure the future by securing that spike. I'd written that Eloise carried that railroad spike back and forth with her every day, made a special little bag for it so it was easier to tote and harder to lose. Her ears had been even more attentive, her senses far more in tune with what was around her, searching as she did for his aroma, his presence, for Jacob's return.

I felt just like her. My novel was tucked in my satchel. I planned to continue reading every chance I got, needing to hurry while refusing to cheat. I didn't want to miss anything Raymond may have added in the little notes he'd made in the margins as the book neared its end. Changes, turning my story into his—maybe even ours—more so than Eloise's and Jacob's. I couldn't stand to lay it down. I worried this tale would go on without me. I held the satchel on my lap and watched, watched everyone who boarded the train, and everyone who got off. Just in case. I stood when it stopped and studied the faces lined on the platforms. When none of them were his, I went on my way, hoping if he was there I'd find him. His drawings, his notes, all led me to believe he was. Was here somewhere. At least he had been, until he met David.

****

"Up for a bridge meeting?" Mr. Wilson asked as soon as I reached my desk.

"Of course," I answered with even more eagerness than I had at other times. I was on a mission now, one of discovery instead of one of avoiding being discovered.

Harvey shook his head. "You amaze me. How can you be so enthusiastic with all that wedding agenda looming over your head?"

Five days. I looked at him, my satchel dangling from my hand. Five days. It was soon. It was ahead, not overhead. I looped the strap over my shoulder. "I'm okay. I'm ready to go."

"Okay, then," he said, still shaking his head. "Guess your mother's a super woman. She must be shouldering one heck of a load for you."

I smiled. "Yes, thank goodness for my mother."

I found myself marking in the margins of my notes, the way I'd done before, as characters sprang up in my mind. It was the same thing Raymond had been doing in my book as it neared the end. I reached down and patted my satchel. It was still there, safe and sound, my book, his drawings, the rest of his story.

No one in or around any of the bridge sites we visited escaped my scrutiny. Even while taking notes and creating character sketches, I paid attention to details—names, faces, and body statures that came within my range. If he was there, I'd find him. If I was there, I trusted he'd find me. He'd want to. Or at least he had wanted to.

My margins became crowded with small sketches, small descriptions, tiny character profiles and comments they'd make if I let them loose in a novel. I'd drawn a bridge in the upper corner, the way Raymond drew them, the way Mr. Wilson approved of. I ran my pencil over the lines, darkening them, strengthening the bridge so that it stood out.

I heard my name, and I glanced up. Men were looking at me, a smile on Mr. Wilson's face. "I'm afraid I'm going to lose her soon," he said. "She sure has a knack for what we're doing, picked it up quickly. She already seemed to understand what I was talking about before we even met."

I blushed as the men nodded. I'd seen most of them before, but one or two were new. This was a gathering of engineers and city managers. Mr. Wilson was going big now, ready to spring from the newest bridge being planned to laying the groundwork for future bridges to be built in the city.

"So you're to be married soon," one commented.

I blushed more, and nodded.

"I'm going to have to meet her fiancé," Mr. Wilson said. "Maybe convince him she's too valuable an asset for me to let go of."

My fiancé. My cheeks burned hotter. I hadn't thought of David all day. He'd been in the foreground, a direction I was heading. I was maneuvering through the next five days with wide swipes, searching through the rubble as I went, leaving no stone unturned or in the way until I got there.

"Like that little drawing there on the corner of her page." Mr. Wilson nodded toward my pad. "That little bridge. It's like she knew what I was talking about before I ever had a chance to explain it to her."

"Your father work on bridges?" one of the men asked.

I shook my head. "He's a metal worker, though," I offered. "Just small metal items, nothing to do with construction."

"You must have inherited some of his know-how." The man chuckled. "Maybe you were meant to be a boy. And bridges would have been your passion. Building them, not just taking notes about them."

I smiled a half smile. Martha Haynes. Martha Haynes. Martha Haynes. That's what I'd thought I was meant to be. A girl passionate about a man who built bridges and writing my own words about him. And me. And us. That's what I had thought I was meant to be.

Chapter 44

Looking at David was like looking at a stranger. Talking to him was like talking to a stranger when he appeared at my door that evening, ready to take me to dinner with the pastor and his wife, a relaxed way of ironing out last-minute details before the wedding. Pastor Reynolds said he'd found this worked well for his soon-to-be-married couples, took some of the strain off the last few days, let them relax and stand back enough to think clearly about what else needed to be done.

David held my coat as we prepared to leave my house. I missed the sleeve with my right arm. He lowered the coat while I raised my arm, and I missed again. "I'm sorry. Try again?"

He raised the coat while I shot lower with my arm, my hand bumping into the side seam and missing the sleeve again.

We weren't in harmony. There was distance between us, some of it created by reading my book again, doing all the things I should have done long before now. Some of it the pressure of a wedding in too few days. "I'll just put it on myself," I said. David let go of my coat, and I slid each arm in and buttoned it.

David smiled when I finished, the same way he always did. I listened as he walked through his usual niceties with my parents, saying just the right things before we left. He recited his normal pleasantries with me as we drove—how his day went, and asking about mine. Five days—for his sake, for Mama's, for Daddy's. For mine—I had five days to figure out what love really was. Five days was not enough time.

Pastor Reynolds and his wife were waiting for us when we walked into the restaurant. David's hand rested at the small of my back as he directed me to the table where they sat. He took my coat and hung it on the back of my chair before he scooted it out, and let me settle in before he helped me slide it nearer the table. I thanked him. I smiled. The way a wife should smile, the way a wife should look, the things she should say. I listened, I chatted, I did everything right, like trying to hit the sleeve. I made all the proper small talk until we ordered and the subject matter changed.

"We're borrowing extra chairs from the Methodist Church down the street," the pastor said. David nodded, and they eased into a discussion of numbers, as well as the arrangement of the chairs. David and the pastor were on neighboring sides of our square table, something I hadn't noticed until I felt the pastor's wife's hand rest on top of my own.

I looked to my side at her. She leaned close. The men's discussion faded into the background. "Do you have any questions, dear?" she whispered. "Of a womanly nature, I mean."

They'd done this before, the pastor and his wife. I hadn't realized it at first, but their strategy was clear to me now. David was likely aware of it before we came in, knowing I'd be seated near the pastor's wife so she could ask me this question five days before we were to be married.

I stared at her, but I could hear the men. They seemed, or were pretending to be, unaware of her personal question, their numbers and impersonal arrangements volleying back and forth between them.

"Your husband did his best to cover everything, I think."

She smiled. The sort of smile that was meant to encourage me and make allowances for him. "He's very thorough," she said, "especially about spiritual matters. But not so much about the intimate details, the way a woman thinks, if you know what I mean."

The thousand replies I could have given, the multitude of questions I needed real answers to, sprang up from my gut. Each one wanted a voice. I clenched my teeth to keep the frenzy inside. I stared at her and nodded, refusing to look down or away. Refusing to cry.

"Men aren't always aware of romantic things," she said. "Now, my husband has been a good student of how to love me the way that's important to me, and I'm grateful for that. But even though he meant well, we didn't start out with anything in that area in common—except for inexperience. Our expectations and ideas of intimacy—oh, my, they couldn't have been farther apart."

The questions, the replies, the turmoil churning inside of me stopped. Everything quieted. "You said romantic," I leaned her way and whispered. "Romance is real? It's normal and okay?"

She frowned, tilted her head back, and studied me, then laughed. "Why, of course it's real and normal. That's the way we women were designed, so no use denying it." Her head tipped near mine again, and with her elbow propped on the table she spoke behind one hand. "But they don't always understand that, or how it's done." She shifted her eyes toward David and her husband, before she looked back to me. "That's why I'm offering to help you. Not just now, but any time, even after you're married. They aren't wired like we are, so there's some give and take. And I'm warning you, sometimes it will seem like you're the one doing all of the giving, and it will feel like work instead of love."

That's what Mama had said. Love was giving. Love was work. I looked at David. He had all that in him, but I'd never seen or felt any romance. He'd work, and he was committed. I'd work, and he wanted me to be committed. I looked at the pastor's wife. Was there a time when her heart beat like a caged bird in her chest, wanting so very much to sing?

"Where does romance come in? Romance is part of love, right? I mean, shouldn't I feel romantic, even with all of the work and commitment?" I whispered.

I didn't understand the magnitude of the pain that must have been in my eyes until I saw it reflected in hers. I saw myself nestled there, and I felt sympathy from her hand as she patted mine. "I know about that book you wrote," she said as the men continued to drum out facts and figures from their corner of the table. "I didn't read it, but I know it was about romance. Just going by what I heard, I'd say you wrote about the dreamy side of it, the part about falling in love, or at least feeling like you did. But not so much about the day-to-day choices that follow falling in love, the sort of choices marriages are made of. Romance like you wrote about is something that sends a woman's emotions into a tailspin, gets her heart started as she moves into the deeper things."

I settled back in my chair. "So you were romantically excited about Pastor?" I whispered. "Or was it pretty much just nuts and bolts from the beginning?" Or something more crucial, like a railroad spike, a tie that held everything together because in your heart you wanted it held together?

"Of course I felt romantic about him." She laughed. "We collided like two sparking magnets, uncontrollably drawn to each other. It was wonderful and fiery, and just the right fuel to get the engine started. The heat of those first sparks melded us together, got us to and through the points where someone had to throw coal on the fire to keep the steam coming. Gotta have the romance, and then keep it moving forward."

Our food arrived. She and I straightened in our chairs. David and Pastor continued to talk around the waiter's hands as he placed plates in front of us. The food smelled and looked wonderful. This was more than a diner, it was a nice restaurant, maybe not as nice as the one I'd seen downtown, but close. I gazed around at the other tables to see who else was there, what sort of people were out tonight, what sort of culture we were dining in.

Most of the tables were small, the right size for couples, or four at the most. The atmosphere was quiet, semi-elegant, the sort of dim lighting that encouraged romance. There were couples all around, next to each other wherever they could be, or only a corner between them, not the expanse of a table. I studied each one, watched how they shared, how they spoke, how they leaned into each other to make the meal an experience, not just a dietary ritual.

"Like that," the pastor's wife said nearby. "That's romance. And the seed of love."

Chapter 45

"Well, I think we're ready," David said as he drove me home. "Tomorrow, it's four more days. Hard to believe, isn't it?"

I nodded, shook my head, then nodded again. I wasn't sure which question I was answering, his or mine. Was it hard to believe, or was I ready? Were we ready?

David rambled on and explained the details of what he and the pastor had decided—numbers, timing, locations, sequence. I thought we'd already worked those details out, but the way David talked, he'd taken care of it all tonight, and I had nothing left to do except wait four days. Four days until my next duty—walk down the aisle and say, "I do."

"How about tomorrow evening you come over to the house?" he asked. "We'll bring most of your clothes over, and whatever else you want to keep. Just leave behind enough clothing and toiletries to get you through the wedding and the next few days. Speaking of that, have you packed for the honeymoon yet?"

"Pack?" I stared through the windshield and watched as he turned into my parents' drive, glad it was dark enough he couldn't see my surprise. Pack and move. It wasn't like I hadn't thought about it before. I just hadn't when there were only four days left to do it in. "I'll just set my honeymoon things aside and pack them the night before the wedding," I said as he shut off the engine. "They won't get crinkled that way."

I felt his approval, sensed the slow nod of his head beside me. "Good idea. But after supper tomorrow, let's do everything else I said."

I tried to imagine emptying my room, the space I'd grown up in and lived in all my life. David was taking over, making the way for me; he was doing everything Mama said a good husband would do. "Thank you," I said, "for making sure these details are taken care of."

"That's my job." He sounded pleased with himself.

He got out of the car and came around to open my car door for me. We walked toward the house, my feet heavy and slow. I lifted each foot as I lagged behind, then marched with a sharp step as I caught up with David.

"What's wrong?" David peered down at me. "You have a rock in your shoe or something?"

"No, sorry, I'm fine. Just tired. Fell behind, that's all."

"Understandably tired." He found my hand and laced his fingers through mine. I waited for him to squeeze it. I wanted him to tie our fingers together instead of leaving them untied. We had contact. I wanted connection. Maybe when intimacy was proper, after the wedding, in four more days starting tomorrow, he would turn his contact into connection.

I closed the front door behind David after he said goodnight, as he returned to his car. I took a deep breath as I shut it between us, then pressed against it. Sometimes I watched him drive away, stood there so I could wave if he turned. I heard him start his car and listened to the hum of his engine soften as he drove away. The wood felt cool on my face, driving out the flush that had grown there during the evening. It felt good. I turned my head and cooled the other cheek also, chilling the turmoil that had risen to the surface.

"Goodnight," I said outside my parents' bedroom door.

"Goodnight, Martha," my mother called from their room. "By the way, did David tell you the news?" The door opened. Daddy was sitting up in bed, leaning against their headboard with a newspaper in his lap while Mama peered around the door, little curls pinned all over her head.

"What news?"

"No need to bring that up now," my father said, peering at my mother beneath his brows. "She has enough on her mind."

Mama waved him off. "But it's good news." She turned back to me, a smile on her face. "David asked to be a partner in your father's business the other day. Of course your father is accepting his offer. That means someday it will be his. Well, both of yours. I can't believe David didn't tell you."

My father settled farther back into his pillow. He looked at me for a second, then down at whatever he'd been reading on his lap.

"He did mention it, but it wasn't definite. Daddy?"

"It's not settled... There's a lot to consider..." He looked at me, and I saw that considering in his eyes.

"It is so settled," Mama chimed in. "At least it will be. David's idea to buy into your father's business is a marvelous one. It'll all be in the family that way."

I watched my father take the paper off his lap and set it on the nightstand next to the bed. He scooted farther under the blankets and pressed his head deeper into the pillow. "Best get some rest, little girl."

I backed away from their doorway, Mama's grin disappearing behind the door as she slid it closed. I could hear my father tell her she should have kept David's offer quiet, said nothing until it was definite, if it ever was. Mama's excitement wasn't to be daunted, even when he added, "A lot could go wrong." She overrode my father's tentativeness with happy sounds, chatter about the wedding, my gown, and how wonderfully things were turning out.

They were counting on me. Everyone was. I walked to my room, leaving Mama's happy chatter behind.

Chapter 46

I didn't change into my nightgown when I closed my bedroom door behind me. I stayed in my clothes, slipped off my shoes, and sat on my bed, leaning back against my headboard. I glanced at my nightstand.

It would be better for everyone if I never knew. Never questioned what love was, what romance was, just committed myself to being a good wife to the man who planned to someday own my father's business. A good daughter. A good person who never looked back at *Love on a Train*.

Or forward to any other sort of writing.

The bleeding was there in those thoughts. Red agony seeping from a heart with nowhere to go. I took my book from the drawer of my nightstand and laid it on my lap. *Love on a Train.* My heart pounded out one beat—one isolated pump—at the inkling Raymond had come back for me. It beat once again with the notion he'd tried to tell me as much by turning my book into our story.

I ran my finger around the book's cover. It was possible Raymond was just being an artist and my friend. That this book was nothing more than his way of sharing with me one last time—his love of art entwined with my love of words—to say thank you and goodbye. I swung my feet over the edge of my bed and slid them back into my shoes.

The immediate demands were so great—the wedding, and the number of lives involved—these were where my attention should be. But there was still the past. Where my heart continued to beat. I rose to my feet, my book in my hand. My words, my story, my heartache that wouldn't go away. I glanced at the cover. At her.

As I studied her, the face so similar to mine, a sheen glanced off her picture, highlighting her image from the lamplight. Small lines appeared, nearly invisible depressions etched around her face. I tilted the book and looked closer. Tiny grooves, small indentations I hadn't noticed before, were dug like troughs around her features.

I held the book close, leaned near the lamp, and tilted it every direction while I studied the lines. I traced them with my finger around her face, around her nose, her chin, and parts of her eyes. I did it again. I pressed harder, then I lifted the book and held it so the lamp's light hit at just the right angle.

There I was. This was no longer her. It was me. Raymond had made pencil marks in the cover, just slight enough I hadn't noticed before. He'd changed her face to mine, covering over what had been to show what was. Or would be. What he may have felt at the time he added to this book. What he possibly wanted and really was trying to tell me.

I dropped back onto my bed. What he'd wanted and tried to tell me—until he met David.

I stared around my room. He'd come back. For me, not just to share the book with me? Had Raymond really intended to make amends if he could, and start fresh? With me? But realized he couldn't, when David met him outside the bookstore? Had David said something that caused Raymond to think it was too late for him? That I'd given myself to another?

I had. I had given myself to another. Just not the way I'd given myself to him.

I jumped up. Karen was right. Even if the opportunity to give myself to Raymond was gone forever, I had to go on. Daddy had to go on. His business had to go on. This was the real reason I could never respond to Mills and Boon's offers for more books. I wasn't finished with *Love on a Train*. I couldn't do another book, another life, go on to another love, until the first one was settled. For me. No matter what Raymond or his other her had done, I needed to know and face the facts and move on.

I slipped from my room and crept down the stairs. I went to the phone and called David.

"Hello?" he answered at last.

"David?" I whispered.

"Martha? Are you okay? I thought you were tired. You should be in bed and asleep by now."

I could hear the reprimand in his voice. I bit my lower lip so I wouldn't just apologize and hang up. "I was gathering a few things for us to move tomorrow," I lied. "Thought I'd get a head start on it." I paused, but he said nothing, so I continued. "I came across that book that man gave you a long time ago. The one at my book signing. Remember?"

The silence on the other end was louder than my pulse hammering against my eardrums. Waiting for David to respond felt like waiting for a volcano to erupt. I finally heard a whistle, a slow release of air.

"Your book is a thing of the past. I thought you'd

thrown that copy away a long time ago. If he didn't come back for it, he clearly didn't care. And neither should you."

"Maybe I should throw it away." I held the book as I spoke, my grip on it growing tighter. I cradled the earpiece against my ear and ran a finger over the lines Raymond had drawn on the cover. I couldn't see them, or the likeness of me in the dark, but I could feel it all. "Except I feel obligated to get it back to him. He did entrust it to me. Well, to you, actually."

David was quiet. Trust was important to him. I could feel the deliberation in his thoughts, the determination to be trustworthy even if it was to do something he thought was immoral.

"I wondered if you had any clues about this man. Like anything he said about himself? Where he worked? Something in particular he reacted to that you may have said?"

"I'll have to think about it," he finally said.

Five days.

I needed something more than "I'll have to think about it." I needed to know if Raymond was wearing construction clothing, if anyone else was with him or even nearby, how he looked when he first walked up, how he looked when he walked away... "Which way did he go?" I asked.

"What? Why does that matter? You need to get to bed. If I remember anything I'll let you know, but pretty much I took it out of his hands, and then he was gone. Just take it back to the bookstore and leave it there. That's where he would come to get it if he really wants it. Which, apparently, he doesn't."

"Thank you," I said.

"What?"

"I said, 'thank you.' Goodnight."

"Get some sleep. We'll worry about your room tomorrow night."

David hung up, and so did I. I tiptoed back upstairs with my book, slipped into my room, and returned to my spot on the bed. I ran my hand over its cover and opened it. And began to read where I'd left off.

Chapter 47

Raymond's notes were there in the margins and in between lines, little alterations that changed my story just enough that the fictitious happy ending I'd crafted melted away and another one began to take its place. Real this time, at least real as he saw it or had maybe expected it to turn out. Not real as it actually had after he'd walked away from the bookstore, leaving this book in David's hands.

"That cup's design is so beautiful." Eloise admired *the tea set in the store owner's hands. "It's from England, isn't it? Their work is so lovely, even their art and their literature..."*

"Eloise," the owner interrupted. *"You can see this design?"*

Eloise stopped. She looked at the cup in the owner's hands and then into the owner's face. She smiled. It grew into a grin. "I can." She laughed. "Why, it has pink flowers, a faint green vine, and small dabs of petals dancing around the rim." She grasped her face with both hands. "How did I not realize I could see? Did it just happen?"

The owner set the teacup down and turned to Eloise. They stood face to face, then hand in hand as the owner laced her fingers through Eloise's. "I don't know," the woman said. "But my guess is you learned to move within your restrictions so well that you no longer struggled." She nodded at Eloise's eyes, then toward her feet, where her shoe was packed full of Mama's padding. "You became so capable that you glided into seeing as smoothly as if you were seeing all along."

Eloise let go of the owner's hands and lifted the teacup from the shelf. The cup was delicate and beautiful; she'd always known that without seeing it. Maybe the owner was right. She gazed around the store, picking out minor nuances she'd only been able to imagine until now. They were there, everything she'd sensed but never could prove.

As she held the cup next to her, the scent of him returned. It had been there so many times, yet she'd never found him. Never was able to see him—until now. She turned in a small circle, studying the people who were around her as she did. Tall, short, men, women... And him. Not far away, watching her, only a few customers between them.

Her heart raced. She set the teacup back on the shelf, never taking her eyes off him. He might vanish if she did, disappear into darkness along with everything else she'd lost sight of for far too long.

I stopped reading. That was my story, part of the fictitious happy ending I'd written, surrounded by words and suggestions of Raymond's that I'd passed over. I went back then, to the first paragraph, and looked at what he'd written, the way he saw Eloise and Jacob coming back together for the first time.

Instead of Eloise, he'd written my name. There it was, "Martha," penned above my character's name. Instead of in a store holding a teacup, I was on a train holding a notepad. It was blank, until I began to notice things—people, actions, characters in motion—bringing my writer's senses to life. Just as it had in spurious notes and sketches at bridge meetings, and at my wedding shower. Little pieces of my ability to see the way a writer could. It was as if Raymond knew. It was as if he'd seen me, and written me into my own story, turning my fiction into truth.

I clapped a hand over my mouth, holding back the gasp I didn't want my parents to hear, as I stared at more of his notes. There, where Eloise was awakened to sight and sensed Jacob again—Raymond gave her my name. And he called Jacob by his own name, Raymond. He wrote that he entered the train while I had my head down, scratching out characters and stories on the pad. I sensed him, picked up on his presence, and felt him nearby. I spotted him then, his head towering above the others. I set my pad and my pencil aside on the seat next to me and stood. He came my way, and I never took my eyes off him. He approached me, the way Eloise approached Jacob. Until...

"Excuse me," Eloise said to the last person between her and Jacob. They moved aside, and there he was, tall, handsome, everything that quickened her heart. A gentle fondness shone in his eyes, gaiety, exuberance beyond what she'd at one time thought was there for her. She paused, one last step still between them, enough space to find out if anything, or everything, had changed. Was he someone else's, or was he...

It was a chore to keep my eyes on my words. I wanted to read only Raymond's. But he was clever, he'd inserted his so skillfully that it made my words critical. They were entwined, his and mine. I couldn't read one without the other.

My heart hammered, sounding like a racehorse's hooves as it drove me on with such power I was certain my parents could hear it. I slid under my covers and drew the blanket up over my chest. I held it there, muffling my heartbeat so no one would know.

I resumed reading, his words this time. My name, his name, the last passenger moving out from between us. He looked at my pad and pencil in the seat beside me. He leaned around me and picked them up. He smiled down at me as he turned the page on my pad and drew what was next, how he saw things from then on. He finished and turned the pad my way.

I flipped over the page in my book, the great bangs of my heart lifting the covers. There it was, another drawing... Actually, only half of it. One corner was torn away.

I remembered David saying Raymond had flipped through the book after David said who he was and that he could get it signed. But David had taken it from him when Gretchen stuck her head out the door. Maybe Raymond didn't want me to have the book anymore at that point. Or maybe he had, but with this picture torn in half.

I looked down at what he had drawn. It was the statue again, the one of the bride he'd sketched earlier. She was on her pedestal and her shapeless, lifeless exterior was crumbling away. I could see my features beneath, my face emerging in real life, pushing away the stone as my arm reached out toward a hand. His hand, most likely, but I couldn't tell. He'd torn the groom's top half away, left the bottom half and an arm.

I was his work of art, just like I'd thought he was mine.

Or was to have been.

If Raymond hadn't met the man I was planning to marry.

Chapter 48

I closed the book. That was the end. The end except for the face of the groom and Jacob's confession to Eloise that it wasn't her lack of sight but his that had taken him away. It wasn't her inability to run the way she wished but his that had kept him away too long.

I thought of my characters. I thought of myself and Raymond as I ran my hand over the book's surface again, the smooth surface, the penciled lines where Raymond had changed the sketched profile from hers to mine. No matter how much I stared at the cover and the back of my hand passing over it, it was Raymond's face I saw.

I stood and tucked the book into my satchel. When David came to move my things from this house to his—ours—I didn't want to give up the book. I'd think of something to tell him about what I'd done with it. Maybe that I had indeed taken it back to the bookstore. But I had to hide it. I couldn't let him see it. Not now, not ever.

I crawled into bed with my clothing on. Four more days, beginning tomorrow morning. Four more days.

****

I stood at my desk, ready and waiting when Mr. Wilson strode up. "You're ready?" he asked, frowning. "How did you know we were going to have a meeting today? I hadn't even told you yet. In fact, I didn't even know until last night."

I hadn't known. He was right. I was just trying to be ready for anything. Everything. Four days. Hardly enough time to settle my future once and for all, but enough time that if I didn't, it would fall into place on its own and happen to me.

"I was wondering…" I began.

"They were supposed to come here," Mr. Wilson glanced toward Mr. Arnold's office then back at me. "At least they were originally planning to do that, when they called me at home last night, but that all changed. I got a call early this morning, and we're going to their attorney's office instead."

I nodded and tucked my pad and my pencils next to my book, inside my satchel. "I'm ready to go," I said, and this time I led him to the car.

I'd been to this attorney's office before, but it had been a while. I made the rounds, shaking hands, letting Mr. Wilson introduce and re-introduce me to each of the men and the one other secretary, all lining the room. We settled around a central table, me between Mr. Wilson and the attorney who'd called the meeting. There was tension in the air. There often was at these meetings. As gentle as Mr. Wilson was, there was always a war. A man's war, even on home ground, even in construction that sometimes felt more like destruction. I pulled my pad from my satchel, set it on the table in front of me, and dug out a pencil.

"You're the girl who draws little bridges, aren't you?" The attorney craned his neck my direction and peered at some of the old drawings on the front page of my pad.

"Just a few," I smiled, a flush warming my cheeks.

I flipped the front page of my pad over and saw more bridges. I flipped the second and the third pages, and several more until I came at last to a clean page.

"Just a few? Looks to me like you should be drawing our blueprints for us." He laughed, the sort of laugh that cut away at some of the tension. I ran my hands over the clean page, picked up my pencil, and smiled at him.

The meeting was about a proposed bridge, one that would be a sister bridge to another just being started in another state. Mr. Wilson wanted contracts on both, if he could manage it, which explained some of the new faces and the serious looks around the table.

I refrained from drawing little bridges in the margins of my page, aware of the attorney at my side. I focused on the meeting, the discussion of that bridge and this one, taking down everything that was said, occasionally touching my satchel to make sure my book was still there.

They deliberated the different terrain in the other state, the soil, the rock formations, the slope of the ground, things that weren't considerations in the flatter plains of Kansas City. Drawings were passed between the men, even a few photos Mr. Wilson had paid to have taken. A man I hadn't met before spoke of the geology of that state, using terms I'd never heard, so I broke them into syllables to make sure I spelled them as accurately as I could. The older, familiar terms were abundant, but easy. Breaking ground, elevations, dynamite, moving earth…terms Raymond had used when his eyes danced with excitement. Those were the things he did, rearranged the scenery to fit the bridge. The same way he, as an artist, arranged everything on paper to support his art.

The door to the meeting room opened, and one of the young women from the office came through with a tray of cookies and rolls, a young man following behind with a pot of coffee, some cups and saucers. Their intrusion broke the concentration in the meeting, brought with it a much-needed breath of fresh air. I laid my pencil beside my pad and leaned back in my chair.

"Keeping up?" the attorney at my side asked. He settled back in his seat also, looking relieved.

I rubbed my hands together and massaged my fingers. "I think so. A few new terms, but I think I have everything right."

He nodded. I could see the same kindness in his eyes I saw in Mr. Wilson's. They were businessmen first, but they were people underneath. I laid a hand on my satchel, felt my book beneath. "Can I ask you a question?"

"Certainly, but I'm not sure I'll know the answer. Some of those terms were new to me, also."

"Not about the terms," I said, lowering my voice and twisting his way so no one else could hear. "It's about the bridge construction itself."

He raised his eyebrows.

"I met a man who did this sort of work once," I said. "A long time ago. That's where I learned about bridges. He did some of the work you're talking about. I wondered…"

The attorney's brows pinched together. "Really? And who was that? Maybe I know him."

I felt the flush on my cheeks. "His name was Raymond. Raymond Haynes," I said even lower.

The attorney's face twisted into a thoughtful

contortion, brows settling into a pondering pose, his eyes taking on that faraway look as he searched for Raymond's name. I waited. I wrapped my arms across the front of my chest to keep my heart from flying out onto my lap.

"No, can't say as I've met him. Carl," the attorney called across the table. "Did you ever hear of a worker named Raymond Haynes?"

My eyes grew wide. I kept my gaze fixed on the attorney, too humiliated to look across the table at Carl, or whoever else was listening now. In the silence where Carl deliberated, I heard his slow nod. I finally peeked his direction, keeping my face and my embarrassment as hidden as I could. Mr. Wilson had included Carl in several of his meetings. Carl was an engineer who had been working bridges for years. He knew everyone and everything, according to Harvey. As recognition spread across Carl's face and he began to nod, my cheeks burned, and I swiveled his direction.

"Yes, I know who you're talking about," Carl said, swallowing a bite of a roll. "Tall fellow, great worker, always happy." Carl tapped his lips with a finger. "He left... He was on that Madison job and then went somewhere to get his bride. She was someone he'd met during the war, or maybe while he was in training."

"And so that's where you learned to draw those little bridges," the attorney cut in. He turned my way and smiled.

I forced a nod.

"That's who we need working for us again," Carl continued from across the table. He took another bite of his roll and stared into space. "He was like you, Wilson. He would get this." Carl nodded toward the blueprints scattered around the table.

Harvey looked up, his roll untouched, coffee cooling in its cup. Blueprints and notes were spread around him, his hair spiked in front where he'd been running his fingers through it. "Pardon?"

"I said you need to find that Haynes guy, if he's around. He thought like you do. Guess he saw some of that same construction when he was overseas. Good man." Carl dug back into his roll.

"I've heard about him. Someone mentioned him before. Anyone know where he is?" Harvey asked, glancing around the table, but he looked back at the drawings in front of him when no one replied.

I gripped the edge of my book through the satchel. I waited for someone to chime in, say that Raymond was back, he hadn't married after all, and they could find him for Mr. Wilson. Everyone chewed while they thought, occasional sips of coffee interspersed with the sound of a pencil on paper as the secretary transcribed some of her earlier notes. Through it all my heart slammed into my ribcage. I waited. I willed someone to speak, looked from face to face, and watched the discussion of Raymond drift away. Then he was gone. As quickly as he'd been deemed a hero, he was forgotten.

"I have to go there. No way around it." Mr. Wilson's hand slapped the table. "I'm going to Illinois and look at this other bridge. Got to."

The discussion revived, cups and saucers were scooted aside along with Raymond. I took notes, transcribed words that were nearly illegible from my tremors. So close. Raymond had been right there at the table, alive in Carl's memory, and then gone. Again.

Just like from the train, from my life, and torn from my book. At least I thought that was him. I needed to know for sure.

Chapter 49

Mr. Wilson steered with one hand, his mind clearly far away. In Illinois, no doubt. I glanced out the side window. I was focused the way he was—letting the scenery pass by while my thoughts ran toward a different view, the one of Carl's face as he'd spoken about Raymond. I analyzed his expression, separated every word, searched for clues, for indications where Raymond might be. There was nothing. I released a deep sigh the same moment Mr. Wilson did.

"I'm leaving for Illinois today. It's not that far, so I'll take the train. I know you're getting married soon...what is it, two days?"

"Four," I answered.

"Four..." He thought after saying it, and I could see four days looking a lot different to him than two. "Four. I know this is selfish, but maybe you could go with me. We could fly, instead. Make a quick trip of it. I could look things over this evening, even. Or maybe first thing in the morning and we could fly back. You could be here by tomorrow afternoon..."

Illinois. Another bridge site. Another possible place Raymond may be. I mulled everything over. My wedding, Mama, David, my father's business... I gripped the edge of my book through the satchel. "David wanted to move my things to his house...I mean our house...this evening."

Mr. Wilson slumped in his seat. He stared straight ahead as he continued to steer with one hand. "My wife would absolutely hang me if she knew I asked a soon-to-be bride to make a business trip more important than her impending wedding." He shook his head. "And she'd be right. I'm sorry. You have far too much going on to be flying anywhere, unless it's for your honeymoon."

I watched his head continue to wag from side to side as he reprimanded himself. I glanced ahead, color and warmth draining from my face, leaving my skin cool as it went. Harvey wasn't the one who needed to be reprimanded. Four days until my wedding. Four days until my honeymoon. It wasn't enough time to turn me into the sort of woman Mama wanted me to be.

"I should probably get ready for my wedding while you're gone." I glanced to the side at Mr. Wilson. "While you're in Illinois, I'll take that time to finish what I need to, if that's okay."

Mr. Wilson's sigh deepened, and he nodded. "Of course. That's the right thing to do. You take that time and take care of the last-minute details so your wedding is perfect. I'll see you after your honeymoon, all right?" He glanced my way.

I nodded. Then I smiled, the list of what I needed to do exploding in my head. It wasn't a normal pre-wedding list, but it was mine. "I'll transcribe these notes from today when we get back to the office, so you can have them while I'm gone."

"I'd appreciate that. You've been an excellent right-hand man." He grinned. "You'll be impossible to replace someday."

Someday. I had no idea what that someday would

look like. Wouldn't have any idea until I got through the next four days. I glanced out the window and pondered my list. Mama'd done her part to get things ready. So had David. So had Karen, and Ida Mae, and Pastor Reynolds. There was only one thing left to do, the thing on my list, and only I could do it. I had to. And I would, as soon as I handed today's notes to Mr. Wilson.

Chapter 50

I found Karen at her desk. I knew the place she worked, but never went there, since we were both employed the same hours every day. The main receptionist pointed me in the right direction, and I saw Karen, her head bent over figures, working as a bookkeeper for the bank.

I walked up to her, one hand fishing into my satchel until I stood in front of her. When Karen looked up there should have been surprise, maybe even a silent, "Oh, no," in her expression, but there wasn't. Instead, I saw in her eyes what I felt in mine—the deep question that needed an answer. In four days.

I opened my book to the last page, the last picture Raymond had drawn. I held it up, turned it for her to see. The bride and the groom. The faceless groom, the one that was torn away.

Karen stared at his drawing, then she glanced up at me. She didn't have to say what I already knew, but she said it anyway. "I'll cover for you."

"Thank you." I closed the book, slid it into my satchel, and wove back between the desks near hers. I didn't turn around. I knew she had my back. And my front. And my heart. She was my true maid of honor, and I had my list of one thing to complete in four days.

Chapter 51

I went to the bookstore and found my friend
Gretchen waiting on a customer. I milled around not too
far from the two of them until they finished.

"Your book has been a tremendous seller," she
said, her eyes alight as she approached me. "I had to
order more, in fact, and everyone asks when you're
going to write the next one."

The scent of so many books made my head spin,
made the thought of a second book seem possible and
right. I loved the smell of words on a page. It was as
electrifying to me as the downtown city streets had
been at night. I drew in a deep breath. "If I do write
another, you plus Mills and Boon will be the first to
know."

"Do a sequel," she said, straightening a row of
books. "I don't know how you do a sequel to a love
story, but there has to be a way."

"It would have to pick up where the first story left
off," I said, more to myself than to Gretchen. And the
first story left off the moment I saw her photo, the
moment he went his way and I tried to go mine. That's
where my first story ended. What Raymond had added
in drawings and changes was the beginning of the
second. "Speaking of my book, do you remember the
man who dropped one off for me to sign when I was
here? He gave it to David, who handed it to you?"

Gretchen looked at me for a second, then nodded. "Yes, yes, I do remember. I don't really remember the man as much as the event, though. Tall, dark hair. Rather good-looking, I think. But I was focused more on David than him."

Tall. Dark hair. Rather good-looking. Raymond. I pulled the book from my satchel and held it for her to see. "This is that book," I said, clamping it tight in my fingers. I didn't want her to take it and see his illustrations. There was no reason for her to take it, but I knew she might. I brought it here to jar her memory, so touching it would be automatic. I stuffed it back into my satchel, her gaze trailing after it until it disappeared. "Has he been back asking for it?"

She shook her head. "No, I'd have told you if he had. And I asked John to watch out for him, also. Funny that man would ask for you to sign it, then disappear."

"I want to make sure he gets it back, if that's possible," I said. My gaze traveled around the store as if he were there, or as if I could conjure up some memory of that day, force him to reappear, if only for one quick question. "Soon."

Gretchen frowned. "I'm not sure how we can find him."

"Can you remember anything else about him? Which direction he went? What he was wearing? The expression on his face?"

She frowned more, and shook her head. "I wish I could." Gretchen began to move toward the front door. I walked behind her. I could tell she was on the scent of him, following a faint memory and trying to get close long after the trail had gone cold. She stopped near the door. I stood back half a step so as not to interfere. She looked through the front glass, stared where I assumed David and Raymond had stood.

"Let's see." She tugged at her chin. "David was right there." She pointed to an area in front of the store. "And the other man…he was over there. Yes, he was looking through the front window before I stuck my head out the door. That's how I know he was nice-looking. My goodness, I can't believe how much I really did see but forgot." She turned to me, a grin on her face. "David snatched the book from his hands, and I came back inside after telling them to come on in."

"I guess the man must have been kind of surprised David grabbed it like that."

Gretchen shrugged. "Maybe not, if he'd come here to have it signed anyway." She turned back toward the front window, tugging at her chin again as she stared out to the sidewalk. "Let's see…what was he wearing…" Her forefinger worked over the tip of her chin as she frowned. "I just don't know." She shook her head. "But I would guess he walked that way." She pointed to her left, not the direction I'd walk to the train station but more the direction of other shops and cafés. "At least he was angled that way when I stepped back inside."

I followed her invisible picture of that afternoon. In my mind, Raymond hadn't had work clothes on, an outfit distinctive enough Gretchen would most likely remember. I could imagine his glance to the inside of the bookstore, maybe hoping to see me. He'd illustrated my book, given me several pictures worth thousands of words that told me he had come back for me. But then—he'd disappeared. Again.

"Thanks," I said. The bubbled image of Raymond

popped and was gone.

"I'm sorry I can't remember more," Gretchen said. "John's not here now, but when he gets back I'll ask him if he's heard from the man, just to be sure. Maybe John forgot to tell me." She didn't sound hopeful. "But I will keep the book here, if you want me to. Just in case."

I shook my head. Not just as my reply, but also as for what to do next. I didn't know. I didn't know whether to go forward or backward. "Thank you, but I'll hold onto it. Just let me know if he ever comes back for it." Which he wouldn't. I was sure of that.

"Don't go yet," Gretchen said. "I have another request from Mills and Boon, and some money for you. Like I said, this book is selling so well John is happy to give you some of the proceeds. You really need to write another." She darted to the back and returned with an envelope that was fairly thick with bills, along with Mills and Boon's letter. She laughed when she saw the "Wow" on my face. "One more book," she said again, "and you'll be rich!"

Rich enough to make it on my own as a writer, if I had to? I thumbed through the bills. At least rich enough to accomplish my list. I stuffed the envelope into my pocketbook.

As the bookstore's door closed behind me, I turned left, headed the direction Raymond had probably gone weeks ago, hoping for the best. I trailed past stores, small restaurants, and vacant lots. I listened to voices, inhaled every odor, kept my eyes moving. Just in case. My feet hurt, my stomach growled. I stopped near a small café and sat on a bench across the sidewalk from it. Men and women passed back and forth in front of me—couples, businessmen, women with children. It was the life I was supposed to live in four days. I wasn't supposed to be a spectator to it, or a writer of it. I was supposed to be one of them.

I kicked my shoes off and wiggled my toes. A passing boy laughed and pointed me out to his mother. I slid my shoes back on and twisted on the bench, looked farther down the walk and wondered. Raymond was probably back on the west coast. I was engaged. Wasn't that good enough? I looked up toward the sky. "God, isn't that good enough?"

The arch of the bridge Raymond had been working on glimmered in the sunlight above the buildings as I stared at the heavens. It beamed supreme in its artistic flair. I stood. The bridge tugged me like a magnet, and I walked that way. Like Eloise, each step I took was measured with deliberation, making sure I didn't fall.

I broke through the last block of buildings, rounded a corner, and there it was. Raymond's bridge, the Madison Bridge. I stood on the last sidewalk before it and stared. Stared at the height Raymond said was good, peered underneath at the type of girding Mr. Wilson approved of. This might be as close as I was going to get to Raymond. This might be as close as I was going to get to my answer.

I stared at his work, drank in every bead, every angle, every slope of the ground that echoed him. I stepped forward. I'd touch what he'd done. And if there was no answer, I'd go home.

I walked across a small drive to the parking lot Mr. Wilson and I had left the car in and that I had once crossed on my own, then over the brown grass I'd been on four times now. There was more of it than there had been, the rough ground flattened by the occasional rain, bare spots almost nonexistent where patches of weeds and grass crept closer together. I stepped into the bridge's shadow, the rumble of traffic above and trains below making the world feel like one giant earthquake. In spite of the noise, in spite of the vibrations and the gloominess underneath, I moved closer. I had to touch it. I had to feel what he had done.

The sound of traffic above became almost deafening as I stood alongside the nearest pillar. It was far larger than I'd noticed before, and I marveled at the weight and pressure it bore. I stretched one arm out and laid my hand against its side, the vibration traveling through my arm like electricity, the rhythm of what Raymond had built touching everything inside as well as outside of me.

I stood there, letting my teeth jar together until I dropped my hand to step away, looking up at the undergirding. At the things Mr. Wilson paid attention to that made a bridge better and stronger and more reliable than older bridges. I ran my gaze over every line. I would draw it again. Every detail, the same way Raymond would. As I looked back over the construction and followed the trail of steel down the pillar, I spotted a flaw—a gouge, something I couldn't imagine Mr. Wilson, or Raymond, or even Jacob, would allow. I stepped to the pillar and stretched upward, strained with my fingers to see how deep the gouge was, but it was just beyond my reach. I glanced around for rocks to stack that I could stand on, studied the earth piled behind it, wondering if I could climb part way up the nearest slope and stretch around the beam. A loop of wire lay on the ground not far from where I stood, rusting, probably left over from the bridge's construction days. I brushed it off, bent one end so I could thread it into the hole as I stood on my toes, and gauge how deep the flaw was. I stretched and struggled, pushed until I maneuvered the wire in as far as it would go, marked with my eyes the depth it went, and drew it out. A shred of paper came with it. A small piece, folded, and ragged around the edges.

I let the paper flutter to the ground as I studied the end of the wire. I measured the flaw to be about one inch deep. Mr. Wilson would have something to say about this. I folded the wire into sections, snatched up the scrap of paper, and shoved both into my pocket. I'd throw them away, keep Raymond's bridge pristine.

I looked up one last time at what Raymond had helped build, and began the walk back to the train station. Eventually David would show up to move my things. I needed to arrive home the same time I always did. I felt like a horse running on two tracks at the same time. One track was four days long, and it led to a normal life, the one I was supposed to live with David. Forever. The other track… It consisted of one task, the one thing on my list, and I had no idea how long that track would run. One day? Two days? If it ran four or more, that race was over.

I quickened my pace. I had to be sure to catch my train.

Chapter 52

Mama was standing on the front porch when I came up the sidewalk, her hands planted on her hips. I slowed, took smaller steps, gauged her mood as I eased her direction.

"David's in there," she announced as I hit the bottom step.

"That's good," I said, advancing with one foot to the first step. "He wanted to eat before we begin moving some of my things to his house." I made the top step and had set one foot on the porch when she moved in front of me.

"He's in there waiting for you, expecting his bride-to-be to come home and help him move her things not to *his* house but to the house that's to belong to both of you, together."

"Mama," I said, maneuvering around her until I was on the porch. "Mama, all of that's true. He's here, I'm here on time, we'll eat, and we'll move. Why are you so upset?"

"Because..." She leaned closer and lowered her voice. "Because of a phone call I got right before your fiancé got here." She raised a finger and pointed it at my nose. "From that bookstore where your book is."

My skin turned cold as blood drained to my feet. I reached for the nearest porch post and held on. "Gretchen said sales were good. Is that the problem?"

"That's not what she called about, and you know it."

I swallowed as Mama moved even closer.

"She said to tell you he had come by after all." Mama's eyes were near mine, her breath heating my face. "I've always known there was a 'he' out there somewhere. I want you to tell me right now who he is. Then you need to march in there and tell David. David's a good man. He deserves to know the truth."

I saw beyond Mama's anger. Somehow my gaze traveled past the fury in her eyes, straight to her fear. I never thought of Mama as afraid, beyond the worry her daughter would be a spinster, there'd be no grandchildren, Mama'd be ostracized for my book-writing sins, and our family looked down on forever. What I saw was the fear of something else, something bigger than all the rest. Something that had maybe put her on the soapbox my whole life, preaching against everything I'd ended up doing anyway.

"Well?" she pressed.

I glanced at the house where David was. She was right. He was a good man, and he did deserve to know. But even I didn't know, didn't know what was true or what to tell him. I had four more days. I had a list. I looked Mama in the eye.

"Mama, that man Gretchen was talking about is a fellow who handed a book to David. David said the man wanted it signed for his wife or girlfriend, David didn't know which. I waited around all day, signing books, thinking that man would come back to the store for his, but he never did. Since David is moving my things tonight, I went through some of my stuff last night. And that book... Well, I still had it, so I took it

274

back to the bookstore today so the man could get it if he came by. Gretchen said he never had. Guess she was wrong. Maybe he talked to John, instead, and she didn't know about it." I spoke in a level tone, a tone so smooth I amazed myself. My chest hurt. My lips quivered. But I refused to bite them.

Mama's eyes narrowed for a moment, but then some of the venom went out of her stance. "Well, he must not have wanted that book too badly. Otherwise, he would have stayed until you signed it." Her chin jutted forward. "That should tell you something."

It did. Everything she said reminded me of what I'd thought all this time. Raymond really didn't care. Not enough to stay, not enough to come back. But he had cared enough to draw pictures for me, and those pictures plus his ending had made my heart beat like nothing else ever had.

"He waited an awfully long time to come back, too. Gretchen said it was about two weeks ago John remembered the guy coming back in. He asked if you'd left the book there for him or taken it with you. John told him you had it, but he could get it from you."

"But John didn't," I said. "He never even tried to get it from me."

Mama looked to the side, her eyes passing from the porch swing to the rocker sitting nearby. "He might have," she said. "He did call here once and ask for you."

"You didn't tell me?" My voice ranged high, striking a pitch even tinnier than hers sometimes did.

"You know good and well that book of yours is bad for you and David. I thought John was calling about another signing. Or even worse, writing another

275

book. I wanted no part of it, and neither should you, so I just forgot about his call."

All of the color that had left me returned. It rose from the bottom of my feet, coursed through my veins, all the way upward until it reached my face. I felt red rage, I felt my cheeks enflame. "Mama, how could you!"

"Me? How could I? What about him? The guy didn't come back for it except that one time."

The wind seeped from my fury, the blood ebbed out of my face. I felt it trickle downward toward the porch floor, taking everything with it, all feeling, all hope. Tears welled in my eyes. Mama spotted them the same moment I felt them. Her brow furrowed, and a war took place on her face—the righteous mother against the caring one. I wanted to run. I didn't care which mother won. No matter which woman survived, I would lose, anyway. The first tear spilled over. As the second followed, I turned. I looked at the front door. I couldn't go in there. I whirled back toward the steps and started down.

I was yanked to a stop before I hit the second step, Mama's fingers wrapped tight around my arm. I glanced up, her face a blur through my tears. "Let go of me, Mama."

She tugged me upward with such force I stumbled back onto the porch. I wrenched my arm as I gained my balance, but she held on tight.

"Listen to me," she said. Her face swam in front of me. I reached into my pocket for a handkerchief, the coiled wire raking across my skin. I yanked my hand out, the wire and paper coming with it, the wire clattering across the wooden porch, and the paper drifting away. "I know you don't understand me, or everything I do, but listen to me and let me explain."

She let go of my arm then, bent over for the wire, and turned and scooped up the paper just before the breeze blew it into the yard. She held both in her hands. I expected her to drill me over what they were, find some reason to see them as suspicious, but she didn't. She was looking at them but not seeing them. She was sorting through thoughts, instead of through the trash that had fallen from my pocket.

"I want you to understand…" She looked up. She twisted the coil of rusty wire in her hands as she looked at me. I'd never seen Mama's eyes so naked before, without the covering of duty. They were truly windows to her soul, and I wished daylight would linger so I could peer further into her, past the fear to a place I'd never seen before. "I never should have married anyone else, no one but your father, and I'm glad I didn't. He was the right man for me." She glanced at the front door. She listened, maybe she was making sure no one was listening back or coming out in the middle of what she had to say. It remained closed, and it seemed quiet on the other side. And quiet on our side. Quieter than she'd ever been.

"Mama…" I swiped my sleeve across my eyes and leaned close to her.

"Like I said, he was the right man, and I'm not sorry I married him. Anyone else…no matter who, or what I felt…would have been a mistake. A mistake I never want you to make, either."

In the silence that followed, I heard her true admission. She'd married a man she didn't love, not the way she'd wanted to love, but what she'd learned to accept instead. Those quieter confessions—the "anyone else," the "no matter who," the "no matter what she felt," were still there. There must have been another. What she didn't say and what I couldn't see in her gaze suggested there had been. I wondered if Daddy knew. If that was why he stayed so quiet, and why she didn't. I looked at the door, thinking about our two Davids on the other side of it. Her David and mine. Two good men, two good providers. A door closed between us.

I watched Mama twist and untwist the wire, the rust leaving orange powder on her fingers and palms. I reached down and took it from her. If she knew where I'd gotten it and why, she'd only feel worse. She'd relive some heartache I wasn't sure she could withstand.

I wanted to tell Mama it was all right, that I understood, because I did. My heart broke for the woman inside her, the woman I never even knew was there. My heart broke for my own wounds, also, a heart that couldn't possibly be broken any more. I laid a hand on her shoulder, slid it down to her arm, and I squeezed.

The front door opened, a slow swing to the inside. Neither Mama nor I looked to see which David was standing there. Maybe both of them. We just stared at each other, then down at our hands. I held onto the wire so she wouldn't take it back and twist it again. The scrap of paper appeared in her palm as she undid a fist. It traveled to her fingertips and she rubbed its folded sides together.

"Thank you for telling me, Mama." I whispered so the Davids wouldn't hear. She nodded. I felt it, a broken admission above fingers that couldn't stop fidgeting.

"Everything all right?" It was my David. I looked to the doorway where he stood behind the screen. Daddy—Mama's David—stood back, his face looking over my David's shoulder. Standing back because he still wasn't sure after all these years. My heart broke for him also. For all the years they'd been in a marriage that was good. Good because they'd made it that way by hard work and commitment.

I looked at my David. I could see his frown through the screen. Not upset, just wondering. Maybe not sure, since I hadn't been sure the whole of our engagement. "We'll be right in," I said.

He said, "Okay," and closed the door. I could feel him near it still, on the other side and unsure. Like my father.

Mama pressed the wad of paper into my hand with the wire. "I just wanted you to know," she said. She straightened, drew herself up. "Throw that trash away. And I don't want to know where you got it or why you're carrying it around." She held her hands over mine, the trash cupped between them. "Just do what's right," she said, soft again. "Just do what you know is best."

We walked inside together then, past the two Davids and into the kitchen to get supper on the table.

"Need to wash our hands," Mama said, clapping hers together to beat the rust off her skin. I trailed her to the sink and set the wire and paper aside as she ran the water. "I'll get rid of those things first," she said, "or our hands will just get all rusty again." She carried them to the wastebasket while I ran my hands under the water. I waited to hear the wire hit the basket, hear her footsteps as she came back to my side to share the soap with me. But I heard nothing. She was quiet, so I turned. She dropped the wire into the basket and puzzled over the paper that lay open in her hands. "You draw this?" she asked and held it up for me to see. "It's quite good."

I shook the water off my hands and stepped her way. I could see the top of a man sketched onto the paper. Black hair, tanned skin, suit jacket and tie… It was torn off at his waist. It was Raymond. It was my groom. Part of the answer I'd hoped to find.

Chapter 53

I became a spectator to my own life as I watched my clothing, my keepsakes, and my extra toiletries being layered into boxes, baskets, and bags.

"You need this?" David asked. Again. He held up a stuffed doll and gave it a little wave in the air. Its head flopped from side to side, its body hovering the direction of my wastebasket and then the direction of the box in which David was stacking the things I'd take to his house. She was the first doll I remember receiving, and I watched the doll's indecision on which way to go. I walked across the room and snatched her from his grasp. "Why'd you do that?" He gave me a sharp look. "You could just tell me yes or no."

I hugged the doll to my chest and went back to my closet. I kept her pinned close with one arm while I sorted through hangers of clothing I wouldn't need in the next few days with the other. David resumed organizing my blanket trunk behind me. I could hear his exasperation in the short spurts of breath that kept time with his arranging.

Daddy was taking my desk apart on one side of my room while Mama went through what I'd kept stored in its drawers nearby. Pieces of me were being disassembled and redefined so they could be reassembled at David's. I had no idea when that would happen, but I had a fear of how it would. I'd be put together differently. The way David wanted me, the way I was supposed to be. I could tell by the parts of me he suggested leaving behind. When he finished reassembling me as his wife, I wouldn't look the same anymore. Forever.

With my doll pressed to my side, I bent down, retrieved the brown suit I'd put in a stack to go to David's. I started a new pile with it, extracting three more outfits with my free hand and laying them on top of the brown suit. I went to my dresser and removed undergarments, pajamas, and my anklet where my money was hidden. My book money. I tucked it inside my pajamas and brought everything over to the small stack. No one was watching, everyone absorbed in their own dismembering of my history, everyone with their own idea of what I'd be recreated to be. I went to my satchel and laid it on top of my newest pile, pressed down on it, my book inside, the crown to my list.

"I'm finished," Mama said. I glanced at my empty desk drawers, wondering how it could be she'd managed to remove me from them. I looked at the stacks she'd made—ink, pens, and pencils lined up on a neat pile of empty pads of paper. Not far from that lay a disorderly heap—pages of short stories, first draft of *Love on a Train*, and little character sketches I'd done before and since. I caught Mama's eye, saw her insistence I keep that mound away from David. I walked over, stood in front of her, and shook my head.

"Those can stay here for now, Mama, but they're not to be destroyed."

"Well, I don't know where you plan to put them. You can't leave them just lying out in the open."

I bent over and shuffled my work into a neat stack.

I set my doll on top and scooped everything into my arms. I straightened, balancing the load as I looked at Mama. "Would you get the attic door, please?"

I saw the refusal on Mama's face as she crossed her arms. The attic was the far north, according to Mama. Full of spiders and rodents, a place none of us dared to go, except her. And even then she raised a ruckus whenever she made the trip up there.

"It's there or with me," I said, nodding toward my boxes for David's house. She turned. I could hear the grind of her reluctance as I followed her out of my room and to the attic's narrow wooden door at the end of the upstairs hallway. Mama opened the door but didn't step aside. "Mama…"

"Those won't survive the far north," she said as I squeezed past her and took the first step. "It's full of mice, and they'll chew those to bits."

"I'm not throwing them away, Mama, so it's up here or at David's."

"Fine, then. Just leave them on the stairs, and I'll put them in a box for you tomorrow."

"I'll do it. Thank you anyway." I climbed the narrow stairs, one step at a time, leaning against the wall as I went. A string dangled somewhere near the top, attached to a single bulb for light, a bulb I prayed worked. I set my stack on the floor when I reached the top and swung my arms through the air until I felt the string. I pulled. A cone of soft light lit me, my papers, the dusty floor, and the top step where I stood.

"Just set them right there at the top of the stairs and come back down here and help," Mama said from below. I heard her foot on the first step. "I'll move them later to a box. I promise."

"No, I'll find a safe place to put them," I called down. "You go ahead. I won't be long."

"There's too much you can trip over in the dark," she warned. "I'll stay close here until you're done."

"Mama, I'll be fine."

"No, I insist."

I heard the fear in her voice, the same fear I'd seen in her eyes on the porch, earlier. I looked down the steps at her. She'd come up another step. "I'll just set them on top this nearest stack of boxes, okay? As long as there aren't mouse droppings on it."

"Okay, then come right back down. To help."

I watched her descend the couple of steps she'd taken. The attic door closed partially after she went through it, and I heard Mama take halting footsteps away. I turned to the attic and stood at the outer perimeter of the cone of light, letting my eyes adjust to the darkness as I searched for the nearest stack of boxes. I saw shelves along one wall, and a couple of tiny windows on two others. Boxes, weighed down with time, were slumped in teetering stacks here and there throughout, just as I remembered seeing the one time I'd followed Mama up the stairs as a girl. I walked to the nearest clump of boxes and ran my hand over its dusty surface, clearing my way through ancient cobwebs, cringing at the thought of mouse droppings, wishing the top one might be open and have enough space for my work.

"Desk is done," I heard my father's voice say through the attic floor. He was not far away below me, and I realized my room was beneath a nearby cluster of boxes.

"And all emptied," Mama replied. "Not much in

there she needed to take with her, anyway."

I left my papers on the stack I'd just cleared and crept to where their voices were. I slid my hands down the stack of boxes above them and squatted near the floor.

"She probably won't make a lot of use of the desk," David said. I heard his footsteps below me. "I'll pay the bills and work at mine. I suppose she could make her grocery lists at this desk."

I rested my palms on the floor, dirty splinters jabbing my fingers.

I heard pieces of my desk being clumped together. By the soft grunts I knew it was my father who was doing it. I crouched with my ear nearer the floor, wondering whether my desk was being left behind or sent to David's. For a different purpose than it had here. Wooden desk legs clattered against each other. Daddy puffed as he gathered them into a group, and then I heard him leave my room. My desk was going. Going to David's for me to make grocery lists on.

"How about these pictures?" David asked. I mentally ran over every wall in my room, recalling pictures of me, my childhood, Karen, and tons of drawings in childlike style.

I could imagine Mama taking a visual tour around my room also. Probably most, if not all, of those pictures would stay. They were her memories, too, hers and Daddy's, not just mine.

"Maybe a scrapbook of them?" David asked. Mama didn't answer.

Daddy reentered the room. I heard him lift the top of my desk and tug it out the door. No one offered to help him; he labored on his own while the other two stayed behind. I tried to envision my desk at David's house. My clothing, my doll, a scrapbook of my history all neatly filed away.

"She'll be a good wife," Mama said after Daddy was gone. "Even I had some adjusting to do after we got married." Mama's voice had a fleeting wistful tone. She cleared her throat. "But, of course, I did it pretty quick."

"It would be easier for her if she left most of this here," David replied. I could imagine him looking around my room. "I mean, she needs her clothing, but even that is mostly work clothes. And she won't need them after she starts raising our family. As for the rest of it, she'll be making new memories, adult ones, and there won't be time for any of what I see here."

It was like attending my own funeral. I heard the eulogy over who I was, and the pronouncement of what I would hopefully be once I got my wife wings and halo. No one was mourning, except me. I felt the cry of death. The end of what I was, what I thought I'd be, the end of the dreams that were supposed to carry pieces of me into my new future.

I leaned against the nearest stack of boxes, hearing and feeling my dreams being torn away the same way Raymond's picture of himself as a groom had been.

The tower of boxes teetered as I slouched against it, a slow collapse toward the wall. I stood, groped for the top box, and tried to hold the stack straight, but I was too late. I stiffened my arms toward the wall to brace for the impact as the boxes tipped with me. The heel of my palms struck the edge of a board mounted to the wall, my skin raking across the board's surface. My hands, like plows, shoved against whatever had been sitting on that board, pushing it all aside.

My fingers burned, my palms stung, my teeth jarred when my hands finally slammed into the outer wall. The boxes leaned with me, both of us dangling at a forty-five degree angle. I bit my lip, held back a groan, and listened. Footsteps left my room. The attic door opened all the way, and a shaft of light beamed up the steps.

"What's going on up there?" Mama called. "You should be back down here by now." I heard her shoe hit the first step.

"I'm okay, Mama. I just cleared a place for my writing, and a box slipped. I'll be right there."

She stayed where she was. So did I, afraid to breathe, afraid to move lest everything crash to the floor.

"David's ready to take this load to your house."

"Okay," I called, my fingers throbbing.

"Then come on down."

"Yes, Mama."

"What else do we need to get?" It was my father's voice below me, back from carrying the pieces and parts of my desk downstairs. I listened. I heard Mama mumble something, take a couple of steps away from the attic door, and then she was gone. Back to my room with David and my father.

With the extra light, I studied the crumpling boxes I was leaning against, and the edge of the board my hands had skidded across. The board was built as a shelf, hidden behind the boxes, and sturdy enough to catch me and hold the things I'd accidentally knocked aside. I inched my hands backwards across its surface, collecting more tiny splinters and bumping against those things. I braced one hand at the board's front edge, gripped the top of the boxes with the other, and slowly pulled the stack toward me until I had my footing and the boxes were upright. I gently let go and slid around them, bracing them as I did. I felt along the board for the items I'd upset, seeing in the dim light what I couldn't see before. A candle. A lighter. A book.

I gathered them together and tiptoed to the top of the stairs beneath the cone of light. The candle was covered with dust, but it had been used at one time, its wick black and charred. I shook the lighter. It was empty, so I set it aside. I blew the top layer of dust off the book, and wiped away what remained with my arm. It was a novel. An old story. An old love story from the look of the title and the picture on the front. The spine creaked as I pried it open, a musty odor wafting upwards. Tiny print on pages almost orange with age made it impossible to read as I fanned the sheets from one side to the other.

Small items tucked here and there between the pages caught my eye. I stopped at one and removed it. A photo of a young man. I held it near the light. I had no idea who he was, so I put him back and searched until I found more—more pictures, little mementoes from places like soda fountains, and letters. One-page letters, barely more than notes—*Dear Ann, meet me at the tree. I love you, Jim.*

Then at the very back, behind all the notes from Jim to Ann about meetings and a secret love, I saw an envelope. Inside it was an invitation, a wedding invitation. A plain printed card that announced Jane Meadows would wed Jim Carsten. I had no idea who Jim Carsten was, or Jane Meadows. But I knew Ann.

She was my mother. Jane must have been Mama's "her." A different her from the woman Mama had expected to marry the man who made her heart beat red. I stuffed each item back into the book and closed it tight. I held it against my chest, and carried it to where I'd found it. I set the book, the candle, and the empty lighter back where they had been. Touched them one last time, then turned.

I secured the boxes in front of her…the old her she'd kept hidden after she found herself in this sensible marriage. I went back to the top of the stairs, stopping at the box where I'd laid my first draft of *Love on a Train*, my other stories, characters that would never be born if I stored them away from light. And relegated them only to candlelight.

I glanced back to where Mama's old life was hidden as I turned off the attic light. "Let those love now, who never loved before; let those who always loved, now love the more," I whispered in the darkness. "For you, Mama. And you, Daddy. And also for me."

Chapter 54

Long after my things had been set in a corner at David's house, long after I'd said all the right things and made Mama and David pleased, long after David said, "Goodnight," and "Only three more days starting tomorrow," did my heart begin to beat again. It resurrected, thud by thud, as I dragged it out of the morgue it had fallen into, promising it we would find life. Somehow. I tiptoed back to the attic after my parents had gone to bed, wrapped my arms around my writing and my doll, and carried them downstairs to the front door. I returned to my room, grabbed the few outfits I'd set aside, my undergarments, my nightgown, my anklet with my money, and my satchel, and brought them downstairs also.

I stood at the front door, my things near my feet, and waited. A car pulled into the drive and the engine shut off. Footsteps came quietly toward the house, up the front steps, and onto our porch. I waited for the knock. Three taps, a pause, and one more tap. It was our secret knock, one Karen and I had created ages ago, one we hadn't used since we were girls.

I unlatched the door and drew it open, holding it tight so it wouldn't make a sound. Karen stood outside the screen, a large suitcase in one hand, a small one in the other. When the door was all the way opened we did the same with the screen door, easing it her way until

Karen and her luggage slipped through.

"Thank you," I mouthed in the low light as she set both suitcases on the floor. She nodded. She opened one and I opened the other. I pointed to the stack of papers and my doll. She picked them up and brought them to the small suitcase. She laid them inside and latched it without a sound.

Together we fit my clothing and my satchel into the other suitcase. I included my pocketbook, a few toiletries, a small amount of food I'd taken from Mama's cupboard. We looked at each other after the large suitcase was latched.

We stood, I put on my coat, walked to Daddy's chair and made sure my note was secured under his ashtray. He'd spot it in the morning. He'd show Mama. They'd think I'd gone to work early and after work would go to Karen's to go over last-minute wedding details. They'd tell David. There would be relief over my diligence, even if Mama and David wouldn't appreciate I wasn't there for supper.

We took the luggage out to the front porch, and I locked the door behind me. We set the screen door gently in its place, never making a sound. We stood facing each other, the luggage at our feet.

"Three more days plus tonight," I whispered. Karen nodded. We each lifted one suitcase and trailed down the front stairs to her car.

We loaded the luggage without a sound and slipped into the front seat. "Your car smells..." I paused as I closed the car's door. "Good." I glanced Karen's way. Like an expert, she started the car and backed it into the street. "One of your riders? Or should I say, is he one of your fares?"

"Let's just say business is good." She smiled as she watched the street ahead. "Now, let's get onto the scent you're really following."

Chapter 55

Trains held different crowds at night than they did in the daytime. The vibrations felt harsher and the hum sounded louder with fewer people to absorb them. I stared at a black window as night time passed by. I was too afraid to look at the other passengers, all of them men, all of them watchful. Night streamed past, my large suitcase on the floor beside my feet, bumping against my legs, a reminder to me and an advertisement to the other passengers that I was far from home.

Mr. Wilson had called from Illinois in the evening. I hadn't thought much about it as I answered his questions regarding old notes about bridges. He'd found me at home, after our dinner and before we'd packed up my room. His concern, the glitch he'd discovered upon arriving in Illinois, had been lost in the evening activities, drowned out by the shock of seeing myself taken apart and carried away. Seeing Mama's life the same way, stuffed into a novel of promise, long since burned out and dead.

"Carl came with me," Mr. Wilson had said. "And I'm glad he did. He knows more about the process than any engineer I've worked with yet. He knows most of the guys here, it turns out. A huge benefit for me, but still, without some of the history Kansas City put us through and what we learned from it, this trip won't be as simple as I'd thought. I'm heading back tonight, he's coming in the morning after he meets with the crews one more time. Oh, and by the way, have a happy wedding. When is it again? Five days?"

Mr. Wilson was either on his way back to Kansas City by now or was already there. He wouldn't know I crossed his path, followed him to Illinois instead of staying home like I should, getting ready for my wedding. It was Carl I wanted to see. If he was finding men in Illinois he'd known, maybe he or someone there could help me. I watched the night speed by, forcing myself to stay awake.

I knew enough about the bridge project Mr. Wilson was working with to be able to tell a cab driver where I needed to go. The sun had been up long enough that men would be at the site, most probably already working, and hopefully Carl would be there, too.

Long gone were the days I shied away from bridge sites. No longer did I hedge and stumble around them like Eloise with her one bad leg. "Thank you," I said to the driver as I paid him. He drove away as I stood near the construction project, my suitcase in my hand.

There was very little done so far on this particular bridge. Very little excavation, only piles of dirt, rocks, and beams. I could imagine how Raymond would see these fragments as a future work of art. He'd see the bridge in its completion, each line and each rivet in its place, each beam just as it should be.

"Can I help you, ma'am?"

I hadn't even noticed the man next to me, where he'd come from or how long he'd been there. He had a pencil balanced behind one ear, a pocket stuffed full of papers, a leathery look to his skin.

"I'm looking for Carl Lancaster," I said. "He was

here with Harvey Wilson. I work for Mr. Wilson."

The misgiving in the man's eyes diminished, the annoyance at a woman being on site began to disappear. "You're just in time. Carl is finishing up, hoping to catch the next train out."

I followed the man over uneven earth. He took it like a mountain goat. I did my best, knowing it was far better than I'd done my first two times at a site.

Carl's eyes widened when I walked up. He scratched his head, looking baffled as if he'd traveled time or space and wasn't sure how he'd done it.

"I know this is a surprise," I jumped in, fighting down the flush I felt creeping into my cheeks. The men who were gathered around him eased back as if I had a disease. They formed a half circle around Carl, leaving me standing alone. "Even Mr. Wilson wasn't expecting me. Is he still here?"

Carl shook his head. "No, he went back last night. Didn't he call you? I thought he did."

I nodded. "Yes, he did. And he mentioned possibly going back last night, but I was hoping he might still be here." I mentally recalled the behaviors Mama'd taught me meant someone was telling a lie. Fidgeting hands, shuffling feet, avoiding eye contact, fingers over the mouth instead of speaking directly. I met Carl's gaze, gripped my suitcase with both hands, and cemented my feet to the ground. "But since I didn't catch him, I'll just give you copies of the information he wanted."

I set my suitcase down and took two folded papers from inside my jacket. I'd written them out on the train, working hard to keep the bump and vibration out of my scrawls. I handed them to Carl. "Here is what Mr. Wilson and I talked about. I thought of a few extra comments later and included them. I didn't know how to contact him, but I knew they were important enough to both of you I should bring them up."

Carl, and the men with him, frowned at me. "Aren't you getting married or something?"

I nodded. "I'm making this trip up here part of my wedding agenda also."

Carl frowned more and scratched the hair beneath his hat.

"It's the only way my mother and fiancé would let me come. We were in dire need of Haskins napkins. Ruby Red. We were short seven sets. I suppose we could have used plain cream-colored ones, but, well, it's my wedding, and I wanted red. That red in particular, so I thought coming up here would give me a chance to get those napkins and hand this paperwork over to you at the same time. You wouldn't happen to know where the Haskins…" I waved the papers toward him with my outstretched arm.

Carl shook his head. I tried not to smile as he shoved my napkin question aside. He took the notes and glanced at them, zeroing in on the main points. I watched his expression shift from skepticism to surprise to interest. "These are good," he said, looking up at me. The other men huddled nearer, glancing down at the pages, then up at me. "This is what Harvey wanted to know."

"I thought you could use them," I said. I stood quietly while the men discussed the notes, grimy fingers pointing at the pages and the few sketches I'd made. I didn't fidget. I kept the suitcase against my legs so I wouldn't tap my foot. Carl handed the notes off to the men, who walked away with them, pointing at rubble and mounds of dirt, their vision coming to life.

"Thank you," Carl said, stepping near me. He brushed off one hand and extended it my direction. "If they can use what Harvey learned in Kansas City, it may keep us from wasting a lot of time up here."

I nodded, made sure my suitcase was secure, and shook his hand.

"It's beautiful," I said, gazing around at the nothing that was there. "I mean, I've learned enough from Mr. Wilson to understand what's coming."

Carl lifted his hat and ran his fingers through strands of hair, his gaze following mine at the empty expanse. "Got a good crew here, and plenty of funding. If Harvey's plans go through, this should be a real beaut and last forever. It will prove his ideas are right. It will make the war worth it for him in the end." He dropped his hat back onto his head.

I glanced at Carl and thought of the war, the effect it had on families, the strange things it made men do. And Karen. "I'm glad," I said. "I'm glad there's a crew to make this come true for Mr. Wilson. Not many of the men here yet, I see." I passed my gaze over the clusters of men here and there, searching for one in particular who'd also been through that war—tall, lean, dark-haired, and handsome.

One of the men approached us as we panned the crew, doing the mountain goat walk over rough terrain. We watched as he headed our way.

"Thought we'd get together in about ten minutes," he said to Carl when he stopped near us. "Ma'am," he said to me, tipping his head. I nodded and smiled.

"This is Martha Cole," Carl said. "She works back in Kansas City with Harvey Wilson. She brought those notes up for me that the guys took over there." Carl pointed at a huddle of men, still holding onto the papers I'd given Carl. "This is Everett," Carl nodded toward the man. "He's been working bridges since birth."

"Happy to meet you, Everett. I know a few things about bridges," I said, shaking Everett's hand. "Learned my first little bit from a man in Kansas City named Raymond Haynes. You probably don't know him, but he worked on the Madison Bridge down there."

I watched Everett's face. I prayed he'd correct me, make this trip worthwhile, and say he did know Raymond. Not only knew him but also knew where he was. And why. And with whom. He nodded as he released my hand. "Haynes…"

"Yeah, tall, thin fellow," Carl added. "Good-natured, good worker…"

"Sure, I might know who you mean. Dark hair, took off to get married or something like that, right?"

My feet began to sink into the ground. First my feet, then my ankles. The earth was swallowing me as I dropped into the netherworld.

Carl nodded. "That's right."

"But after that," I cut in. My voice sounded like a croak. I cleared my throat and tried again. "I mean he came back. After going away to get married, he came back to Kansas City. Right?"

The men frowned. Marriage data meant nothing to them. Their worlds revolved around steel and cement. They turned toward the piles of beams and thought.

"Jackson hired him to work a bridge. Let's see, that was about two months ago." Everett rubbed his chin. "Was glad to get Haynes, I remember that."

"Which bridge was that?" I glanced at the piles of

beams also, telling my heart to be still.

"A ways east of Kansas City, but not as far as Lexington."

East of Kansas City. There was no stopping my heart. Raymond was near, an easy train ride from Illinois.

"That bridge finished?" Carl cut in.

I glanced at the sky, gauged where the sun was, and wondered when the next train south would leave.

"Almost. Down to the finishing touches."

I looked at Everett. Raymond wasn't a finishing-touches worker, except in his art. He was a ground breaker, a construction worker, not a painter or any of the niceties that came at the end.

"It's almost finished?" My voice croaked again, my eyes felt wide and hot.

"We're trying to hire most of those guys to come here, if we can get them to move this far."

"Maybe you can get Haynes." Carl crossed his arms and smiled.

Everett shook his head. "Probably not. He took off again, it seems. Something about things not working out like he thought, so he was going back, I think. Don't know for sure. But anyway, not sure where to find him anymore."

"I need to get to the train station," I said. "And I have a lot to do before that. Is there a way you can call for a driver?" My voice trembled. My hands did, too, as I lifted my suitcase.

"Oh, yeah, your napkins. What was it you said? Hopkins?"

"Haskins. Ruby Red." I wanted to run one hand over my mouth, shuffle my feet, glance away, and fidget…but more than anything I wanted to cry, to run, to just admit it was all lies. But I couldn't. "Yes, I'll go there first."

"Tell you what. How about I take you to this napkin place. It's the least I can do after what you did for me. This little meeting won't take long, and you'll be on the first possible train back to Kansas City after you get what you need." Carl looked pleased.

"Oh, no. I couldn't. I won't subject you to Ruby Red anything." I forced a smile, gripping my suitcase handle tighter. "If you could just call for a driver, I'll be fine. Thank you, though."

Carl scratched his head. "I have to go to the station myself anyway. Are you sure?"

"I'm positive. If you saw how long it took me to find the right red back in Kansas City, you never would have offered." I stretched my smile farther, held my feet still, kept my eye contact steady.

"Well, okay, then. Everett, will you make the call for the lady?"

Everett nodded and walked away. I had no idea where he'd go for a phone. I just wanted him to hurry. I told Carl goodbye as calmly as I could. I trembled from head to toe as I walked to where I had been dropped off this morning, my suitcase beating against my leg, my heart hammering against my ears.

When at last the construction site was behind me, Carl back with the men, and me out of their view, I cried. I let tears fall, something forbidden at job sites, let them trickle down my cheeks and onto my brown suit.

Chapter 56

Two more days, two more days, two more days. The rhythm of the train chugged out the reminder. After today, when tomorrow dawned, I'd have two more days. Two more days. Two more days.

I stared at the train's black window, just as I'd done on my way to Illinois. Now I was traveling west into Kansas City, a futile trip to the bridge east of there behind me.

I'd brought enough of my book earnings to take me to California, if that's what I had to do. I had plenty of cash but was short on time. I'd gone to Raymond's last known bridge site. I'd eaten a sandwich at the depot in Illinois, caught the first train southeast, and slept from Illinois to there.

I dragged my suitcase with me to a spot near the site and tucked it behind a bush. I walked to the bridge, praying it wouldn't be Jackson I ran into. I wanted to avoid him, in case he spoke with Carl at some point. I preferred to ask any other man who wouldn't care who I was or why I was there, maybe even be miffed that a woman was where construction was going on.

I chose a filthy man, his work clothes almost in tatters. He was passing not far from where I stood as he toted an empty pail to a waiting truck.

"Excuse me," I called. He frowned when he spotted me. "I'm looking for a Mr. Haynes," I said.

"His first name is Richard. No, sorry, it's Raymond. I'm just the delivery person. In any case, I have paperwork for him from his attorney's office." I planted my feet next to each other and stood. I pressed my hands against my sides so they wouldn't fidget, and I kept my focus on the man. "Is Mr. Haynes working here?"

The man tossed the pail onto the truck's bed and sauntered my way. "Haynes." He scratched his chin the way they all did, as he gazed back at the job site. "Nope, I think I know who you're talking about. No, he's gone. Won't be back, either."

I took the news without a flinch, even though it felt like a blow. "I was afraid of that. Any idea where I can find him?"

The man shook his head, frowned more, and said he could ask around for me.

"That's all right. I...I mean, we'll try somewhere else."

"I really didn't know him. But he was a good drawer, I remember that."

"He drew?"

"Now and then. Yeah, I remember. He drew the bridge, what it would look like. He did a good job of it, too, even though it wasn't nearly done." The man looked at me, his eyes lighting up. "He drew you, too. Yeah, he drew pictures of you. Funny, I thought he was drawing his girlfriend, but you work for his attorney, you say? Guess you must look like her or something, because now that I think about it, seems someone said something about him getting married."

"Thank you," I said, backing away. "Thank you for your time."

I'd nearly stumbled as I turned back toward my suitcase. If I fell, I knew I'd never get back up.

Two more days, two more days, two more days. The train tried to lull me to sleep, but it couldn't. I stared at the black window, telling the man with the black hair goodbye.

Chapter 57

"Land sakes, you look awful!" Mama clapped a hand against her chest after I dragged out of bed and stumbled downstairs in the morning.

My train hadn't arrived in Kansas City until four o'clock in the morning. I'd staggered home with my suitcase and crept up the stairs to my bed. Daddy's usual morning noises stirred me in my sleep, but it was Mama's, "Two more days," outside my bedroom door that brought me out of it.

I lay there listening to them, Daddy getting dressed, Mama heading downstairs to make breakfast. I could hear the hurry in her footsteps, the footsteps I was about to follow. When their noises were far away, I sat up in bed. Two more days. Tomorrow was my last day before I married David. Today was my two more days.

I stood, opened Karen's suitcase, and stared at my clothing. And my satchel.

I set my dirty clothing aside to be washed and put away the remainder. Two outfits and leftover book money. Enough to get me to California or through the next two days, whichever I'd needed to do. As things had turned out, the outfits were all I needed to get me through the next two days. I lifted my satchel, opened it, and took the book from inside. *Love on a Train*. It could live in an attic near a burned-out candle and an empty lighter the rest of its life, or I could end its life today. I opted for neither. I would take it to Karen's to add to my other stories she'd taken with her in the smaller suitcase. They'd all have to go eventually. I'd decided I couldn't end up like Mama with my story always somewhere over my head, my life an unhappy reminder one floor below.

I tumbled into a kitchen chair while Mama let out another near-yelp. "What happened to you?" She patted her chest. "You been out all night?"

"No, of course not." I struggled to my feet, searched the cabinet for a coffee cup, then helped myself to some of Daddy's coffee.

Mama stood there, assessing me. "I think I need to call Beverly," she said. "Cancel your hair and all your fixing up for the wedding day and do them tomorrow instead. You'll scare David to death tomorrow night at your rehearsal."

"Maybe just a nap, instead," I suggested. If I slept through until tomorrow, slept my two last days away, I wouldn't make any more mistakes. I'd feel no pain, and I could wake up refreshed and ready, ready to be David's wife.

"No time for naps," Mama said, glancing at Daddy, who'd been sitting quietly in the chair across the table from me, then back at me. "Too much to do. Why, we've got to get your dress here, and set up for the dinner tomorrow night after the rehearsal. You can help me make sandwiches. Gladys was going to help, but her son's got the measles, and I don't want her touching any of the food."

Mama rambled on. I listened but didn't hear. Daddy and I stared at one another over our cups' brims and through the coffee's steam.

"You ready for this?" he asked when Mama finally paused.

I set my cup down. I nodded as I watched the rising steam. I'd have to give up coffee after this. Not because of David, but because of me. It was tied to being a writer, just like having a cigarette would have been. Coffee would be a constant reminder of what had been, could have been, but never would be again. From tomorrow on, the only writing I would do was to make lists. Grocery lists.

"I'm ready," I said, looking up at him.

"You're not ready at all," Mama cut in. "Not until we get you dolled up and all of the other things I just mentioned done. You should have been writing them down. Here, let me get you some paper and you can make a list."

Mama disappeared, then returned with a small tablet and a pencil. "Write down what you need to get done. I'll add the rest."

I stared at the pad while she bustled away. Daddy sipped his coffee across from me. I scooted my cup aside and began my new writing career, only one word coming to mind, the one thing that had been on my list since Harvey told me he was going to Illinois.

I wrote it down, and Daddy stood. "I'll help you with whatever it is you've got to do, little girl," he said. I nodded, and trailed him to my room.

"I recall doing this for your mama," Daddy said, standing next to me in my doorway. "Eons ago, right before we got married, we packed up what little she owned and moved it to the house we first lived in."

Daddy and I stood side by side, both of us smelling like fried ham and eggs, Mama still downstairs cleaning up after our breakfast. Those were the same sounds she'd been making for years, but this morning they were faster, with a more determined clank to the pans.

"Mama sounds...excited," I said.

Daddy nodded. "She's setting great store by your wedding day."

"You'd think it was hers instead of mine," I said. "I mean, she's actually put more into this than I have. And I'm sorry about that, Daddy. I know I've been a strain to you, not always cooperating the way Mama says I should. I...I didn't mean to be so..."

Daddy put a hand on my shoulder. We both stared around my room. It looked like it had been pillaged by thieves. "What's that?" he asked, pointing at Karen's suitcase still on my floor. My eyes fully opened for the first time this morning. I'd meant to close it and hide it under my bed.

"Um, that's Karen's," I said. "She loaned it to me. In case I needed it. You know, to put things in. To move..."

Daddy walked over to the suitcase and stared down into it before he glanced up at me. He looked tired, like I was. Both of us exhausted from a wedding—me from mine, and him from his. "I didn't realize years ago when we took your mama's things apart and carried them to our new place that we were dismantling her. Somehow, we never got her put together right again. I don't know what we did wrong, but it was probably my fault. I tried everything I knew, but nothing ever worked. The other night, you looked just like she did then. I could have been packing up your mother all over again, when I looked at you. You're all piled up in a corner over there at David's right now, and I want to make sure you get put back together the right way. The way you want." He looked back down at the suitcase. "I don't want you to live dismantled your whole life, like I think your mother has. I'd rather see you not married at all than like that."

Less than two days. Day after tomorrow. The day after tomorrow I was to become Mrs. David Tidwell. And today, Daddy was giving me permission to be sure. I'd been so unsure. Completely unsure. I'd scoured my options and reasons and motives, looking for a way to be sure, but it was never there. Whether I left David for Raymond, or Raymond for David, or both for no one didn't matter. I'd needed that chance to stand back and see each, see myself, see how I really felt, but that chance never happened like it should. Just pieces. And fragments. Obstacles and opposition that never fit together. Not in so few days.

"It's okay, Daddy. I'm okay." I kept from biting my lips. I kept my hands at my sides, my feet planted flat, and my eyes on Daddy's. "I know what I have to do."

"You know what you have to do, do you?" Mama marched into my room, the pad of paper waving in her hand. "I told you to make your list. You call this a list?" Mama held the pad, one finger tapping on the single word I'd written.

Lie.

"What do you mean, 'Lie'?" Mama's voice hit that unsteady yodel.

I felt Daddy's eyes on me.

"I meant lie down," I said, swiping a hand over my mouth and shuffling my feet. "When I get the chance. That's all."

"I'm helping her so maybe she'll have the chance to do just that," Daddy told Mama as he took my one-word list from her hands. Mama eyed us both, and marched back down the stairs. He stuffed the pad into his pocket. "I told you I'd help with your list, and I will. And I'm starting here." He closed Karen's suitcase and slid it under my bed.

Chapter 58

Organ music filled the sanctuary as Pastor Reynolds stood at the front of our church, lining us up, pointing which way each of us should go tomorrow during the wedding. Stand here, do this now and that then, face this way, and walk that direction. We were a dizzied circus of baffled performers.

"Even though it's a small wedding," he said, clapping his hands together, "we still want the ceremony to be dignified. For instance, the boy with the rings, send him down the aisle first. Wait until he's at the front of the church before sending the flower girl."

We nodded. People scurried into place. David was already where he was supposed to stand, his best man positioned slightly behind him. I could see David drawing mental maps, backing the pastor with suggestions, making sure everyone was in the right place at the right time. I moved farther down the aisle from the heat of the activity, my father sticking at my side.

"Next we want Karen to walk to the front," Pastor Reynolds continued. "Go ahead and practice it now, Karen. And take your time. Walk as if you're the bride, because, after all, you're her maid of honor; you're the closest we will come to her until she steps into view."

Karen had been standing off to the side, near a man I didn't know. His hair was sandy-colored and straight, his face pleasant, his expression comfortably attentive. He placed one hand at the small of her back as she stepped around him to head toward the back of the sanctuary, the other resting on a cane as he repositioned himself after she passed. *William,* she mouthed as she threaded between two rows of pews, coming toward me and my father. "Thank God I learned to drive," she slowed enough to whisper as she walked by us. I glanced across the sanctuary at William. I saw on him what showed on Mr. Wilson and on Raymond. He was back from the war, finding his way, finding a new life and a new way to live it. Just like Karen was finding.

Karen disappeared at the back of the sanctuary, then reappeared at the entrance to the aisle. I watched her pause and steal a glance William's way. His gaze was fixed on her, a gaze I'd written about and felt once myself. When he shifted his weight to reposition the cane, I thought of Eloise's shoe, her temporary blindness, the opposition Karen had to overcome when she learned to drive. I thought of red.

"Head this way," David called. He waved an arm to usher Karen forward. I looked from William to Karen as she started toward the front, a slow and elegant pace I knew I couldn't match. "Thirteen, fourteen..." David's voice broke my spell. I turned his direction and saw him watching Karen's feet, calculating her every move, his head bobbing as he counted each step.

"Over here," Pastor Reynolds said when she reached the front, David finishing with a definitive "twenty-eight steps." The two men aligned her, and she turned to me and smiled, then glanced to the side at William again.

"Now for the good part," the pastor said. He stared at me. I stared back.

"Martha," David said, a slight lilt in his tone.

I looked from Pastor to him. "Yes?"

He shooed me with his fingers. "Go on, you're the good part. Go to the end of the aisle so you can walk this way."

I pointed to my chest. "Me?"

Daddy took me by the elbow, pivoted us toward the back, and escorted me out of the sanctuary. My face flushed as I realized what everyone must be thinking. I was acting like a spectator when I was really the show. I was the good part.

"I'm so silly, Daddy. Everyone must think I've lost my mind."

Daddy didn't answer me. He just kept walking, leaving the sanctuary farther and farther behind. We passed through the foyer and came to the church's front door. I watched his hand grasp the door's handle.

"Daddy, they're going to think we've both lost our minds." I laid my hand over his and looked to the side, up at his face. At his profile, as he stared straight ahead, looking at the church doors, closed in front of us. "Daddy?"

"You're not the good part, Martha." He finally turned my way. "You're the best part. And I want to be sure you know that. I'm not lying down on that, either."

"What?"

"No lie." He let go of my elbow and faced me. "And I don't want you to have to lie, either. Not tell one or live one."

I realized then that he'd been looking at me like this for years. At Mama, too. He'd been looking at her

312

through the same eyes, eyes that understood what they really didn't.

"Martha?" David's voice called from the front of the sanctuary.

I realized the organist was playing the bride's march as Daddy and I continued to stare at one another. I wanted to tell Daddy that sometimes you have to lie, like Mama had to all these years to him, like he had to, to himself. Like all of the lies I'd told the past few days to accomplish nothing other than to lead me to one more.

"Martha, are you coming?" David called again.

Lying didn't make me the best part, it didn't make me what Karen had wanted me to be, or what she'd become. It just made me a part. The part I was supposed to be. "Let's go, Daddy. Everyone's waiting."

We marched at a slow pace to the mouth of the aisle, where we turned and paused. Arm in arm, we faced the pastor, David, his best man, Karen, and my mother—who wasn't supposed to be standing near Karen but was. The organist increased her volume, and the church vibrated. Like a train. Like a train in the night when no one was there and the seat next to you was empty. I tugged my father's arm. He stepped forward, the two of us together, down the aisle toward David. The music vibrated through me. I felt it resonate in every fiber. I looked ahead at my husband-to-be, let the chords buoy me, create an emotional sensation, the first I'd ever felt around him. Maybe for him. I squeezed my father's arm as I watched David's face. If this feeling could continue, if it could just be the seed of some sort of love.

David's lips moved, and I smiled. His head dipped

with each word he said to himself as we drew nearer. I tried to read his lips, look for the movements that formed the word, "love," but his head was tilted too far down, his focus on my feet. Nineteen. Twenty. Twenty-one. Daddy and I drew closer, near enough I could see David mouth the numbers, his head bobbing with each one and each step. Seven steps from my fiancé, I stopped. David stopped counting. He looked up and frowned.

Watch me, I mouthed. I pointed to my face. We started forward, again, David's eyes on mine. When at last Daddy and I reached him, David stiffened and aligned himself at my father's other side.

The music slowed as we stood there, mellowed to soft chords until it stopped. Mama made a noise as the last chord faded. Karen led her to the nearest pew and sat her there. I stared straight ahead, like what I would do tomorrow. What I would do forever.

"Of course I won't do the actual ceremony," the pastor said. "I'll ask who gives this woman, after which you can join your wife," he said to my father. My father let go of my arm and disappeared behind me as David stepped into his place. "Then," the pastor continued, "I'll ask if anyone has just cause why this union shouldn't take place, talk a little about love and commitment, we'll do the vows, exchange the rings, and finally…the kiss. The thing everyone waits for." He grinned at us. I wondered if David was grinning, but I didn't look to see. "We can practice that part. It's a little risky to actually say vows tonight, or pronounce you husband and wife, but the kiss is fine if you want to. Go ahead."

David moved at my side. He edged closer, and I

felt his hand on my arm. I glanced in his direction, my eyes widening as his face inched near. I closed my eyes, felt his lips against mine. I waited, wondering if there would be more, some emotional sensation like before. Like when Raymond had kissed me so long ago on the train. David pulled away. The breath I'd felt on my upper lip was gone. Chords from the organ shook the church, I jumped, Mama yelped, and the pastor laughed.

"Good thing we practiced that part," the pastor shouted over the pounding organ. "Looks like the two of you needed it. Now you'll turn to the crowd. I'll introduce you as Mr. and Mrs. David Tidwell, and you'll exit the sanctuary. Head on out to the vestibule and form a line so people can file past and congratulate you, then be off to the reception."

Mama jumped up. She began chatting about pictures, the flowers, where the gifts should be placed, and who would be working the reception area. David was listening. These were details we'd discussed thousands of times. I let her ramble, I let him nod. Less than one more day. Less than one more day. Tomorrow. Martha Haynes. Martha Haynes. Martha Haynes. Martha Tidwell. Martha Tidwell. Martha Tidwell.

Chapter 59

I stared out the train's window, Kansas City passing by. At least the segment from where I got on to the station where I'd get off and head to my job. I'd let Mr. Arnold know I was ready to come back to work, if he'd please tell Mr. Wilson. He said Mr. Wilson had been impatiently waiting, worried I wouldn't come back at all, so he'd be thrilled to know I was finally ready. Mr. Arnold congratulated me, told me to take my time in the morning, they'd all be happy to see me when I got there.

I'd seen this same scenery thousands of times, so many that I didn't even really think about it as it passed. A blur of buildings and people and street lamps, familiar stops, familiar faces, all a part of the blur. "Ma'am." "Miss." "Good morning." I nodded and smiled, most of these people had become like family, nameless faces that knew my face as well as I knew theirs.

I stretched my fingers in my lap. I hadn't taken notes for so long they felt stiff and awkward, like they'd forgotten how to hold a pencil and take dictation of someone else's words. The train slowed as I stretched and spread my fingers, watching the reflection of my face appear and disappear over and over in the window as the train glided past dark buildings near the upcoming station.

We came to a stop. People got on and people got off. I listened. Footsteps, voices, bags and coats brushed by. Then we started up again, chugged forward. My reflection back again. I smiled. It felt like I'd been around the world on a train, far more than having just fallen in love.

The buildings became closer and taller. The main station was coming near. I gathered my satchel and my bag, my satchel lighter now, with only my lunch in it. The vibrations waned, and the squeal of the wheels increased. I scooted to the edge of the seat and waited. When it stopped, I stood, along with several others. My first day back. There would be questions, sly looks, silly giggles from my coworkers. I braced myself. I was ready. After all, we'd all adjust. I had.

"You have a nice day, miss," the porter said as I passed him, leaving the car.

"Thank you. You too. See you this evening." I stepped down onto the platform and turned to the left for my job.

"Miss! Miss! I almost forgot." The porter bounded down the steps behind me, he hurried my direction, his arm outstretched. "I was supposed to give this to you," he panted. I took a small envelope from his hands. "Have a good day, miss."

I watched him hustle back to the train and jump on. The door closed behind him and the train chugged forward. I turned back toward work, stuffed my bag and satchel under one arm, and opened the envelope as I went.

A few handwritten pages were inside. At the top of the first page I saw, *Love on a Train—Epilogue.* I frowned. I stopped walking. People brushed past me as

I stood in the middle of the sidewalk staring at pages I hadn't written. I thought of Amelia and other women I'd signed my book for. I thought of Karen, and even David's mother, wondering who had done this. I bit my lips together, pressed them into a taut line, wishing I knew what David's mother's handwriting looked like.

"Excuse me." More people brushed past. I glanced around and to the side. I spotted a bench near the storefronts. I wove through the crowd and took a seat there, settled my bags on my lap, and looked at *Love on a Train—Epilogue.*

"Someone once said it's easier to stop loving than it is to stop hating. Love is a passion more easily destroyed, whereas hatred rolls like an insatiable fire raging beyond control." Jacob wanted to tell Eloise that. He wanted to whisper it in her ear, but she was too far back. There was one more person, one who at the last minute had stepped between them. He stretched, he craned. She was so near, yet so far. "Some say love is fragile and therefore easy to destroy." He wanted to ask her if hers was still there or if it had crumbled in his absence. He waited, he watched her, he leaned around the person between them, who was always there.

The person spoke then, spoke to Eloise. She paused and listened to the person, who led her away. Jacob raised his hand so she could see, but she couldn't. Or she didn't. The other person filled her sight, filled her ears, and then she was gone.

I stared at the page and flipped it over. My happy ending was gone, the fictional one I wrote. This one was too real. This one hurt. No one would buy this story; everyone already lived it. I glanced at the second page, not sure I wanted to read more.

Jacob watched her go. Maybe Eloise's love hadn't gone away. Maybe her attention was only being transferred to another. She disappeared into the crowd. He lowered his hand. Either way, it didn't matter. She was gone.

He waited for his love to die, like they said it would. He took hammers to it. He tried to reshape it and bend it, even fuse it to fit another, but it wouldn't budge. They were wrong, whoever they were that said love was easy to destroy. It wasn't. Not for him. Not ever.

The handwriting was familiar. I studied the slants and curves of the letters. Whoever it was, they'd written a bittersweet ending, one they'd meant to be about Jacob and what he had experienced, but I knew it was about Eloise, instead. And me. I, too, had learned that love, real love, was impossible to destroy.

I flipped the page over, thinking that was the end, but on the back was a sketch. It was of me. It was my profile. And below it was written, "Want to see a picture of the girl I wish I could marry? All my best to you always, Eloise. Ever yours, Jacob."

The pages quivered in my hands. I tried to refold them, press them into halves and quarters, but my fingers trembled, and the pages creased where they hadn't been creased before. I stuffed them into my satchel and looked every direction. He had to be somewhere.

Instead of continuing toward work, I turned back to the station. My steps were clipped at first, then my stride stretched longer and grew quicker. I was running by the time I reached the station. I stopped on the platform and stared at the next train's windows, just like Raymond had in his drawings.

I stretched to my toes and strained to see better, just in case he was there. Somewhere. His height, his dark hair, eyes that I'd never forget.

Everyone on and off the train looked different from him, all the same. Same average height, same light hair, same distracted expressions as they rushed toward whatever it was that called them. And their faces—all the same—none of them sharp, dark, and handsome like his.

My heart slowed, settled down to a steady rhythm. Steady but strong. Beating like it used to, like it was supposed to, like I always wanted it to. Until he had gone.

Passengers gathered around me, waiting for another train. Others squeezed past, making last-minute leaps onto the train that was waiting. The air changed in the midst of their commotion. The brisk wind that swept along with their rush swirled around me, bringing with it that scent.

His scent. The one I could never forget.

I breathed. I drew in the aroma of the man I'd loved. Really loved. I understood that at last.

I dropped to the flat of my feet, afraid if I moved, I'd lose it. Not just the scent of him, but him. I inhaled as I stood there, drank in as much of him as I could, and held on to what little of him I had.

"Martha."

The last time I'd heard his voice, he disappeared. There it was again, behind me now, so near I could feel the vibration of his tone, even above the waiting train.

"Don't turn around. Just hear me out, and after that

I promise I'll go."

I closed my eyes and continued to breathe, drawing in what I could, praying this was real and not just a dream.

He came nearer. I could feel him. I was Martha Cole on the train again, my heart pounding, my hands rearranging my skirts so I could feel the nearness of his body. The dark ruddiness of his complexion came close—I could see it even with him behind me. The gentleness I'd noticed the first moment I saw him wrapped around me, held me, kept me from stumbling past as I had before.

"I realized too late it was you. Not her. I thought at first it was that you were so like her. Every time I looked at you I thought it was her I was seeing. But it wasn't. It was you all along. I just didn't know that until I saw her again and realized she was tied to the war, to my need for someone to be there to bring me back. Nothing more. I felt so bad when I first understood. I almost went through with the wedding for fear of letting her down. But the less of you that was there, the less of me that was there, also. And the less I became of what she wanted. I told her, then. I took back the illusion we'd both built. That's all it was in the end, an illusion, a dream. Without love."

Tears came to my eyes as he sketched another thousand words that revealed my heart, also. He drew the two of us with his nearness, the soothing vibration of his voice, the painful words he chose. We were so close, so very much the same, yet so far.

"The time I returned here, that's when I met your fiancé. Your husband now. There no going back and no going forward for me. I'd reached my end because you'd reached yours, and I had nowhere to go."

"No going back?" I asked. "You didn't go back? To her?"

I felt him come even closer. "No," he said. "Of course not. And I'm only here now so you know that. So you don't read your book, see the changes I made, and wonder. I owe you more than I can ever repay for the way you hurt, and the way I caused that hurt. I'm sorry, Martha. I'm sorry to her because I made a foolish mistake. And I'm sorry to you because you loved freely and I was too late to realize that I did, also. I wish you all the happiness you wanted in your life. With him."

It was as if we'd become one all over again in that moment, in those few words, in the nearness but farness of how we stood.

When he moved away, I felt it. I felt the familiar rending of one being ripped apart where there was no seam, no joint. It was a rending of unity and sameness, a whole.

I whirled then. But he wasn't there. The crowd had filled the space between us, their browns, their indistinctive heights and faces blocking my view. I looked through them, over them, and around them for dark hair on a head higher than theirs, for nearly coal black eyes I would spot if only he'd turn just one more time.

Then it was there. Black hair that caught a sheen in the morning light.

I wove through the crowd, I begged their pardon as I squeezed them aside until I was close. I stretched my arm forward, my hand near his back, my fingers close to his jacket when he stopped. I stopped behind him. I dropped my arm, and for a moment we just breathed.

"You're not married? You really didn't go back for her?" I asked. I saw his shoulders shift, I felt their tautness as he turned.

"No, I didn't." His face was as I remembered, yet more. Handsome, but with heartache, deeper grooves softened by love. And the loss of it. "I couldn't. I couldn't have just a marriage. I had to have love."

"Me, too," I said.

"What?"

"I couldn't have just a marriage. I had to have love. Real love. The way I knew it should be."

He took a step forward, and so did I. His arm bridged the span between us, our hearts already there. His fingers touched my hand. They were warm; they created a sensation in me, a desire to laugh, to love, to do all the things a wife or woman in love should want to do. A desire to write. When I looked into his eyes I saw my next story. I saw my happy ending, the one Mama said could never be.

"You didn't marry him?"

"I didn't," I said. "It would have been a lie, and that was a list I had to tear up."

A porter called from the train behind us. He gave the final warning as one by one the train's doors began to close. Raymond smiled down at me, a beautiful smile on a beautiful face. He took me by the elbow, the way Daddy had the one and only time I ever walked down the aisle. Before the last door could close, Raymond scooped me up, off my feet, and into his arms.

"Love on a train," he said as he carried me up the steps, "and love off it, this time, too." He stood me in the aisle of the train car and pulled me close.

He kissed me then, picking up where he'd left off

ages ago. I could hear Mama's gasp, in the back of my mind, over the startled applause of those around us. Her reminders of what couldn't and shouldn't be were drowned beneath the smiles and laughter of the other passengers nearby.

Love on a train or off it. Love anywhere. By anyone, even and especially by her and Daddy's only daughter. By me.

A word from the author...

Born and raised in the Midwest, I earned a four-year degree in Medical Technology and have worked in the field of science ever since.

Outside of the laboratory I delve deeply into literature, both reading and writing, my favorite tales involving moral dilemmas and the choices people come up against.

Other hobbies include wildlife photography with the use of trail cameras, shed antler hunting, garden and yard work, and theater.

Connect with Colleen at:
colleenldonnelly@gmail.com
http://colleenldonnelly.wordpress.com
https://twitter.com/ColleenLDonnell/
www.colleenldonnelly.com
https://www.facebook.com/ColleenLDonnelly

~*~

Other Books by Colleen Donnelly
available from The Wild Rose Press, Inc.
MINE TO TELL
ASKED FOR

www.ingramcontent.com/pod-product-compliance
Lightning Source LLC
Chambersburg PA
CBHW071527260626
47170CB00002B/534